THE WONDERFUL ADVENTURES
OF NILS

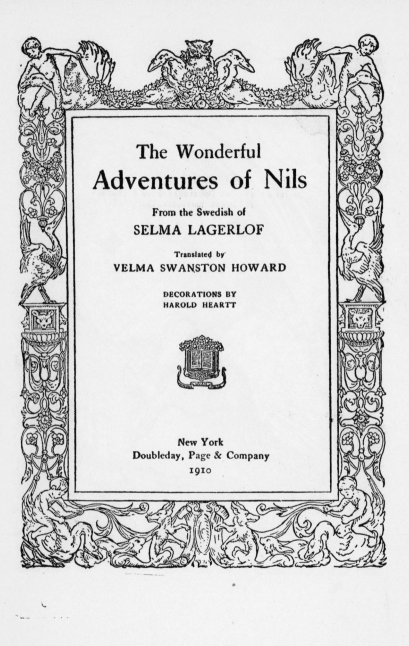

The Wonderful
Adventures of Nils

From the Swedish of
SELMA LAGERLOF

Translated by
VELMA SWANSTON HOWARD

DECORATIONS BY
HAROLD HEARTT

New York
Doubleday, Page & Company
1910

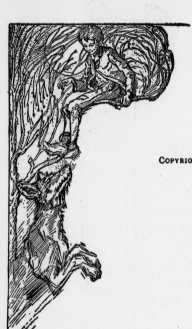

PUBLISHERS' NOTE

"The Wonderful Adventures of Nils" was written for use in schools as "supplementary reading," with the special idea of introducing such subjects as would be educative as well as entertaining to the minds of children from the ages of nine to eleven. The book has been adopted in the public schools of Sweden, but older people have found in it a book of permanent value.

In so far as possible, the translator has faithfully interpreted the author's local and idiomatic expressions.

TRANSLATOR'S INTRODUCTION

THIS book, which is the latest work of Sweden's greatest fiction writer, was published in Stockholm, December, 1906. It became immediately the most popular book of the year in Scandinavia.

Four years ago the author received a commission from the National Teachers' Association to write a reader for the public schools.

She devoted three years to Nature study and to familiarising herself with animal and bird life. She sought out hitherto unpublished folk-lore and legends of the different provinces. These she has ingeniously woven into her story.

The book has been translated into German and Danish, and the book reviewers of Germany and Denmark, as well as those of Sweden, are unanimous in proclaiming this Selma Lagerlöf's best work.

One reviewer has said: "Since the days

of Hans Christian Andersen, we have had
nothing in Scandinavian juvenile literature
to compare with this remarkable book."
Another reviewer wrote: "Miss Lagerlöf has
the keen insight into animal psychology of
a Rudyard Kipling."

Stockholm's *Dagblad* said among other
things: "The great author stands as it
were in the background. The prophetess
is forgotten for the voices that speak through
her. It is as though the book had sprung
direct from the soul of the Swedish nation."

Sydsvenska Dagbladet writes: "The signifi-
cant thing about this book is: while one
follows with breathless interest the shift-
ing scenes and adventures, one learns many
things without being conscious of it. . . .
The author's imagination unfolds an almost
inexhaustible wealth in invention of new,
and ever-changing adventures, told in such a
convincing way that we almost believe them.
. . . As amusement reading for the
young, this book is a decided acquisition.
The intimate blending of fiction and fact is
so subtle that one finds it hard to distinguish

where one ends, and the other begins. It
is a classic. . . A masterwork."

From *Gefle Posten:* "The author is here—
as always, the great story-teller, the greatest, perhaps, in Scandinavian literature since
the days of Hans Christian Andersen. To
children whose imaginations have been fos-
tered by Ashbjörnsen, Andersen, and 'Thou-
sand-and-One Nights,' Nils Holgersson will
always be precious, as well as to those of us
who are older."

From *Göteborg Posten:* "Selma Lagerlöf
has given us a good lift onward. She is the
one whom we, in these days, place first and
foremost. . . Among the other work which
she has done for us, and for our children, she
has re-created our geography for us. . . Upon imagination's road she has sought to open
the child-heart to an understanding of animals,
while she tactfully and playfully drops into
little knowledge-thirsty minds a comprehen-
sive understanding of the habits and char-
acteristics of different animals. She carries
us with her . . . and shapes for us—old
and young—a new childhood in tune with the

thought of our time. What does she not touch upon in this wonderful book? . . . As Mowgli, who had the key to all the languages of the Jungle, once found his way to all his little brother and sister-hearts in the great civilised world, so shall the Thumbietot of Swedish fairyland lead many little thirsting child-souls, not only on the highways of adventure, but also upon the road of seriousness and learning."

Another critic says: "Beyond all doubt, 'Nils Holgersson's Journey' is one of the most noteworthy books ever published in our language. I take it, that no other nation has a book of this sort. One can make this or that comment on one and another phase of it, but the whole impresses one as so masterful, so great, and so Swedish, that one lays the book down with a sense of gratitude for the privilege of reading such a thing. There is a deep undercurrent of Swedish earnestness all through this tale of Nils Holgersson. It belongs to us. It is a part of us."

Ny Tid writes: "Selma Lagerlöf's book contains just as much information—no, twice

as much—as the old readers. It acquaints
the children with Sweden's nature; it interests
them in its bird world—both tame and wild;
in its domestic and forest animals, even in
its rats. It explains its vegetation, its soil,
its mountain-formations, its climatic con-
ditions. It gives you customs, superstitions
and the folk-lore in different sections of the
country. It takes in farming industry, manors and factories; cities and peasant-cabins,
and even dog-kennels. It has a word for
everything; an interest in, and for, everything. For, mark you, this book has not
been patched together by the dilettante, by
committees. . . It was written by a
highly gifted, warm-hearted seer, to whom
the child-nature has not been a murky pool
to fish in, but a clear, impressionable mirror.
The author has fulfilled her mission in
a wholly convincing manner. She has
had enough imagination and skill to
blend all the dry travel and nature ma-
terial into the harmonious beauty of fable.
She knew how to combine the useful with
the beautiful, as no pedant of the prac-

tical, or the æsthetic, has ever dreamed it.
She has converted the absorption of knowl-
edge into a child's game—a pleasure. Her
style throughout is the simplest, the most
facile for children to grasp. . . . Her
utterances are hearty without being bois-
terous; most playful and humorous without being loquacious. Her work is a model
text-book; and just therefore, a finished
work of art."

"From *Goteborg Morgon Posten:* "The fame
of her literary greatness goes forward without a
dissenting voice; fills her own land, and travels
far and wide outside its borders. . . Just
as modestly as she points a moral, just so deli-
cately and unobtrusively does she give information. Everything comes to you through the
adventures, or through the concrete images of
imagination's all-compelling form. . . .
No one who has retained a particle of his child
mind can escape the genuine witchery of the
poesy in 'Nils Holgersson.' "

A new history of literature, entitled "Frauen
der Gegenwart", by Dr. Theodore Klaiber,
mentions Miss Lagerlöf as the foremost woman

writer of our time, and says that she is
receiving the same affectionate homage for
her art in other lands, that has been accorded
to her in Sweden.   Dr. Klaiber does not see
in her merely "a dreaming poetess far
removed from the world." He finds her too
forceful and courageous for this.

"But she sees life with other eyes than do
our up-to-date people.   All her world becomes
saga and legend. . . .   More than all other
modern authors, she has that all-embracing
love for everything which never wanes and
never wearies." says Dr. Klaiber.

Torsten Fågelqvist, a well-known Swedish
writer, ends his review of the book with these
remarks: "Our guide is clear-visioned,
many-sided and maternal. She can speak
all languages: the language of animals, and
the language of flowers; but first and last,
childhood's language. And the best of all
is, that under her spell all are compelled to
become children."

VELMA SWANSTON HOWARD.

Comments translated from Swedish and German.

CONTENTS

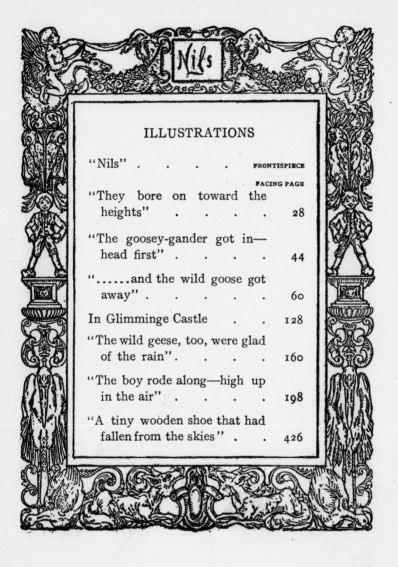

ILLUSTRATIONS

THE WONDERFUL ADVENTURES
OF NILS

I

THE BOY

THE ELF

Sunday, March twentieth.

ONCE there was a boy. He was—let us say—something like fourteen years old; long and loose jointed and towheaded. He wasn't good for much, that boy. His chief delight was to eat and sleep; and after that —he liked best to make mischief.

It was a Sunday morning and the boy's parents were getting ready to go to church. The boy sat on the edge of the table, in his shirt sleeves, and thought how lucky it was that both father and mother were going away, and the coast would be clear for a couple of hours. "Good! Now I can take down pop's gun and fire off a shot, without anybody's meddling interference," he said to himself.

But it was almost as if father should have

3

guessed the boy's thoughts, for just as he was on the threshold—ready to start—he stopped short, and turned toward the boy: "Since you won't come to church with mother and me," he said, "the least you can do, is to read the service at home. Will you promise to do so?" "Yes," said the boy, "that I can do easy enough." And he thought, of course, that he wouldn't read any more than he felt like reading.

The boy thought that never had he seen his mother so persistent. In a second she was over by the shelf near the fireplace, and took down Luther's Commentary and laid it on the table, in front of the window—opened at the service for the day. She also opened the New Testament, and placed it beside the Commentary. Finally, she drew up the big arm-chair, which was bought at the parish auction the year before, and which, as a rule, no one but father was permitted to occupy.

The boy sat thinking that his mother was giving herself altogether too much trouble with this spread; for he had no intention of reading more than a page or so. But now,

for the second time, it was almost as if his
father were able to see right through him.
He walked up to the boy, and said in a severe
tone: "Now, remember, that you are to
read carefully! For when we come back, I
shall question you thoroughly; and if you
have skipped a single page, it will not go well
with you."

"The service is fourteen and a half pages
long," said his mother, just as if she wanted
to heap up the measure of his misfortune.
"You'll have to sit down and begin the reading at once, if you expect to get through with
it."

With that they departed. And as the boy
stood in the doorway watching them, he
thought that he had been caught in a trap.
"There they go congratulating themselves,
I suppose, in the belief that they've hit upon
something so good that I'll be forced to sit
and hang over the sermon the whole time that
they are away," thought he.

But his father and mother were certainly
not congratulating themselves upon anything
of the sort; but, on the contrary, they were

very much distressed. They were poor farmers, and their place was not much bigger than a garden-plot. When they first moved there, the place couldn't feed more than one pig and a pair of chickens; but they were uncommonly industrious and capable folk— and now they had both cows and geese. Things had turned out very well for them; and they would have gone to church that beautiful morning—satisfied and happy—if they hadn't had their son to think of. Father complained that he was dull and lazy; he had not cared to learn anything at school, and he was such an all-round good-for-nothing, that he could barely be made to tend geese. Mother did not deny that this was true; but she was most distressed because he was wild and bad; cruel to animals, and ill-willed toward human beings. "May God soften his hard heart, and give him a better disposition!" said the mother, "or else he will be a misfortune, both to himself and to us."

The boy stood for a long time and pondered whether he should read the service or **not**. Finally, he came to the conclusion

that, this time, it was best to be obedient.
He seated himself in the easy chair, and began
to read. But when he had been rattling
away in an undertone for a little while, this
mumbling seemed to have a soothing effect
upon him—and he began to nod.

It was the most beautiful weather outside!
It was only the twentieth of March; but the
boy lived in West Vemminghög Township,
down in Southern Skåne, where the spring
was already in full swing. It was not as yet
green, but it was fresh and budding. There
was water in all the trenches, and the colt's-
foot on the edge of the ditch, was in bloom.
All the weeds that grew in among the stones,
were brown and shiny. The beech-woods
in the distance, seemed to swell and grow
thicker with every second. The skies were
high—and a clear blue. The cottage door
stood ajar, and the lark's trill could be heard
in the room. The hens and geese pattered
about in the yard, and the cows, who felt
the spring air away in their stalls, lowed
their approval every now and then.

The boy read and nodded and fought

against drowsiness. "No! I don't want to fall asleep," thought he, "for then I'll not get through with this thing the whole forenoon."

But—somehow—he fell asleep.

He did not know whether he had slept a short while, or a long while; but he was awakened by hearing a slight noise back of him.

On the window-sill, facing the boy, stood a small looking-glass; and almost the entire cottage could be seen in this. As the boy raised his head, he happened to look in the glass; and then he saw that the cover to his mother's chest had been opened.

His mother owned a great, heavy, iron-bound oak chest, which she permitted no one but herself to open. Here she treasured all the things she had inherited from her mother, and of these she was especially careful. Here lay a couple of old-time peasant dresses, of red homespun cloth, with short bodice and plaited shirt, and a pearl-bedecked breast pin. There were starched white-linen head-dresses, and heavy silver ornaments and chains. Folks don't care to go about

dressed like that in these days, and several
times his mother had thought of getting rid
of the old things; but somehow, she hadn't
had the heart to do it.

Now the boy saw distinctly—in the glass—
that the chest-lid was open. He could not
understand how this had happened, for his
mother had closed the chest before she went
away. She never would have left that precious chest open when he was at home, alone.

He became low-spirited and apprehensive.
He was afraid that a thief had sneaked his
way into the cottage. He didn't dare to
move; but sat still and stared into the looking-
glass.

While he sat there and waited for the thief
to make his appearance, be began to wonder
what that dark shadow was which fell across
the edge of the chest. He looked and looked
—and did not want to believe his eyes. But
the thing, which at first seemed shadowy,
became more and more clear to him; and
soon he saw that it was something real. It
was no less a thing than an elf who sat there
—astride the edge of the chest!

To be sure, the boy had heard stories about
elves, but he had never dreamed that they
were such tiny creatures. He was no taller
than a hand's breadth—this one, who sat on
the edge of the chest. He had an old,
wrinkled and beardless face, and was dressed
in a black frock coat, knee-breeches and a
broad-brimmed black hat. He was very
trim and smart, with his white laces about
the throat and wrist-bands, his buckled shoes,
and the bows on his garters. He had taken
from the chest an embroidered piece, and sat
and looked at the old-fashioned handiwork
with such an air of veneration, that he did
not observe the boy had awakened.

The boy was somewhat surprised to see the
elf, but, on the other hand, he was not particularly frightened. It was impossible to
be afraid of one who was so little. And since
the elf was so absorbed in his own thoughts
that he neither saw nor heard, the boy thought
that it would be great fun to play a trick on
him; to push him over into the chest and shut
the lid on him, or something of that kind. ''

But the boy was not so courageous that he

dared to touch the elf with his hands, instead he looked around the room for something to poke him with. He let his gaze wander from the sofa to the leaf-table; from the leaf-table to the fireplace. He looked at the kettles, then at the coffee-urn, which stood on a shelf, near the fireplace; on the water bucket near the door; and on the spoons and knives and forks and saucers and plates, which could be seen through the half-open cupboard door. He looked at his father's gun, which hung on the wall, beside the portrait of the Danish royal family, and on the geraniums and fuchsias, which blossomed in the window. And last, he caught sight of an old butterfly-snare that hung on the window frame. He had hardly set eyes on that butterfly-snare, before he reached over and snatched it and jumped up and swung it alongside the edge of the chest. He was himself astonished at the luck he had. He hardly knew how he had managed it—but he had actually snared the elf. The poor little chap lay, head downward, in the bottom of the long snare, and could not free himself.

The first moment the boy hadn't the least idea what he should do with his prize. He was only particular to swing the snare backward and forward, to prevent the elf from getting a foothold and clambering up.

The elf began to speak, and begged, oh! so pitifully, for his freedom. He had brought them good luck—these many years—he said, and deserved better treatment. Now, if the boy would set him free, he would give him an old coin, a silver spoon, and a gold penny, as big as the case on his father's silver watch.

The boy didn't think that this was much of an offer; but it so happened—that after he had gotten the elf in his power, he was afraid of him. He felt that he had entered into an agreement with something weird and uncanny; something which did not belong to his world, and he was only too glad to get rid of the horrid thing.

For this reason he agreed at once to the bargain, and held the snare still, so the elf could crawl out of it. But when the elf was almost out of the snare, the boy happened to think that he ought to have bargained for

large estates, and all sorts of good things. He should at least have made this stipulation: that the elf must conjure the sermon into his head. "What a fool I was to let him go!" thought he, and began to shake the snare violently, so the elf would tumble down again.

But the instant the boy did this, he received such a stinging box on the ear, that he thought his head would fly in pieces. He was dashed—first against one wall, then against the other; he sank to the floor, and lay there—senseless.

When he awoke, he was alone in the cottage. The chest-lid was down, and the butterfly-snare hung in its usual place by the window. If he had not felt how the right cheek burned, from that box on the ear, he would have been tempted to believe the whole thing had been a dream. "At any rate, father and mother will be sure to insist that it was nothing else," thought he. "They are not likely to make any allowances for that old sermon, on account of the elf. It's best for me to get at that reading again," thought he.

But as he walked toward the table, he noticed something remarkable. It couldn't be possible that the cottage had grown. But why was he obliged to take so many more steps than usual to get to the table? And what was the matter with the chair? It looked no bigger than it did a while ago; but now he had to step on the rung first, and then clamber up in order to reach the seat. It was the same thing with the table. He could not look over the top without climbing to the arm of the chair.

"What in all the world is this?" said the boy. "I believe the elf has bewitched both the arm-chair and the table—and the whole cottage."

The Commentary lay on the table and, to all appearances, it was not changed; but there must have been something queer about that too, for he could not manage to read a single word of it, without actually standing right in the book itself.

He read a couple of lines, and then he chanced to look up. With that, his glance fell on the looking-glass; and then he cried aloud: "Look! There's another one!"

For in the glass he saw plainly a little, little creature who was dressed in a hood and leather breeches.

"Why, that one is dressed exactly like me!" said the boy, and clasped his hands in astonishment. But then he saw that the thing in the mirror did the same thing. Then he began to pull his hair and pinch his arms and swing round; and instantly he did the same thing after him; he, who was seen in the mirror.

The boy ran around the glass several times, to see if there wasn't a little man hidden behind it, but he found no one there; and then he began to shake with terror. For now he understood that the elf had bewitched him, and that the creature whose image he saw in the glass—was he, himself.

THE WILD GEESE

THE boy simply could not make himself believe that he had been transformed into an elf. "It can't be anything but a dream —a queer fancy," thought he. "If I wait a

few moments, I'll surely be turned back into a human being again."

He placed himself before the glass and closed his eyes. He opened them again after a couple of minutes, and then expected to find that it had all passed over—but it hadn't. He was—and remained—just as little. In other respects, he was the same as before. The thin, straw-coloured hair; the freckles across his nose; the patches on his leather breeches and the darns on his stockings, were all like themselves, with this exception—that they had become diminished.

No, it would do no good for him to stand still and wait, of this he was certain. He must try something else. And he thought the wisest thing that he could do was to try and find the elf, and make his peace with him.

And while he sought, he cried and prayed and promised everything he could think of. Nevermore would he break his word to anyone; never again would he be naughty; and never, never would he fall asleep again over the sermon. If he might only be a human being once more, he would be such a good and helpful and obedient boy. **But no** matter how much he promised—it did **not** help him the least little bit.

Suddenly he remembered that he had **heard** his mother say, all the tiny folk made **their** home in the cowsheds; and, at once, he concluded to go there, and see if he couldn't find the elf. It was a lucky thing that the cottage-door stood partly open, for he never could have reached the bolt and opened **it;** but now he slipped through without **any** difficulty.

When he came out in the hallway, he **looked** around for his wooden shoes; for in the **house,** to be sure, he had gone about in his stocking-feet. He wondered how he should manage with these big, clumsy wooden shoes; **but** just then, he saw a pair of tiny shoes **on the** doorstep. When he observed that the elf **had** been so thoughtful that he had also bewitched the wooden shoes, he was even more troubled. It was evidently his intention that this affliction should last a long time.

On the wooden board-walk in front **of the** cottage, hopped a gray sparrow. **He had**

hardly set eyes on the boy before he called
out: "Teetee! Teetee! Look at Nils goosey-
boy! Look at Thumbietot! Look at Nils
Holgersson Thumbietot!"

Instantly, both the geese and the chickens
turned and stared at the boy; and then they
set up a fearful cackling. "Cock-el-i-coo,"
crowed the rooster, "good enough for him!
Cock-el-i-coo, he has pulled my comb." "Ka,
ka, kada, serves him right!" cried the hens;
and with that they kept up a continuous
cackle. The geese got together in a tight
group, stuck their heads together and asked:
"Who can have done this? Who can have
done this?"

But the strangest thing of all was, that the
boy understood what they said. He was so
astonished, that he stood there as if rooted
to the doorstep, and listened. "It must be
because I am changed into an elf," said he.
"This is probably why I understand bird-talk."

He thought it was unbearable that the hens
would not stop saying that it served him
right. He threw a stone at them and shouted:
"Shut up, you pack!"

But it hadn't occurred to him before, that he was no longer the sort of boy the hens need fear. The whole henyard made a rush for him, and formed a ring around him; then they all cried at once: "Ka, ka, kada, served you right! Ka, ka, kada, served you right!"

The boy tried to get away, but the chickens ran after him and screamed, until he thought he'd lose his hearing. It is more than likely that he never could have gotten away from them, if the house cat hadn't come along just then. As soon as the chickens saw the cat, they quieted down and pretended to be thinking of nothing else than just to scratch in the earth for worms.

Immediately the boy ran up to the cat. "You dear pussy!" said he, "you must know all the corners and hiding places about here? You'll be a good little kitty and tell me where I can find the elf."

The cat did not reply at once. He seated himself, curled his tail into a graceful ring around his paws—and stared at the boy. It was a large black cat with one white spot on his chest. His fur lay sleek and soft, and shone in the sunlight. The claws were drawn in, and the eyes were a dull gray, with just a little narrow dark streak down the centre. The cat looked thoroughly good-natured and inoffensive.

"I know well enough where the elf lives," he said in a soft voice, "but that doesn't say that I'm going to tell *you* about it."

"Dear pussy, you must tell me where the elf lives!" said the boy. "Can't you see how he has bewitched me?"

The cat opened his eyes a little, so that the green wickedness began to shine forth. He spun round and purred with satisfaction before he replied. "Shall I perhaps help you because you have so often grabbed me by the tail?" he said at last.

Then the boy was furious and forgot entirely how little and helpless he was now. "Oh! I can pull your tail again, I can," said he, and ran toward the cat.

The next instant the cat was so changed that the boy could scarcely believe it was the same animal. Every separate hair on his body stood on end. The back was bent; the

legs had become elongated; the claws scraped the ground; the tail had grown thick and short; the ears were laid back; the mouth was frothy; and the eyes were wide open and glistened like sparks of red fire.

The boy didn't want to let himself be scared by a cat, and he took a step forward. Then the cat made one spring and landed right on the boy; knocked him down and stood over him—his forepaws on his chest, and his jaws wide apart—over his throat.

The boy felt how the sharp claws sank through his vest and shirt and into his skin; and how the sharp eye-teeth tickled his throat. He shrieked for help, as loudly as he could, but no one came. He thought surely that his last hour had come. Then he felt that the cat drew in his claws and let go the hold on his throat.

"There!" he said, "that will do now. I'll let you go this time, for my mistress's sake. I only wanted you to know which one of us two has the power now."

With that the cat walked away—looking as smooth and pious as he did when he first appeared on the scene. The boy was so crestfallen that he didn't say a word, but only hurried to the cowhouse to look for the elf.

There were not more than three cows, all told. But when the boy came in, there was such a bellowing and such a kick-up, that one might easily have believed that there were at least thirty.

"Moo, moo, moo," bellowed Mayrose. "It is well there is such a thing as justice in this world."

"Moo, moo, moo," sang the three of them in unison. He couldn't hear what they said, for each one tried to out-bellow the others.

The boy wanted to ask after the elf, but he couldn't make himself heard because the cows were in full uproar. They carried on as they used to do when he let a strange dog in on them. They kicked with their hind legs, shook their necks, stretched their heads, and measured the distance with their horns.

"Come here, you!" said Mayrose, "And you'll get a kick that you won't forget in a hurry!"

"Come here," said Gold Lily, "and you shall dance on my horns!"

"Come here, and you shall taste how it felt when you threw your wooden shoes at me, as you did last summer!" bawled Star.

"Come here, and you shall be repaid for that wasp you let loose in my ear!" growled Gold Lily.

Mayrose was the oldest and the wisest of them, and she was the very maddest. "Come here!" said she, "that I may pay you back for the many times that you have jerked the milk pail away from your mother; and for all the snares you laid for her, when she came carrying the milk pails; and for all the tears which she has stood here and wept over you!"

The boy wanted to tell them how he regretted that he had been unkind to them; and that never, never—from now on—should he be anything but good, if they would only tell him where the elf was. But the cows didn't listen to him. They made such a racket that he began to fear one of them would succeed in breaking loose; and he

thought that the best thing for him to do,
was to go quietly away from the cowhouse.

When he came out, he was thoroughly
disheartened. He could understand that no
one on the place wanted to help him find
the elf. And little good would it do him,
probably, if the elf were found

He crawled up on the broad hedge which
fenced in the farm, and which was overgrown
with briers and lichen. There he sat down
to think about how it would go with him, if
he never became a human being again. When
father and mother came home from church,
there would be a surprise for them. Yes,
a surprise—it would be all over the land; and
people would come flocking from East Vemminghög, and from Torp, and from Skerup.
The whole Vemminghög township would come
to stare at him. Perhaps father and mother
would take him with them, and show him at
the market place in Kivik.

No, that was too horrible to think about.
He would rather that no human being should
ever see him again.

His unhappiness was simply frightful! No

one in all the world was so unhappy as he. He was no longer a human being—but a freak.

Little by little he began to comprehend what it meant—to be no longer human. He was separated from everything now; he could no longer play with other boys, he could not take charge of the farm after his parents were gone; and certainly no girl would think of marrying *him*.

He sat and looked at his home. It was a little log house, which lay as if it had been crushed down to earth, under the high, sloping roof. The outhouses were also small; and the patches of ground were so narrow that a horse could barely turn around on them. But little and poor though the place was, it was much too good for him *now*. He couldn't ask for any better place than a hole under the stable floor.

It was wondrously beautiful weather! It budded, and it rippled, and it murmured, and it twittered—all around him. But he sat there with such a heavy sorrow. He should never be happy any more about anything.

Never had he seen the skies as blue as they were to-day.   Birds of passage came on their travels.   They came from foreign lands, and had travelled over the East sea, by way of Smygahuk, and were now on their way North. They were of many different kinds; but he was only familiar with the wild geese, who came flying in two long rows, which met at an angle.

Several flocks of wild geese had already flown by.   They flew very high, still he could hear how they shrieked: "To the hills! Now we're off to the hills!"

When the wild geese saw the tame geese, who walked about the farm, they sank nearer the earth, and called: "Come along! Come along! We're off to the hills!"

The tame geese could not resist the temptation to raise their heads and listen, but they answered very sensibly: "We're pretty well off where we are. We're pretty well off where we are."

It was, as we have said, an uncommonly fine day, with an atmosphere that it must have been a real delight to fly in, so light and

bracing. And with each new wild geese-flock that flew by, the tame geese became more and more unruly. A couple of times they flapped their wings, as if they had half a mind to fly along. But then an old mother-goose would always say to them: "Now don't be silly. Those creatures will have to suffer both hunger and cold."

There was a young gander whom the wild geese had fired with a passion for adventure. "If another flock comes this way, I'll follow them," said he.

Then there came a new flock, who shrieked like the others, and the young gander answered: "Wait a minute! Wait a minute! I'm coming."

He spread his wings and raised himself into the air; but he was so unaccustomed to flying, that he fell to the ground again.

At any rate, the wild geese must have heard his call, for they turned and flew back slowly to see if he was coming.

"Wait, wait!" he cried, and made another attempt to fly.

All this the boy heard, where he lay on

the hedge. "It would be a great pity,"
thought he, "if the big goosey-gander should
go away. It would be a big loss to father and
mother if he was gone when they came home
from church."

When he thought of this, once again he
entirely forgot that he was little and helpless.
He took one leap right down into the goose-
flock, and threw his arms around the neck
of the goosey-gander. "Oh, no! You don't
fly away this time, sir!" cried he.

But just about then, the gander was considering how he should go to work to raise
himself from the ground. He couldn't stop
to shake the boy off, hence he had to go
along with him—up in the air.

They bore on toward the heights so rapidly, that the boy fairly gasped. Before he
had time to think that he ought to let go his
hold around the gander's neck, he was so high
up that he would have been killed instantly,
if he had fallen to the ground.

The only thing that he could do to make
himself a little more comfortable, was to try
and get upon the gander's back. And there

"They bore on toward the heights"

he wriggled himself forthwith; but not without considerable trouble. And it was not an easy matter, either, to hold himself secure on the slippery back, between two swaying wings. He had to dig deep into feathers and down with both hands, to keep from tumbling to the ground.

THE BIG CHECKED CLOTH

THE boy had grown so giddy that it was a long while before he came to himself. The winds howled and beat against him, and the rustle of feathers and swaying of wings sounded like a whole storm. Thirteen geese flew around him, flapping their wings and honking. They danced before his eyes and they buzzed in his ears. He didn't know whether they flew high or low, or in what direction they were travelling.

After a bit, he regained just enough sense to understand that he ought to find out where the geese were taking him. But this was not so easy, for he didn't know how he should ever muster up courage enough to look down. He was sure he'd faint if he attempted it.

The wild geese were not flying very high because the new travelling companion could not breathe in the very thinnest air. For his sake they also flew a little slower than usual.

At last the boy just made himself cast one glance down to earth. Then he thought that a great big rug lay spread beneath him, which was made up of an incredible number of large and small checks.

"Where in all the world am I now?" he wondered.

He saw nothing but check upon check. Some were broad and ran crosswise, and some were long and narrow—all over, there were angles and corners. Nothing was round, and nothing was crooked.

"What kind of a big, checked cloth is this that I'm looking down on?" said the boy to himself without expecting anyone to answer him.

But instantly, the wild geese who flew about him, called out: "Fields and meadows. Fields and meadows."

Then he understood that the big, checked

cloth he was travelling over was the flat
land of southern Sweden; and he began to
comprehend why it looked so checked and
multi-coloured. The bright green checks he
recognised first; they were rye fields that
had been sown in the fall, and had kept themselves green under the winter snows. The
yellowish-gray checks were stubble-fields—
the remains of the oat-crop which had grown
there the summer before. The brownish
ones were old clover meadows: and the black
ones, deserted grazing lands or ploughed-up
fallow pastures. The brown checks with
the yellow edges were, undoubtedly, beech-
tree forests; for in these you'll find the big
trees which grow in the heart of the forest
—naked in winter; while the little beech-
trees, which grow along the borders, keep
their dry, yellowed leaves way into the spring.
There were also dark checks with gray centres:
these were the large, built-up estates encircled by the small cottages with their blacken-
ing straw roofs, and their stone-divided land-
plots. And then there were checks green in
the middle with brown borders: these were

the orchards, where the grass-carpets were
already turning green, although the trees and
bushes around them were still in their nude,
brown bark.

The boy could not keep from laughing
when he saw how checked everything looked.

But when the wild geese heard him laugh,
they called out—kind o' reprovingly: "Fertile
and good land.   Fertile and good land."

The boy had already become serious.
"To think that you can laugh; you, who
have met with the most terrible misfortune
that can possibly happen to a human being!"
thought he.   And for a moment he was pretty
serious; but it was n't long before he was
laughing again.

Now that he had grown somewhat accustomed to the ride and the speed, so that he
could think of something besides holding
himself on the gander's back, he began to
notice how full the air was of birds flying
northward.   And there was a shouting and
a calling from flock to flock.   "So you came
over to-day?" shrieked some.   "Yes," answered
the geese.   "How do you think the spring's

getting on?" "Not a leaf on the trees and ice-cold water in the lakes," came back the answer.

When the geese flew over a place where they saw any tame, half-naked fowl, they shouted: "What's the name of this place? What's the name of this place?" Then the roosters cocked their heads and answered: "Its name's Lillgarde this year—the same as last year; the same as last year."

Most of the cottages were probably named after their owners—which is the custom in Skåne. But instead of saying this is "Per Matssons," or "Ola Bossons," the roosters hit upon the kind of names which, to their way of thinking, were more appropriate. Those who lived on small farms, and belonged to poor cottagers, cried: "This place is called Grainscarce." And those who belonged to the poorest hut-dwellers screamed: "The name of this place is Little-to-eat, Little-to-eat, Little-to-eat."

The big, well-cared-for farms got high-sounding names from the roosters—such as Luckymeadow, Eggberga and Moneyville.

But the roosters on the great landed estates were too high and mighty to condescend to anything like jesting. One of them crowed and called out with such gusto that it sounded as if he wanted to be heard clear up to the sun: "This is Herr Dybeck's estate; the same this year as last year; this year as last year."

A little further on strutted one rooster who crowed: "This is Swanholm, surely all the world knows that!"

The boy observed that the geese did not fly straight forward; but zigzagged hither and thither over the whole South country, just as though they were glad to be in Skåne again and wanted to pay their respects to every separate place.

They came to one place where there were a number of big, clumsy-looking buildings with great, tall chimneys, and all around these were a lot of smaller houses. "This is Jordberga Sugar Refinery," cried the roosters. The boy shuddered as he sat there on the goose's back. He ought to have recognised this place, for it was not very far from his home.

Here he had worked the year before as a watch boy; but, to be sure, nothing was exactly like itself when one saw it like that—from up above.

And think! Just think! Osa the goose girl and little Mats, who were his comrades last year! Indeed the boy would have been glad to know if they still were anywhere about here. Fancy what they would have said, had they suspected that he was flying over their heads!

Soon Jordberga was lost to sight, and they travelled toward Svedala and Skaber Lake and back again over Görringe Cloister and Häckeberga. The boy saw more of Skåne in this one day than he had ever seen before —in all the years that he had lived.

Whenever the wild geese happened across any tame geese, they had the best fun! They flew forward very slowly and called down: "We're off to the hills. Are you coming along? Are you coming along?"

But the tame geese answered: "It's still winter in this country. You're out too soon. Fly back! Fly back!"

The wild geese lowered themselves that they might be heard a little better, and called: "Come along! We'll teach you how to fly and swim."

Then the tame geese got mad and wouldn't answer them with a single honk.

The wild geese sank themselves still lower— until they almost touched the ground—then, quick as lightning, they raised themselves, just as if they'd been terribly frightened. "Oh, oh, oh!" they exclaimed. "Those things were not geese. They were only sheep, they were only sheep."

The ones on the ground were beside themselves with rage and shrieked: "May you be shot, the whole lot o' you! The whole lot o' you!"

When the boy heard all this teasing he laughed. Then he remembered how badly things had gone with him, and he cried. But the next second, he was laughing again.

Never before had he ridden so fast; and to ride fast and recklessly—that he had always liked. And, of course, he had never dreamed that it could be as fresh and bracing as it

was, up in the air; or that there rose from
the earth such a fine scent of resin and soil.
Nor had he ever dreamed what it could be
like—to ride so high above the earth. It was
just like flying away from sorrow and trouble
and annoyances of every kind that could be
thought of.

II

AKKA FROM KEBNEKAISE

EVENING

THE big tame goosey-gander that had followed them up in the air, felt very proud of being permitted to travel back and forth over the south country with the wild geese, and crack jokes with the tame birds. But in spite of his keen delight, he began to tire as the afternoon wore on. He tried to take deeper breaths and quicker wing-strokes, but even so he remained several goose-lengths behind the others.

When the wild geese, who flew last, noticed that the tame one couldn't keep up with them, they began to call to the goose who rode in the centre of the angle and led the procession: "Akka from Kebnekaise! Akka from Kebnekaise!" "What do you want of me?" asked the leader. "The white one will be

left behind; the white one will be left behind."
"Tell him it's easier to fly fast than slow!"
called the leader, and raced on as before.

The goosey-gander certainly tried to follow
the advice, and increase his speed; but then
he became so exhausted that he sank way
down to the drooping willows that bordered the
fields and meadows.

"Akka, Akka, Akka from Kebnekaise!"
cried those who flew last and saw what a hard
time he was having. "What do you want
now?" asked the leader—and she sounded
awfully angry. "The white one sinks to the
earth; the white one sinks to the earth."
"Tell him it's easier to fly high than low!"
shouted the leader, and she didn't slow up
the least little bit, but raced on as before.

The goosey-gander tried also to follow this
advice; but when he wanted to raise himself, he became so winded that he almost
burst his breast.

"Akka, Akka!" again cried those who
flew last. "Can't you let me fly in peace?"
asked the leader, and she sounded even
madder than before.

"The white one is ready to collapse."
"Tell him that he who has not the strength
to fly with the flock, can go back home!"
cried the leader. She certainly had no idea
of decreasing her speed—but raced on as before.

"Oh! is that the way the wind blows,"
thought the goosey-gander. He understood
at once that the wild geese had never intended
to take him along up to Lappland. They
had only lured him away from home in sport.

He felt thoroughly exasperated. To think
that his strength should fail him now, so
he wouldn't be able to show these tramps
that even a tame goose was good for something! But the most provoking thing of all was
that he had fallen in with Akka from Kebnekaise. Tame goose that he was, he had heard
about a leader goose, named Akka, who was
more than a hundred years old. She had such
a big name that the best wild geese in the world
followed her. But no one had such a contempt for tame geese as Akka and her flock,
and gladly would he have shown them that
he was their equal.

He flew slowly behind the rest, while he

deliberated whether he should turn back or continue. Finally, the little creature that he carried on his back said: "Dear Morten Goosey-gander, you know well enough that it is simply impossible for you, who have never flown, to go with the wild geese all the way up to Lappland. Won't you turn back before you kill yourself?"

But the farmer's lad was about the worst thing the goosey-gander knew anything about, and as soon as it had dawned on him that this puny creature actually believed that he couldn't make the trip, he decided to stick it out. "If you say another word about this, I'll drop you into the first ditch we ride over!" said he, and at the same time his fury gave him so much strength that he began to fly almost as well as any of the others.

It isn't likely that he could have kept this pace up very long, neither was it necessary; for, just then, the sun sank quickly; and at sunset the geese flew down, and before the boy and the goosey-gander knew what had happened, they stood on the shores of Vomb Lake.

" They probably intend that we shall spend the night here," thought the boy, and jumped down from the goose's back.

He stood on a narrow beach by a fair-sized lake. It was ugly to look upon, because it was almost entirely covered with an ice-crust that was blackened and uneven and full of cracks and holes—as spring ice generally is.

The ice was already breaking up. It was loose and floating and had a broad belt of dark, shiny water all around it; but there was still enough of it left to spread chill and winter terror over the place.

On the other side of the lake there appeared to be an open and light country, but where the geese had lighted there was a thick pine-growth. It looked as if the forest of firs and pines had the power to bind the winter to itself. Everywhere else the ground was bare; but beneath the sharp pine-branches lay snow that had been melting and freezing, melting and freezing, until it was as hard as ice.

The boy thought he had struck an arctic wilderness, and he was so miserable that he wanted to scream. He was hungry too.

He hadn't eaten a bite the whole day. But where should he find any food? Nothing eatable grew on either ground or tree in the month of March.

Yes, where was he to find food, and who would give him shelter, and who would fix his bed, and who would protect him from the wild beasts?

For now the sun was away and frost came from the lake, and darkness sank down from heaven, and terror stole forward on the twilight's trail, and in the forest it began to patter and rustle.

Now the good humour which the boy had felt when he was up in the air, was gone, and in his misery he looked around for his travelling companions. He had no one but them to cling to now.

Then he saw that the goosey-gander was having even a worse time of it than he. He was lying prostrate on the spot where he had alighted; and it looked as if he were ready to die. His neck lay flat against the ground, his eyes were closed, and his breathing sounded like a feeble hissing.

"Dear Morten Goosey-Gander," said the boy, "try to get a swallow of water! It isn't two steps to the lake."

But the goosey-gander didn't stir.

The boy had certainly been cruel to all animals, and to the goosey-gander in times gone by; but now he felt that the goosey-gander was the only comfort he had left, and he was dreadfully afraid of losing him.

At once the boy began to push and drag him, to get him into the water, but the goosey-gander was big and heavy, and it was mighty hard work for the boy; but at last he succeeded.

The goosey-gander got in head first. For an instant he lay motionless in the slime, but soon he poked up his head, shook the water from his eyes and sniffed. Then he swam, proudly, between reeds and seaweed.

The wild geese were in the lake before him. They had not looked around for either the goosey-gander or for his rider, but had made straight for the water. They had bathed and primped, and now they lay and gulped half-rotten pond-weed and water-clover.

"The goosey-gander got in—head first"

The white goosey-gander had the good fortune to spy a perch. He grabbed it quickly, swam ashore with it, and laid it down in front of the boy. "Here's a thank you for helping me into the water," said he.

It was the first time the boy had heard a friendly word that day. He was so happy that he wanted to throw his arms around the goosey-gander's neck, but he refrained; and he was also thankful for the gift. At first he must have thought that it would be impossible to eat raw fish, and then he had a notion to try it.

He felt to see, if he still had his sheath-knife with him; and, sure enough, there it hung— on the back button of his trousers, although it was so diminished that it was hardly as long as a match. Well, at any rate, it served to scale and cleanse fish with; and it wasn't long before the perch was eaten.

When the boy had satisfied his hunger, he felt a little ashamed because he had been able to eat a raw thing. "It's evident that I'm not a human being any longer, but a real elf," thought he.

While the boy ate, the goosey-gander stood silently beside him. But when he had swallowed the last bite, he said in a low voice: "It's a fact that we have run across a stuck-up goose folk who despise all tame birds."

"Yes, I've observed that," said the boy.

"What a triumph it would be for me if I could follow them clear up to Lappland, and show them that even a tame goose can do things!"

"Y-e-e-s," said the boy, and drawled it out because he didn't believe the goosey-gander could ever do it; yet he didn't wish to contradict him. "But I don't think I can get along all alone on such a journey," said the goosey-gander. "I'd like to ask if you couldn't come along and help me?" The boy, of course, hadn't expected anything but to return to his home as soon as possible, and he was so surprised that he hardly knew what he should reply. "I thought that we were enemies, you and I," said he. But this the goosey-gander seemed to have forgotten entirely. He only remembered that the boy had but just saved his life.

"I suppose I really ought to go home to father and mother," said the boy. "Oh! I'll get you back to them some time in the fall," said the goosey-gander. "I shall not leave you until I put you down on your own doorstep."

The boy thought it might be just as well for him if he escaped showing himself before his parents for a while. He was not disinclined to favour the scheme, and was just on the point of saying that he agreed to it— when they heard a loud rumbling behind them. It was the wild geese who had come up from the lake—all at one time—and stood shaking the water from their backs. After that they arranged themselves in a long row —with the leader-goose in the centre—and came toward them.

As the white goosey-gander sized up the wild geese, he felt ill at ease. He had expected that they should be more like tame geese, and that he should feel a closer kinship with them. They were much smaller than he, and none of them were white. They were all gray with a sprinkling of brown. He

was almost afraid of their eyes. They were
yellow, and shone as if a fire had been kindled
back of them. The goosey-gander had always
been taught that it was most fitting to move
slowly and with a rolling motion, but these
creatures did not walk—they half ran. He
grew most alarmed, however, when he looked
at their feet. These were large, and the soles
were torn and ragged-looking. It was evident that the wild geese never questioned
what they tramped upon. They took no
by-paths. They were very neat and well
cared for in other respects, but one could see by
their feet that they were poor wilderness-folk.

The goosey-gander only had time to whisper
to the boy: "Speak up quickly for yourself,
but don't tell them who you are!"—before
the geese were upon them.

When the wild geese had stopped in front
of them, they curtsied with their necks
many times, and the goosey-gander did like-
wise many more times. As soon as the
ceremonies were over, the leader-goose said:
"Now I presume we shall hear what kind of
creatures you are."

"There isn't much to tell about me," said the goosey-gander. "I was born in Skanor last spring. In the fall I was sold to Holger Nilsson of West Vemminghög, and there I have lived ever since." "You don't seem to have any pedigree to boast of," said the leader-goose. "What is it, then, that makes you so high-minded that you wish to associate with wild geese?" "It may be because I want to show you wild geese that we tame ones may also be good for something," said the goosey-gander. "Yes, it would be well if you could show us that," said the leader-goose, "We have already observed how much you know about flying; but you are more skilled, perhaps, in other sports. Possibly you are strong in a swimming match?" "No, I can't boast that I am," said the goosey-gander. It seemed to him that the leader-goose had already made up her mind to send him home, so he didn't much care how he answered. "I never swam any farther than across a marl-ditch," he continued. "Then I presume you're a crack sprinter," said the goose. "I have never seen a tame goose run, nor have

I ever done it myself," said the goosey-
gander; and he made things appear much
worse than they really were.

The big white one was sure now that the
leader-goose would say that under no cir-
cumstances could they take him along. He
was very much astonished when she said:
"You answer questions courageously; and
he who has courage can become a good travelling companion, even if he is ignorant in the
beginning. What do you say to stopping
with us for a couple of days, until we can
see what you are good for?" "That suits
me!" said the goosey-gander—and he was
thoroughly happy.

Thereupon the leader-goose pointed with
her bill and said: "But who is that you
have with you? I've never seen anything
like him before." "That's my comrade,"
said the goosey-gander. "He's been a goose-
tender all his life. He'll be useful all right to
take with us on the trip." "Yes, he may be
all right for a tame goose," answered the wild
one. "What do you call him?" "He has
several names," said the goosey-gander—

hesitatingly, not knowing what he should hit upon in a hurry, for he didn't want to reveal the fact that the boy had a human name. "Oh! his name is Thumbietot," he said at last. "Does he belong to the elf family?" asked the leader-goose. "At what time do you wild geese usually retire?" said the goosey-gander quickly—trying to evade that last question. "My eyes close of their own accord about this time."

One could easily see that the goose who talked with the gander was very old. Her entire feather outfit was ice-gray, without any dark streaks. The head was larger, the legs coarser, and the feet were more worn than any of the others. The feathers were stiff; the shoulders knotty; the neck thin. All this was due to age. It was only upon the eyes that time had had no effect. They shone brighter—as if they were younger—than any of the others!

She turned, very haughtily, toward the goosey-gander. "Understand, Mr. Tame-goose that I am Akka from Kebnekaise! And that the goose who flies nearest me—to the

right—is Iksi from Vassijaure, and the one
to the left, is Kaksi from Nuolja! Understand, also, that the second right-hand goose
is Kolmi from Sarjektjakko, and the second,
left, is Neljä from Svappavaara; and behind
them fly Viisi from Oviksfjällen and Kuusi
from Sjangeli! And know that these, as
well as the six goslings who fly last—three to
the right, and three to the left—are all high
mountain geese of the finest breed! You
must not take us for land-lubbers who strike
up a chance acquaintance with any and everyone! And you must not think that we permit anyone to share our quarters, that will
not tell us who his ancestors were."

When Akka, the leader-goose, talked in
this way, the boy stepped briskly forward.
It had distressed him that the goosey-gander,
who had spoken up so glibly for himself,
should give such evasive answers when it
concerned him. "I don't care to make a
secret of who I am," said he. "My name is
Nils Holgersson. I'm a farmer's son, and,
until to-day, I have been a human being;
but this morning—" He got no further.

As soon as he had said that he was human the leader-goose staggered three steps backward, and the rest of them even farther back. They all extended their necks and hissed angrily at him.

"I have suspected this ever since I first saw you here on these shores," said Akka; "and now you can clear out of here at once. We tolerate no human beings among us."

"It isn't possible," said the goosey-gander, meditatively, "that you wild geese can be afraid of anyone who is so tiny! By to-morrow, of course, he'll turn back home. You can surely let him stay with us overnight. None of us can afford to let such a poor little creature wander off by himself in the night—among weasels and foxes!"

The wild goose came nearer. But it was evident that it was hard for her to master her fear. "I have been taught to fear everything in human shape—be it big or little," said she. "But if you will answer for this one, and swear that he will not harm us, he can stay with us to-night. But I don't believe our night quarters are suitable either for him or you, for we intend to roost on the broken ice out here."

She thought, of course, that the goosey-gander would be doubtful when he heard this, but he never let on. "She is pretty wise who knows how to choose such a safe bed," said he.

"You will be answerable for his return to his own to-morrow."

"Then I, too, will have to leave you," said the goosey-gander. "I have sworn that I would not forsake him."

"You are free to fly whither you will," said the leader-goose.

With this, she raised her wings and flew out over the ice and one after another the wild geese followed her.

The boy was very sad to think that his trip to Lappland would not come off, and, in the bargain, he was afraid of the chilly night quarters. "It will be worse and worse," said he. "In the first place, we'll freeze to death on the ice."

But the ganᴏer was in a good humour. "There's no danger," said he. "Only make haste, I beg of you, and gather together as much grass and litter as you can well carry."

When the boy had his arms full of dried grass, the goosey-gander grabbed him by the shirt-band, lifted him, and flew out on the ice, where the wild geese were already fast asleep, with their bills tucked under their wings.

"Now spread out the grass on the ice, so there'll be something to stand on, to keep me from freezing fast. You help me and I'll help you," said the goosey-gander.

This the boy did. And when he had finished, the goosey-gander picked him up, once again, by the shirt-band, and tucked him under his wing. "I think you'll lie snug and warm there," said the goosey-gander as he covered him with his wing.

The boy was so imbedded in down that he couldn't answer; and he was nice and comfy. Oh, but he was tired!—And in less than two winks he was fast asleep.

NIGHT

It is a fact that ice is always treacherous and not to be trusted. In the middle of the night the loosened ice-cake on Vomb Lake

moved about, until one corner of it touched
the shore. Now it happened that Mr. Smirre
Fox, who lived at this time in Övid Cloister
Park—on the east side of the lake—caught
a glimpse of that one corner, while he was out
on his night chase. Smirre had seen the wild
geese early in the evening, and hadn't dared
to hope that he might get at one of them,
but now he walked right out on the ice.

When Smirre was very near to the geese,
his claws scraped the ice, and the geese awoke,
flapped their wings, and prepared for flight.
But Smirre was too quick for them. He
darted forward as though he'd been shot;
grabbed a goose by the wing, and ran toward
land again.

But this night the wild geese were not alone
on the ice, for they had a human being among
them—little as he was. The boy had awakened when the goosey-gander spread his wings.
He had tumbled down on the ice and was
sitting there, dazed. He hadn't grasped the
whys and wherefores of all this confusion, until
he caught sight of a little long-legged dog
who ran over the ice with a goose in his mouth.

In a minute the boy was after that dog, to try and take the goose away from him. He must have heard the goosey-gander call to him: "Have a care, Thumbietot! Have a care!" But the boy thought that such a little runt of a dog was nothing to be afraid of and he rushed ahead.

The wild goose that Smirre Fox tugged after him, heard the clatter as the boy's wooden shoes beat against the ice, and she could hardly believe her ears. "Does that infant think he can take me away from the fox?" she wondered. And in spite of her misery, she began to cackle right merrily, deep down in her windpipe. It was almost as if she had laughed.

"The first thing he knows, he'll fall through a crack in the ice," thought she.

But dark as the night was, the boy saw distinctly all the cracks and holes there were, and took daring leaps over them. This was because he had the elf's good eyesight now, and could see in the dark. He saw both lake and shore just as clearly as if it had been daylight.

Smirre Fox left the ice where it touched the
shore. And just as he was working his way
up to the land-edge, the boy shouted to him:
"Drop that goose, you sneak!" Smirre didn't
know who was calling to him, and wasted no
time in looking around, but increased his
pace.

The fox made straight for the forest and the
boy followed him, with never a thought of the
danger he was running. On the contrary, he
thought all the while about the contemptuous
way in which he had been received by the
wild geese that evening; and he made up his
mind to let them see that a human being was
something higher than all else created.

He shouted, again and again, to that dog,
to make him drop his game. "What kind of
a dog are you, who can steal a whole goose and
not feel ashamed of yourself? Drop her at
once! or you'll see what a beating you'll get.
Drop her, I say, or I'll tell your master how
you behave!"

When Smirre Fox saw that he had been mistaken for a scary dog, he was so amused that
he came near dropping the goose. Smirre

was a great plunderer who wasn't satisfied
with only hunting rats and pigeons in the
fields, but he also ventured into the farm-
yards to steal chickens and geese. He knew
that he was feared throughout the district;
and anything as idiotic as this he had not
heard since he was a baby.

The boy ran so fast that the thick beech-
trees appeared to be running past him—backward, but he caught up with Smirre. Finally,
he was so close to him that he got a hold on
his tail. "Now I'll take the goose from you
anyway," cried he, and held on as hard as
ever he could, but he hadn't strength enough
to stop Smirre. The fox dragged him along
until the dry foliage whirled around him.

But now it began to dawn on Smirre how
harmless the thing was that pursued him.
He stopped short, put the goose on the ground,
and stood on her with his forepaws, so she
couldn't fly away. He was just about to bite
off her neck—but then he couldn't resist the
desire to tease the boy a little. "Hurry off
and complain to the master, for now I'm
going to bite the goose to death!" said he.

Certainly the one who was surprised when he saw what a pointed nose, and heard what a hoarse and angry voice that dog which he was pursuing had,—was the boy! But now he was so enraged because the fox had made fun of him, that he never thought of being frightened. He took a firmer hold on the tail, braced himself against a beech trunk; and just as the fox opened his jaws over the goose's throat, he pulled as hard as he could. Smirre was so astonished that he let himself be pulled backward a couple of steps—and the wild goose got away. She fluttered upward feebly and heavily. One wing was so badly wounded that she could barely use it. In addition to this, she could not see in the night darkness of the forest but was as helpless as the blind. Therefore she could in no way help the boy; so she groped her way through the branches and flew down to the lake again.

Then Smirre made a dash for the boy. "If I don't get the one, I shall certainly have the other," said he; and you could tell by his voice how mad he was. "Oh, don't you

" ......and the wild goose got away"

believe it!'' said the boy, who was in the best
of spirits because he had saved the goose.   He
held himself fast by the fox-tail, and swung
with it—to one side—when the fox tried to
catch him.

There was such a dance in that forest that
the dry beech-leaves fairly flew! Smirre swung
round and round, but the tail swung too;
while the boy kept a tight grip on it, so the
fox couldn't grab him.

The boy was so gay after his success that,
in the beginning, he only laughed and made
fun of the fox.   But Smirre was persevering
—as old hunters generally are—and the boy
began to fear that he should be captured in the
end.

Then he caught sight of a little, young
beech-tree that had shot up as slender as a
rod, that it might soon reach the free air
above the canopy of branches which the old
beeches spread over it.

Quick as a flash, he let go of the fox-tail
and climbed the beech tree.   Smirre Fox was
so excited that he continued to dance around
after his tail for a long time.

"Don't bother with the dance any longer!"
said the boy.

But Smirre couldn't endure the humiliation of his failure to get the better of such a
little tot, so he lay down under the tree, that
he might keep a close watch on him.

The boy didn't have any too good a time
of it where he sat, astride a frail branch.
The young beech did not, as yet, reach the
high branch-canopy, so the boy couldn't get
over to another tree, and he didn't dare to
come down again. He was so cold and numb
that he almost lost his hold around the
branch; and he was dreadfully sleepy; but
he didn't dare fall asleep for fear of tumbling
down.

My! but it was dismal to sit in that way the
whole night through, out in the forest! He
never before understood the real meaning
of "night." It was just as if the whole world
had become petrified, and never could come
to life again.

Then it commenced to dawn. The boy
was glad that everything began to look like
itself once more; although the chill was

even sharper than it had been during the night.

Finally, when the sun got up, it wasn't yellow but red. The boy thought it looked as though it were angry and he wondered what it was angry about. Perhaps it was because the night had made it so cold and gloomy on earth, while the sun was away.

The sunbeams came down in great clusters, to see what the night had been up to. It could be seen how everything blushed—as if they all had guilty consciences. The clouds in the skies; the satiny beech-limbs; the little intertwined branches of the forest-canopy; the hoar-frost that covered the foliage on the ground—everything grew flushed and red. More and more sunbeams came bursting through space, and soon the night's terrors were driven away, and such a marvellous lot of living things came forward. The black woodpecker, with the red neck, began to hammer with its bill on the branch. The squirrel glided from his nest with a nut, and sat down on a branch and began to shell it. The starling came

flying with a worm, and the bulfinch sang in the tree-top.

Then the boy understood that the sun had said to all these tiny creatures: "Wake up now, and come out of your nests! I'm here! Now you need be afraid of nothing."

The wild-goose call was heard from the lake, as they were preparing for flight; and soon all fourteen geese came flying through the forest. The boy tried to call to them, but they flew so high that his voice couldn't reach them. They probably believed the fox had eaten him up; and they didn't trouble themselves to look for him.

The boy came near crying with regret; but the sun stood up there—orange-coloured and happy—and put courage into the whole world. "It isn't worth while, Nils Holgersson, for you to be troubled about anything, as long as I'm here," said the sun.

GOOSE-PLAY

Monday, March twenty-first.

EVERYTHING remained unchanged in the forest—about as long as it takes a goose to eat her breakfast. But just as the morning

was verging on forenoon, a goose came flying,
all by herself, under the thick tree-canopy.
She groped her way, hesitatingly, between
the stems and branches, and flew very
slowly. As soon as Smirre Fox saw her, he
left his place under the beech tree, and sneaked
up toward her. The wild goose didn't avoid
the fox, but flew very close to him. Smirre made
a high jump for her but he missed her; and
the goose went on her way down to the lake.

It was not long before another goose came
flying. She took the same route as the first
one; and flew still lower and slower. She,
too, flew close to Smirre Fox, and he made
such a high spring for her, that his ears
brushed her feet. But she, too, got away from
him unhurt, and went her way toward the
lake, silent as a shadow.

A little while passed and then there came
another wild goose. She flew still slower and
lower; and it seemed even more difficult for
her to find her way between the beech-
branches. Smirre made a powerful spring!
He was within a hair's breadth of catching her;
but that goose also managed to save herself.

Just after she had disappeared, came a
fourth. She flew so slowly, and so badly,
that Smirre Fox thought he could catch
her without much effort, but he was afraid of
failure now, and concluded to let her fly past—
unmolested. She took the same direction
the others had taken; and just as she was
come right above Smirre, she sank down so
far that he was tempted to jump for her. He
jumped so high that he touched her with his
tail. But she flung herself quickly to one
side and saved her life.

Before Smirre got through panting, three
more geese come flying in a row. They flew
just like the rest, and Smirre made high
springs for them all, but he did not succeed
in catching any one of them.

After that came five geese; but these flew
better than the others. And although it
seemed as if they wanted to lure Smirre to
jump, he withstood the temptation. After
quite a long time came one single goose. It
was the thirteenth. This one was so old that
she was gray all over, without a dark speck
anywhere on her body. She didn't appear to

use one wing very well, but flew so wretchedly
and crookedly, that she almost touched the
ground. Smirre not only made a high leap for
her, but he pursued her, running and jumping
all the way down to the lake. But not even
this time did he get anything for his trouble.

When the fourteenth goose came along,
it looked very pretty because it was white.
And as its great wings swayed, it glistened
like a light, in the dark forest. When
Smirre Fox saw this one, he mustered all his
resources and jumped half-way up to the tree-
canopy. But the white one flew by unhurt
like the rest.

Now it was quiet for a moment under the
beeches. It looked as if the whole wild-
goose-flock had travelled past.

Suddenly Smirre remembered his prisoner
and raised his eyes toward the young beech-
tree. And just as he might have expected—
the boy had disappeared.

But Smirre didn't have much time to think
about him; for now the first goose came back
again from the lake and flew slowly under the
canopy. In spite of all his ill luck, Smirre

was glad that she came back, and darted
after her with a high leap.   But he had been
in too much of a hurry, and hadn't taken the
time to calculate the distance, and he landed
at one side of the goose.   Then there came
still another goose; then a third; a fourth;
a fifth; and so on, until the angle closed in
with the old ice-gray one, and the big white
one.   They all flew low and slow.   Just as
they swayed in the vicinity of Smirre Fox,
they sank down—kind of inviting-like—for
him to take them.   Smirre ran after them and
made leaps a couple of fathoms high—but
he couldn't manage to get hold of a single
one of them.

It was the most awful day that Smirre Fox
had ever experienced.   The wild geese kept
on travelling over his head.   They came
and went—came and went.   Great splendid
geese, who had eaten themselves fat on the
German heaths and grain fields, swayed all
day through the woods, and so close to him
that he touched them many times; yet he
was not permitted to appease his hunger with
a single one of them.

The winter was hardly gone yet, and Smirre recalled nights and days when he had been forced to tramp around in idleness, with not so much as a hare to hunt, when the rats hid themselves under the frozen earth; and when the chickens were all shut up. But all the winter's hunger had not been as hard to endure as this day's miscalculations.

Smirre was no young fox. He had had the dogs after him many a time, and had heard the bullets whizz around his ears. He had lain in hiding, down in the lair, while the dachshunds crept into the crevices and all but found him. But all the anguish that Smirre Fox had been forced to suffer under this hot chase, was not to be compared with what he suffered every time that he missed one of the wild geese.

In the morning, when the play began, Smirre Fox had looked so stunning that the geese were amazed when they saw him. Smirre loved display. His coat was a brilliant red; his breast white; his nose black; and his tail was as bushy as a plume. But when the evening of this day was come,

Smirre's coat hung in loose folds.   He was bathed in sweat; his eyes were without lustre; his tongue hung far out from his gaping jaws; and froth oozed from his mouth.

In the afternoon Smirre was so exhausted that he grew delirious.   He saw nothing before his eyes but flying geese.   He made leaps for sun-spots which he saw on the ground; and for a poor little butterfly that had come out of his chrysalis too soon.

The wild geese flew and flew, unceasingly. All day long they continued to torment Smirre.   They were not moved to pity because Smirre was done up, fevered, and out of his head.   They continued without a let-up, although they understood that he hardly saw them, and that he jumped after their shadows.

When Smirre Fox sank down on a pile of dry leaves, weak and powerless and almost ready to give up the ghost, they stopped teasing him.

"Now you know, Mr. Fox, what happens to the one who dares to come near Akka of Kebnekaise!" they shouted in his ear; and with that they left him in peace.

III

THE WONDERFUL JOURNEY
OF NILS

ON THE FARM

Thursday, March twenty-fourth.

JUST at that time a thing happened in Skåne which created a good deal of discussion and even got into the newspapers but which many believed to be a fable, because they had not been able to explain it.

It was about like this: A lady squirrel had been captured in the hazelbrush that grew on the shores of Vomb Lake, and was carried to a farmhouse close by. All the folks on the farm—both young and old—were delighted with the pretty creature with the bushy tail, the wise, inquisitive eyes, and the natty little feet. They intended to amuse themselves all summer by watching its nimble movements; its ingenious way of shelling

nuts; and its droll play. They immediately
put in order an old squirrel cage with a little
green house and a wire-cylinder wheel. The
little house, which had both doors and windows,
the lady squirrel was to use as a dining room
and bedroom. For this reason they placed
therein a bed of leaves, a bowl of milk and
some nuts. The cylinder wheel, on the other
hand, she was to use as a play-house, where
she could run and climb and swing round.

The people believed that they had arranged
things very comfortably for the lady squirrel,
and they were astonished because she didn't
seem to be contented; but, instead, she sat
there, downcast and moody, in a corner of
her room. Every now and again, she would
let out a shrill, agonised cry. She did not
touch the food; and not once did she swing
round on the wheel. "It's probably because
she's frightened," said the farmer folk. "To-
morrow, when she feels more at home, she
will both eat and play."

Meanwhile, the women folk on the farm
were making preparations for a feast; and
just on that day when the lady squirrel had

been captured, they were busy with an elaborate bake. They had had bad luck with something: either the dough wouldn't rise, or else they had been dilatory, for they were obliged to work long after dark.

Naturally there was a great deal of excitement and bustle in the kitchen, and probably no one there took time to think about the squirrel, or to wonder how she was getting on. But there was an old grandma in the house who was too aged to take a hand in the baking; this she herself understood, but just the same she did not relish the idea of being left out of the game. She felt rather downhearted; and for this reason she did not go to bed but seated herself by the sitting-room window and looked out.

They had opened the kitchen door on account of the heat; and through it a clear ray of light streamed out on the yard; and it became so well lighted out there that the old woman could see all the cracks and holes in the plastering on the wall opposite. She also saw the squirrel cage which hung just where the light fell clearest. And she noticed how the squirrel ran from her room to the wheel, and from the wheel to her room, all night long, without stopping an instant. She thought it was a strange sort of unrest that had come over the animal; but she believed, of course, that the strong light kept her awake.

Between the cow-house and the stable there was a broad, handsome carriage-gate; this too came within the light-radius. As the night wore on, the old grandma saw a tiny creature, no bigger than a hand's breadth, cautiously steal his way through the gate. He was dressed in leather breeches and wooden shoes like any other working man. The old grandma knew at once that it was the elf, and she was not the least bit frightened. She had always heard that the elf kept himself somewhere about the place, although she had never seen him before; and an elf, to be sure, brought good luck wherever he appeared.

As soon as the elf came into the stone-paved yard, he ran right up to the squirrel-cage. And since it hung so high that he could not reach it, he went over to the storehouse after a rod; placed it against the cage, and swung himself up—in the same way that a sailor climbs a rope. When he had reached the cage, he shook the door of the little green house as if he wanted to open it; but the old grandma didn't move; for she knew that the children had put a padlock on the door, as they feared that the boys on the neighbouring farms would try to steal the squirrel. The old woman saw that when the boy could not get the door open, the lady squirrel came out to the wire wheel. There they held a long conference together. And when the boy had listened to all that the imprisoned animal had to say to him, he slid down the rod to the ground, and ran out through the carriage-gate.

The old woman didn't expect to see anything more of the elf that night, nevertheless, she remained at the window. After a few moments had gone by, he returned. He was in such a hurry that it seemed to her as though his feet hardly touched the ground; and he rushed right up to the squirrel cage.

The old woman, with her far-sighted eyes, saw him distinctly; and she also saw that he carried something in his hands; but what it was she couldn't imagine. The thing he carried in his left hand he laid down on the pavement; but that which he held in his right hand he took with him to the cage. He kicked so hard with his wooden shoes on the little window that the glass was broken. He poked in the thing which he held in his hand to the lady squirrel. Then he slid down again, and took up that which he had laid upon the ground, and climbed up to the cage with that also. The next instant he ran off again with such haste that the old woman could hardly follow him with her eyes.

But now it was the old grandma who could no longer sit still in the cottage; but who, very slowly, went out to the back yard and stationed herself in the shadow of the pump to await the elf's return. And there was one other who had also seen him and had become curious. This was the house cat. He crept along slyly and stopped close to the wall, just two steps away from the stream of light. They both stood and waited, long and patiently, on that chilly March night, and the old woman was just beginning to think about going in again, when she heard a clatter on the pavement, and saw that the little mite of an elf came trotting along once more, carrying a burden in each hand, as he had done before. That which he bore squealed and squirmed. And now a light dawned on the old grandma. She understood that the elf had hurried down to the hazel-grove and brought back the lady squirrel's babies; and that he was carrying them to her so they shouldn't starve to death.

The old grandma stood very still, so as not to disturb them; and it did not look as if the elf had noticed her. He was just going to lay one of the babies on the ground so that he could swing himself up to the cage with the other one—when he saw the house cat's green eyes glisten close beside him. He stood there, bewildered, with a young one in each hand.

He turned around and looked in all directions; then he became aware of the old

grandma's presence. Then he did not hesitate long; but walked forward, stretched his arms as high as he could reach, for her to take one of the baby squirrels.

The old grandma did not wish to prove herself unworthy of the confidence, so she bent down and took the baby squirrel, and stood there and held it until the boy had swung himself up to the cage with the other one. Then he came back for the one he had entrusted to her care.

The next morning, when the farm folk had gathered together for breakfast, it was impossible for the old woman to refrain from telling them of what she had seen the night before. They all laughed at her, of course, and said that she had been only dreaming. There were no baby squirrels this early in the year.

But she was sure of her ground, and begged them to take a look into the squirrel cage and this they did. And there lay on the bed of leaves, four tiny half-naked, half-blind baby squirrels, who were at least a couple of days old.

When the farmer himself saw the young ones, he said: "Be it as it may with this; but one thing is certain, we, on this farm, have behaved in such a manner that we are shamed before both animals and human beings." And, thereupon, he took the mother squirrel and all her young ones from the cage, and laid them in the old grandma's lap. "Go thou out to the hazel-grove with them," said he, "and let them have their freedom back again!"

It was this event that was so much talked about, and which even got into the newspapers, but which the majority would not credit because they were not able to explain how anything like that could have happened.

VITTSKÖVLE

Saturday, March twenty-sixth.

Two days later, another strange thing happened. A flock of wild geese came flying one morning, and lit on a meadow down in Eastern Skåne not very far from Vittskövle manor. In the flock were thirteen wild geese, of the usual gray variety, and one white

goosey-gander, who carried on his back a tiny
lad dressed in yellow leather breeches, green
vest, and a white woollen toboggan hood.

They were now very near the Eastern sea;
and on the meadow where the geese had
alighted the soil was sandy, as it usually is
on the sea-coast. It looked as if, formerly,
there had been flying sand in this vicinity
which had to be held down; for in several
directions large, planted pine-woods could
be seen.

When the wild geese had been feeding a
while, several children came along, and
walked on the edge of the meadow. The
goose who was on guard at once raised herself into the air with noisy wing-strokes, so
the whole flock should hear that there was
danger on foot. All the wild geese flew
upward; but the white one trotted along on
the ground unconcerned. When he saw the
others fly he raised his head and called after
them: "You needn't fly away from these!
They are only a couple of children!"

The little creature who had been riding on
his back, sat down upon a knoll on the

outskirts of the wood and picked a pine-cone in pieces, that he might get at the seeds. The children were so close to him that he did not dare to run across the meadow to the white one. He concealed himself under a big, dry thistle-leaf, and at the same time gave a warning-cry. But the white one had evidently made up his mind not to let himself be scared. He walked along on the ground all the while; and not once did he look to see in what direction they were going.

Meanwhile, they turned from the path, walked across the field, getting nearer and nearer to the goosey-gander. When he finally did look up, they were right upon him. He was so dumfounded, and became so confused, he forgot that he could fly, and tried to get out of their reach by running. But the children followed, chasing him into a ditch, and there they caught him. The larger of the two stuck him under his arm and carried him off.

When the boy, who lay under the thistle-leaf saw this, he sprang up as if he wanted to take the goosey-gander away from them;

then he must have remembered how little and powerless he was, for he threw himself on the knoll and beat upon the ground with his clenched fists.

The goosey-gander cried with all his might for help: "Thumbietot, come and help me! Oh, Thumbietot, come and help me!" The boy began to laugh in the midst of his distress. "Oh, yes! I'm just the right one to help anybody, I am!" said he.

Anyway he got up and followed the goosey-gander. "I can't help him," said he, "but I shall at least find out where they are taking him."

The children had a good start; but the boy had no difficulty in keeping them within sight until they came to a hollow where a brook gushed forth. But here he was obliged to run alongside of it for some little time, before he could find a place narrow enough for him to jump over.

When he came up from the hollow the children had disappeared. He could see their footprints on a narrow path which led to the woods, and these he continued to follow.

Soon he came to a cross-road. **Here the** children must have separated, for there **were** footprints in two directions.   The boy looked now as if all hope had fled.   Then he saw a little white down on a heather-knoll, and he understood that the goosey-gander had dropped this by the wayside to let him know in which direction he had been carried; **and** therefore he continued his search.   He followed the children through the entire wood. The goosey-gander he did not see; but whereever he was likely to miss his way, lay a little white down to put him right.

The boy continued faithfully to **follow the** bits of down.   They led him out of the **wood**, across a couple of meadows, up on a road, **and** finally through the entrance of a broad *allée*. At the end of the *alleé* there were gables **and** towers of red tiling, decorated with bright borders and other ornamentations that glittered and shone.   When the boy saw **that** this was some great manor, he thought **he** knew what had become of the goosey-gander. "No doubt the children have carried **the** goosey-gander to the manor and **sold him** there. By this time he's probably butchered," he said to himself. But he did not seem to be satisfied with anything less than proof positive, and with renewed courage he ran forward. He met no one in the *allée*—and that was well, for such as he are generally afraid of being seen by human beings.

The mansion which he came to was a splendid, old-time structure with four great wings which inclosed a courtyard. On the east wing, there was a high arch leading into the courtyard. This far the boy ran without hesitation, but when he got there he stopped. He dared not venture farther, but stood still and pondered what he should do now.

There he stood, with his finger on his nose, thinking, when he heard footsteps behind him; and as he turned around he saw a whole company march up the *allée*. In haste he stole behind a water-barrel which stood near the arch, and hid himself.

Those who came up were some twenty young men from a folk-high-school, out on a pedestrian tour. They were accompanied by one of the instructors. When they were

come as far as the arch, the teacher requested
them to wait there a moment, while he went
in and asked if they might see the old castle
of Vittskövle.

The newcomers were warm and tired; as
if they had been on a long tramp. One of
them was so thirsty that he went over to the
water-barrel and stooped down to drink. He
had a tin box such as botanists use hang-
ing about his neck. He evidently thought
that this was in his way, for he threw it down
on the ground. With this, the lid flew open,
and one could see that there were a few spring
flowers in it.

The botanist's box dropped just in front of
the boy; and he must have thought that here
was his opportunity to get into the castle and
find out what had become of the goosey-
gander. He smuggled himself quickly into
the box and concealed himself as well as he
could under the anemones and colts-foot.

He was hardly hidden before the young man
picked the box up, hung it around his neck,
and slammed down the cover.

Then the teacher came back, and said

that they had been given permission to enter the castle. At first he conducted them no farther than the courtyard. There he stopped and began to talk to them about this ancient structure.

He called their attention to the first human beings who had inhabited this country, and who had been obliged to live in mountain-grottoes and earth-caves; in the dens of wild beasts, and in the brushwood; and that a very long period had elapsed before they learned to build themselves huts from the trunks of trees. And afterward how long had they not been forced to labour and struggle, before they had advanced from the log cabin, with its single room, to the building of a castle with a hundred rooms—like Vittskövle!

It was about three hundred and fifty years ago that the rich and powerful built such castles for themselves, he said. It was very evident that Vittskövle had been erected at a time when wars and robbers made it unsafe in Skåne. All around the castle was a deep trench filled with water; and across this there had been a bridge in bygone days that could be noisted up. Over the gate-arch there is, even to this day, a watch-tower; and all along the sides of the castle ran sentry-galleries, and in the corners stood towers with walls a metre thick. Yet the castle had not been erected in the most savage war times; for Jens Brahe, who built it, had also studied to make of it a beautiful and decorative ornament. If they could see the big, solid stone structure at Glimminge, which had been built only a generation earlier, they would readily see that Jens Holgersen Ulfstand, the builder, hadn't figured upon anything else—only to build big and strong and secure, without bestowing a thought upon making it beautiful and comfortable. If they visited such castles as Marsvinsholm, Snogeholm and Övid's Cloister—which were erected a hundred years or so later—they would find that the times had become less warlike. The gentlemen who built these places, had not furnished them with fortifications; but had only taken pains to provide themselves with great, splendid dwelling houses.

The teacher talked at length—and in

detail; and the boy who lay shut up in the
box was pretty impatient; but he must have
lain very still, for the owner of the box
hadn't the least suspicion that he was carrying
him along.

Finally the company went into the castle.
But if the boy had hoped for chance to crawl
out of that box, he was deceived; for the
student carried it upon him all the while,
and the boy was obliged to accompany him
through all the rooms. It was a tedious
tramp. The teacher stopped every other
minute to explain and instruct.

In one room he found an old fireplace, and
before this he stopped to talk about the
different kinds of fireplaces that had been
used in the course of time. The first indoors
fireplace had been a big, flat stone on the
floor of the hut, with an opening in the roof
which let in both wind and rain. The next
had been a big stone hearth with no opening
in the roof. This must have made the hut
very warm, but it also filled it with soot
and smoke. When Vittskövle was built,
the people had advanced far enough to open

the fireplace, which, at that time, had a wide
chimney for the smoke; but it also took
most of the warmth up in the air with it.

If that boy had ever in his life been cross
and impatient, he was given a good lesson
in patience that day. It must have been a
whole hour now that he had lain perfectly
still.

In the next room they came to, the teacher
stopped before an old-time bed with its high
canopy and rich curtains. Immediately he
began to talk about the beds and bed places
of olden days.

The teacher didn't hurry himself; but then
he did not know, of course, that a poor little
creature lay shut up in a botanist's box, and
only waited for him to get through. When
they came to a room with gilded leather hang-
ings, he talked to them about how the people
had dressed their walls and ceilings ever
since the beginning of time. And when he
came to an old family portrait, he told them
all about the different changes in dress. And
in the banquet halls he described ancient
customs of celebrating weddings and funerals.

Thereupon, the teacher talked a little about the excellent men and women who had lived in the castle; about the old Brahes, and the old Barnekows; of Christian Barnekow, who had given his horse to the king to help him escape; of Margareta Ascheberg who had been married to Kjell Barnekow and who, when a widow, had managed the estates and the whole district for fifty-three years; of banker Hageman, a farmer's son from Vittskövle, who had grown so rich that he had bought the entire estate; about the Stjernsvärds, who had given the people of Skåne better ploughs, which enabled them to discard the ridiculous old wooden ploughs that three oxen were hardly able to drag. During all this, the boy lay still. If he had ever been mischievous and shut the cellar door on his father or mother, he understood now how they had felt; for it was hours and hours before that teacher got through.

At last the teacher went out into the courtyard again. And there he discoursed upon the tireless labour of mankind to procure for themselves tools and weapons, clothes and houses and ornaments. He said that such an old castle as Vittskövle was a mile-post on time's highway. Here one could see how far the people had advanced three hundred and fifty years ago; and one could judge for one-self whether things had gone forward or back-ward since their time.

But this dissertation the boy escaped hear-ing; for the student who carried him was thirsty again, and stole into the kitchen to ask for a drink of water. When the boy was carried into the kitchen, he should have tried to look around for the goosey-gander. He had begun to move; and as he did this, he happened to press too hard against the lid—and it flew open. As botanists' box-lids are always flying open, the student thought no more about the matter but pressed it down again. Then the cook asked him if he had a snake in the box.

"No, I have only a few plants," the student replied. "It was certainly something that moved there," insisted the cook. The student threw back the lid to show her that she was mistaken. "See for yourself—if———"

But he got no further, for now the boy
dared not stay in the box any longer, but
with one bound he stood on the floor, and
out he rushed. The maids hardly had time
to see what it was that ran, but they hurried
after it, nevertheless.

The teacher still stood and talked when he
was interrupted by shrill cries. "Catch him,
catch him!" shrieked those who had come
from the kitchen; and all the young men
raced after the boy, who glided away faster
than a rat. They tried to intercept him at
the gate, but it was not so easy to get a hold
on such a little creature, so, luckily, he got
out in the open.

The boy did not dare to run down toward
the open *allée*, but turned in another direction.
He rushed through the garden into the back
yard. All the while the people raced after
him, shrieking and laughing. The poor little
thing ran as hard as ever he could to get out
of their way; but still it looked as though the
people would catch up with him.

As he rushed past a labourer's cottage, he
heard a goose cackle, and saw a white down

lying on the doorstep. There, at last, was
the goosey-gander! He had been on the
wrong track before. He thought no more of
housemaids and men, who were hounding
him, but climbed up the steps—and into the
hallway. Farther he couldn't come, for the
door was locked. He heard how the goosey-
gander cried and moaned inside, but he
couldn't get the door open. The hunters that
were pursuing him came nearer and nearer,
and, in the room, the goosey-gander cried more
and more pitifully. In this direst of needs
the boy finally plucked up courage and
pounded on the door with all his might.

A child opened it, and the boy looked into
the room. In the middle of the floor sat a
woman who held the goosey-gander tight—
to clip his quill-feathers. It was her children
who had found him, and she didn't want to
do him any harm. It was her intention to
let him in among her own geese, had she
only succeeded in clipping his wings so he
couldn't fly away. But a worse fate could
hardly have happened to the goosey-gander,
and he shrieked and moaned with all his might.

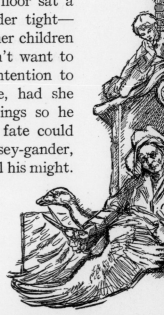

And a lucky thing it was that the woman
hadn't started the clipping sooner. Now
only two quills had fallen under the shears
when the door was opened—and the boy
stood on the door-sill. But a creature like
that the woman had never seen before. She
couldn't believe anything else but that it
was Goa-nisse himself; and in her terror she
dropped the shears, clasped her hands—and
forgot to hold on to the goosey-gander.

As soon as he felt himself freed, he ran
toward the door. He didn't give himself time
to stop; but, as he ran past him, he grabbed
the boy by the neck-band and carried him
along with him. On the stoop he spread his
wings and flew up in the air; at the same time
he made a graceful sweep with his neck and
seated the boy on his smooth, downy back.

And off they flew—while all Vittskövle
stood and stared after them.

IN ÖVID CLOISTER PARK

ALL that day, when the wild geese played
with the fox, the boy lay and slept in a
deserted squirrel nest. When he awoke,

along toward evening, he felt very uneasy.
"Well, now I shall soon be sent home again!
Then I'll have to exhibit myself before father
and mother," thought he. But when he
looked up and saw the wild geese, who lay and
bathed in Vomb Lake—not one of them said
a word about his going. "They probably think
the white one is too tired to travel home with
me to-night," thought the boy.

The next morning the geese were awake
at daybreak, long before sunrise. Now the
boy felt sure that he'd have to go home; but,
curiously enough, both he and the white
goosey-gander were permitted to follow the
wild ones on their morning tour. The boy
couldn't comprehend the reason for the delay,
but he figured it out in this way, that the
wild geese did not care to send the goosey-
gander on such a long journey until they had
both eaten their fill. Come what might, he
was only glad for every moment that should
pass before he must face his parents.

The wild geese travelled over Övid's Cloister
estate which was situated in a beautiful
park east of the lake, and looked very

imposing with its great castle; its well planned court surrounded by low walls and pavilions; its fine old-time garden with covered arbours, streams and fountains; its wonderful trees, trimmed bushes, and its evenly mown lawns with their beds of beautiful spring flowers.

When the wild geese rode over the estate in the early morning hour there was no human being about. When they had carefully assured themselves of this, they lowered themselves toward the dog kennel, and shouted: "What kind of a little hut is this? What kind of a little hut is this?"

Instantly the dog came out of his kennel— furiously angry—and barked at the air.

"Do you call this a hut, you tramps! Can't you see that this is a great stone castle? Can't you see what fine terraces, and what a lot of pretty walls and windows and great doors it has, bow, wow, wow, wow? Don't you see the grounds, can't you see the garden, can't you see the conservatories, can't you see the marble statues? You call this a hut, do you? Do huts have parks with beech-groves and hazel-bushes and trailing vines and oak trees and firs and hunting-grounds filled with game, wow, wow, wow? Do you call this a hut? Have you seen huts with so many outhouses around them that they look like a whole village? You must know of a lot of huts that have their own church and their own parsonage; and that rule over the district and the peasant homes and the neighbouring farms and barracks, wow, wow, wow? Do you call this a hut? To this hut belong the richest possessions in Skåne, you beggars! You can't see a bit of land, from where you hang in the clouds, that does not obey commands from this hut, wow, wow, wow!"

All this the dog managed to cry out in one breath; and the wild geese flew back and forth over the estate, and listened to him until he was winded. But then they cried: "What are you so mad about? We didn't ask about the castle; we only wanted to know about your kennel, stupid!"

When the boy heard this joke, he laughed; then a thought stole in on him which at once made him serious. "Think how many of these amusing things you would hear, if you

could go with the wild geese through the whole country, all the way up to Lappland!" said he to himself. "And just now, when you are in such a bad fix, a trip like that would be the best thing you could hit upon."

The wild geese travelled to one of the wide fields, east of the estate, to eat grass-roots, and they kept this up for hours. In the meantime, the boy wandered in the great park which bordered the field. He hunted up a beech-nut grove and began to look up at the bushes, to see if a nut from last fall still hung there. But again and again the thought of the trip came over him, as he walked in the park. He pictured to himself what a fine time he would have if he went with the wild geese. To freeze and starve: that he believed he should have to do often enough; but as a recompense, he would escape both work and study.

As he walked there, the old gray leader-goose came up to him, and asked if he had found anything eatable. No, that he hadn't, he replied, and then she tried to help him. She couldn't find any nuts either, but she discovered a couple of dried blossoms that hung on a brier-bush. These the boy ate with a good relish. But he wondered what mother would say, if she knew that he had lived on raw fish and old winter-dried blossoms.

When the wild geese had finally eaten themselves full, they bore off toward the lake again, where they amused themselves with games until almost dinner time.

The wild geese challenged the white goosey-gander to take part in all kinds of sports. They had swimming races, running races, and flying races with him. The big tame one did his level best to hold his own, but the clever wild geese beat him every time. All the while, the boy sat on the goosey-gander's back and encouraged him, and had as much fun as the rest. They laughed and screamed and cackled, and it was remarkable that the people on the estate didn't hear them.

When the wild geese were tired of play, they flew out on the ice and rested for a couple of hours. The afternoon they spent in pretty much the same way as the forenoon. First, a couple of hours feeding, then bathing and

play in the water near the ice-edge until sunset, when they immediately arranged themselves for sleep.

"This is just the life that suits me," thought
the boy when he crept in under the gander's
wing. "But to-morrow, I suppose I'll be
sent home."

Before he fell asleep, he lay and thought
that if he might go along with the wild geese,
he would escape all scoldings because he was
lazy.   Then he could cut loose every day, and
his only worry would be to get something to
eat.   But he needed so little nowadays; and
there would always be a way to get that.

So he pictured the whole scene to himself;
what he should see, and all the adventures
that he would be in on.   Yes, it would be
something different from the wear and tear at
home.   "If I could only go with the wild
geese on their travels, I shouldn't grieve because I'd been transformed," thought the boy.

He wasn't afraid of anything—except being
sent home; but not even on Wednesday did
the geese say anything to him about going.
That day passed in the same way as Tuesday;

and the boy grew more and more contented with the outdoor life. He thought that he had the lovely Övid Cloister park—which was as large as a forest—all to himself; and he wasn't anxious to go back to the stuffy cabin and the little patch of ground there at home.

On Wednesday he believed that the wild geese thought of keeping him with them; but on Thursday he lost hope again,

Thursday began just like the other days; the geese fed on the broad meadows, and the boy hunted for food in the park. After a while Akka came to him, and asked if he had found anything to eat. No, he had not; and then she looked up a dry caraway herb, that had kept all its tiny seeds intact.

When the boy had eaten, Akka said that she thought he ran around in the park altogether too recklessly. She wondered if he knew how many enemies he had to guard against—he, who was so little. No, he didn't know anything at all about that. Then Akka began to enumerate them for him.

Whenever he walked in the park, she said, that he must look out for the fox and the

marten; when he came to the shores of the
lake, he must think of the otters; as he sat on
the stone wall, he must not forget the
weasels, who could creep through the smallest holes; and if he wished to lie down and
sleep on a pile of leaves, he must first find
out if the adders were not sleeping their
winter sleep in the same pile. As soon as he
came out in the open fields, he should keep an
eye out for hawks and buzzards; for eagles
and falcons that soared in the air. In the
bramble-bush he could be captured by the
sparrow-hawk; magpies and crows were found
everywhere and in these he mustn't place
any too much confidence. As soon as it was
dusk, he must keep his ears open and listen
for the big owls, who flew along with such
soundless wing-strokes that they could come
right up to him before he was aware of their
presence.

When the boy heard that there were so
many who were after his life, he thought that
it would be simply impossible for him to escape.
He was not particularly afraid to die, but he
didn't like the idea of being eaten up, so he

asked Akka what he should do to protect
himself from the carnivorous animals.

Akka answered at once that the boy should
try to get on good terms with all the small
animals in the woods and fields: with the
squirrel-folk, and the hare-family; with bulfinches and titmice and woodpeckers and
larks. If he made friends with them, they
could warn him against dangers, find hiding
places for him, and protect him.

But, later in the day, when the boy tried
to profit by this counsel, and turned to Sirle
Squirrel to ask for his protection, it was evident that he did not care to help him. "You
surely can't expect anything from me, or the
rest of the small animals!" said Sirle. "Don't
you think we know that you are Nils the goose
boy, who tore down the swallow's nest last
year, crushed the starling's eggs, threw baby
crows in the marl-ditch, caught thrushes in
snares, and put squirrels in cages? You just
help yourself as well as you can; and you may
be thankful that we do not form a league
against you, and drive you back to your own
kind!"

This was just the sort of answer the boy would not have let go unpunished, in the days when he was Nils the goose boy. But now he was only fearful lest the wild geese, too, had found out how wicked he could be. He had been so anxious for fear he wouldn't be permitted to stay with the wild geese, that he hadn't dared to get into the least little mischief since he joined their company. It was true that he didn't have the power to do much harm now, but, little as he was, he could have destroyed many birds' nests, and crushed many eggs, if he'd been a mind to. Now he had been good. He hadn't pulled a feather from a goose-wing, or given anyone a rude answer; and every morning when he called upon Akka he had always removed his cap and bowed.

All day Thursday he thought it was surely on account of his wickedness that the wild geese did not care to take him along up to Lappland. And in the evening, when he heard that Sirle Squirrel's wife had been stolen, and her children were starving to death, he made up his mind to help them. And we have already been told how well he succeeded.

When the boy came into the park on Friday, he heard the bulfinches sing in every bush, of how Sirle Squirrel's wife had been carried away from her children by cruel robbers, and how Nils, the goose boy, had risked his life among human beings, and taken the little squirrel children to her.

"And who is so honoured in Övid Cloister park now, as Thumbietot!" sang the bulfinch; "he, whom all feared when he was Nils the goose boy? Sirle Squirrel will give him nuts; the poor hares are going to play with him; the small wild animals will carry him on their backs, and fly away with him when Smirre Fox approaches. The titmice are going to warn him against the hawk, and the finches and larks will sing of his valour."

The boy was absolutely certain that both Akka and the wild geese had heard all this. But still Friday passed and not one word did they say about his remaining with them.

Until Saturday the wild geese fed in the fields around Övid, undisturbed by Smirre Fox.

But on Saturday morning, when they came out in the meadows, he lay in wait for them,

and chased them from one field to another, and they were not allowed to eat in peace. When Akka understood that he didn't intend to leave them in peace, she came to a decision quickly, raised herself into the air and flew with her flock several miles away, over Färs' plains and Linderödsosen's hills. They did not stop before they had arrived in the district of Vittskövle.

But at Vittskövle the goosey-gander was stolen, and how it happened has already been related. If the boy hadn't used all his powers to help him, he would never again have been found.

On Saturday evening, as the boy came back to Vomb Lake with the goosey-gander, he thought that he had done a good day's work; and he speculated a good deal on what Akka and the wild geese would say to him. The wild geese were not at all sparing in their praises, but they did not say the word he was longing to hear.

Then Sunday came again. A whole week had gone by since the boy had been bewitched, and he was still just as little.

But he didn't appear to be giving himself any extra worry on account of this thing. On Sunday afternoon he sat huddled together in a big, fluffy, osier-bush, down by the lake, and blew on a reed-pipe. All around him there sat as many finches and bulfinches and starlings as the bush could well hold—who sang songs which he tried to teach himself to play. But the boy was not at home in this art. He blew so false that the feathers raised themselves on the little music-masters and they shrieked and fluttered in their despair. The boy laughed so heartily at their excitement, that he dropped his pipe.

He began once again, and that went just as badly. Then all the little birds wailed: "To-day you play worse than usual, Thumbietot?" You don't take one true note! Where are your thoughts, Thumbietot?"

"They are elsewhere," said the boy—and this was true. He sat there and pondered how long he would be allowed to remain with the wild geese; or if he should be sent home perhaps to-day.

Finally the boy threw down his pipe and

jumped from the bush.   He had seen Akka,
and all the wild geese, coming toward him
in a long row.   They walked so uncommonly
slow and dignified-like, that the boy immediately understood that now he should learn
what they intended to do with him.

When they stopped at last, Akka said:
"You may well have reason to wonder at me,
Thumbietot, who have not said thanks to
you for saving me from Smirre Fox.   But I
am one of those who would rather give thanks
by deeds than words.   I have sent word to
the elf that bewitched you.   At first he
didn't want to hear anything about curing
you; but I have sent message upon message
to him, and told him how well you have conducted yourself among us.   He greets you,
and says, that as soon as you turn back home,
you shall be human again."

But think of it!   Just as happy as the boy
had been when the wild geese began to speak,
just that miserable was he when they had
finished.   He didn't say a word, but turned
away and wept.

"What in all the world is this?" said Akka.

"It looks as though you had expected more of me than I have offered you."

But the boy was thinking of the care-free days and the banter; and of adventure and freedom and travel, high above the earth, that he should miss, and he actually bawled with grief. "I don't want to be human," said he. "I want to go with you to Lappland." "I'll tell you something," said Akka. "That elf is very touchy, and I'm afraid that if you do not accept his offer now, it will be difficult for you to coax him another time."

It was a strange thing about that boy—as long as he had lived, he had never cared for anyone. He had not cared for his father or mother; not for the school teacher; not for his schoolmates; nor for the boys in the neighbourhood. All that they had wished to have him do—whether it had been work or play— he had only thought tiresome. Therefore there was no one whom he missed or longed for.

The only ones that he had come anywhere near agreeing with, were Osa, the goose girl, and little Mats—a couple of children who had tended geese in the fields, like himself. But he didn't care particularly for them either. No, far from it! "I don't want to be human," bawled the boy. "I want to go with you to Lappland. That's why I've been good for a whole week!" "I don't want to forbid you to come along with us as far as you like," said Akka, "but think first if you wouldn't rather go home again. A day may come when you will regret this."

"No," said the boy, "that's nothing to regret. I have never been as well off as here with you."

"Well then, let it be as you wish," said Akka.

"Thanks!" said the boy, and he felt so happy that he had to cry for very joy—just as he had cried before from sorrow.

IV

GLIMMINGE CASTLE

BLACK RATS AND GRAY RATS

IN SOUTH-EASTERN SKÅNE—not far from the sea there is an old castle called Glimminge. It is a big and substantial stone house; and can be seen over the plain for miles around. It is not more than four stories high; but it is so ponderous that an ordinary farmhouse, which stands on the same estate, looks like a little children's playhouse in comparison.

The big stone house has such thick ceilings and partitions that there is scarcely room in its interior for anything but the thick walls. The stairs are narrow, the entrances small; and the rooms few. That the walls might retain their strength, there are only the fewest number of windows in the upper stories, and none at all are found in the lower ones.

In the old war times, the people were just as glad that they could shut themselves up in a strong and massive house like this, as one is nowadays to be able to creep into furs in a snapping cold winter. But when the time of peace came, they did not care to live in the dark and cold stone halls of the old castle any longer. They have long since deserted the big Glimminge castle, and moved into dwelling places where the light and air can penetrate.

At the time when Nils Holgersson wandered around with the wild geese, there were no human beings in Glimminge castle; but for all that, it was not without inhabitants. Every summer there lived a stork couple in a large nest on the roof. In a nest in the attic lived a pair of gray owls; in the secret passages hung bats; in the kitchen oven lived an old cat; and down in the cellar there were hundreds of old black rats.

Rats are not held in very high esteem by other animals; but the black rats at Glimminge castle were an exception. They were always mentioned with respect, because they had

shown great valour in battle with their enemies; and much endurance under the great
misfortunes which had befallen their kind.
They nominally belonged to a rat-folk who,
at one time, had been very numerous and
powerful, but who were now dying out.
During a long period of time, the black rats
owned Skåne and the whole country. They
were found in every cellar; in every attic;
in larders and cowhouses and barns; in
breweries and flour-mills; in churches and
castles; in every man-constructed building.
But now they were banished from all this—
and were almost exterminated. Only in one
and another old and secluded place could
one run across a few of them; and nowhere
were they to be found in such large numbers
as in Glimminge castle.

When an animal folk die out, it is generally
the human kind who are the cause of it;
but that was not the case in this instance.
The people had certainly struggled with the
black rats, but they had not been able to do
them any harm worth mentioning. Those
who had conquered them were an animal

folk of their own kind, who were called gray rats.

These gray rats had not lived in the land since time immemorial, like the black rats, but descended from a couple of poor immigrants who landed in Malmö from a Libyan sloop about a hundred years ago. They were homeless, starved-out wretches who stuck close to the harbour, swam among the piles under the bridges, and ate refuse that was thrown in the water. They never ventured into the city, which was owned by the black rats.

But gradually, as the gray rats increased in number they grew bolder. At first they moved over to some waste places and condemned old houses which the black rats had abandoned. They hunted their food in gutters and dirt heaps, and made the most of all the rubbish that the black rats did not deign to take care of. They were hardy, contented and fearless; and within a few years they had become so powerful that they undertook to drive the black rats out of Malmö. They took from them attics, cellars and store-

rooms, starved them out or bit them to death
for they were not at all afraid of fighting.

When Malmö was captured, they marched
forward in small and large companies
to conquer the whole country. It is almost
impossible to comprehend why the black
rats did not muster themselves into a
great, united war-expedition to exterminate
the gray rats, while these were still few in
numbers. But the black rats were so certain of their power that they could not believe
it possible for them to lose it. They sat still
on their estates, and in the meantime the
gray rats took from them farm after farm,
city after city. They were starved out,
forced out, rooted out. In Skåne they had
not been able to maintain themselves in a
single place except Glimminge castle.

The old castle had such secure walls and
such few rat passages led through these, that
the black rats had managed to protect themselves, and to prevent the gray rats from
crowding in. Night after night, year after
year, the struggle had continued between the
aggressors and the defenders; but the black

rats had kept faithful watch, and had fought with the utmost contempt for death, and, thanks to the fine old house, they had always conquered.

It will have to be acknowledged that as long as the black rats were in power they were as much shunned by all other living creatures as the gray rats are in our day— and for just cause; they had thrown themselves upon poor, fettered prisoners, and tortured them; they had ravished the dead; they had stolen the last turnip from the cellars of the poor; bitten off the feet of sleeping geese; robbed eggs and chicks from the hens; and committed a thousand depredations. But since they had come to grief, all this seemed to have been forgotten; and no one could help but marvel at the last of a race that had held out so long against its enemies.

The gray rats that lived in the courtyard at Glimminge and in the vicinity, kept up a continuous warfare and tried to watch out for every possible chance to capture the castle. One would fancy that they should have allowed the little company of black rats to

occupy Glimminge castle in peace, since they
themselves had acquired all the rest of the
country; but you may be sure this thought
never occurred to them. They were wont
to say that it was a point of honour with them
to conquer the black rats at some time or
other. But those who were acquainted with
the gray rats must have known that it was
because the human kind used Glimminge
castle as a grain storehouse that the gray ones
could not rest before they had taken possession
of the place.

THE STORK

Monday, March twenty-eighth.

EARLY one morning the wild geese who stood
and slept on the ice in Vomb Lake were awakened by long calls from the air. "Trirop,
Trirop!" it sounded, "Trianut, the crane,
sends greetings to Akka, the wild goose, and
her flock. To-morrow will be the day of the
great crane dance on Kullaberg."

Akka raised her head and answered at
once: "Greetings and thanks! Greetings and
thanks!"

With that, the cranes flew farther; anu the wild geese heard them for a long while— where they travelled and called out over every field, and every wooded hill: "Trianut sends greetings. To-morrow will be the day of the great crane dance on Kullaberg."

The wild geese were very happy over this invitation. "You're in luck," they said to the white goosey-gander, "to be permitted to attend the great crane dance on Kullaberg!" "Is it then so remarkable to see cranes dance?" asked the goosey-gander. "It is something that you have never even dreamed about!" replied the wild geese.

"Now we must think out what we shall do with Thumbietot to-morrow—so that no harm can come to him, while we run over to Kulla-berg," said Akka. "Thumbietot shall not be left alone!" said the goosey-gander. "If the cranes won't let him see their dance, then I'll stay with him."

"No human being has ever been permitted to attend the Animals' Congress, at Kullaberg," said Akka, "and I shouldn't dare to take Thumbietot along. But we'll discuss this

more at length later in the day. Now we
must first and foremost think about getting
something to eat.''

With that Akka gave the signal to adjourn.
On this day she also sought her feeding-place
a good distance away, on Smirre Fox's account,
and she didn't alight until she came to the
swampy meadows a little south of Glimminge castle.

All that day the boy sat on the shores of a
little pond, and blew on reed-pipes. He was
out of sorts because he shouldn't see the crane
dance, and he just couldn't say a word, either
to the goosey-gander, or to any of the others.

It was pretty hard that Akka should still
doubt him. When a boy had given up being
human, just to travel around with a few wild
geese, they surely ought to understand that
he had no desire to betray them. Then, too,
they ought to understand that when he had
renounced so much to follow them, it was
their duty to let him see all the wonders they
could show him.

"I'll have to speak my mind right out to
them," thought he. But hour after hour

passed, still he hadn't come round to it. It may sound remarkable—but the boy had actually acquired a kind of respect for the old leader-goose. He felt that it was not easy to pit his will against hers.

On one side of the swampy meadow, where the wild geese fed, there was a broad stone hedge. Toward evening when the boy finally raised his head, to speak to Akka, his glance happened to rest on this hedge. He uttered a little cry of surprise, and all the wild geese instantly looked up, and stared in the same direction. At first, both the geese and the boy thought that all the round, gray stones in the hedge had acquired legs, and were starting on a run; but soon they saw that it was a company of rats who ran over it. They moved very rapidly, and ran forward, tightly packed, line upon line, and were so numerous that, for some time, they covered the entire stone hedge.

The boy had been afraid of rats, even when he was a big, strong human being. Then what must his feelings be now, when he was so tiny that two or three of them could overpower him? One shudder after another travelled down his spinal column as he stood and stared at them.

But strangely enough, the wild geese seemed to feel the same aversion toward the rats that he did. They did not speak to them; and when they were gone, they shook themselves as if their feathers had been mud-bespattered.

"Such a lot of gray rats abroad!" said Iksi from Vassijaure. "That's not a good omen."

The boy intended to take advantage of this opportunity to say to Akka that he thought she ought to let him go with them to Kulla-berg, but he was prevented anew, for all of a sudden a big bird came down in the midst of the geese.

One could believe, when one looked at this bird, that he had borrowed body, neck and head from a little white goose. But in addition to this, he had procured for himself large black wings, long red legs, and a thick bill, which was too large for the little head, and weighed it down until it gave him a sad and worried look.

Akka at once straightened out the folds of

her wings, and curtsied many times as she approached the stork. She wasn't specially surprised to see him in Skåne so early in the spring, because she knew that the male storks are in the habit of coming over in good season to take a look at the nest, and see that it hasn't been damaged during the winter, before the female storks go to the trouble of flying over the East sea. But she wondered very much what it might signify that he sought her out, since storks prefer to associate with members of their own family.

"I can hardly believe that there is anything wrong with your house, Herr Ermenrich," said Akka.

It was apparent now that it is true what they say: a stork can seldom open his bill without complaining. But what made the thing he said sound even more doleful was that it was difficult for him to speak out. He stood for a long time and only clattered with his bill; afterward he spoke in a hoarse and feeble voice. He complained about everything: the nest—which was situated at the very top of the roof-tree at Glimminge castle—

had been totally destroyed by winter storms; and no food could he get any more in Skåne. The people of Skåne were appropriating all his possessions. They dug out his marshes and laid waste his swamps. He intended to move away from this country, and never return to it again.

While the stork grumbled, Akka, the wild goose who had neither home nor protection, could not help thinking to herself: "If I had things as comfortable as you have, Herr Ermenrich, I should be above complaining. You have remained a free and wild bird; and still you stand so well with human beings that no one will fire a shot at you, or steal an egg from your nest." But all this she kept to herself. To the stork she only remarked, that she couldn't believe he would be willing to move from a house where storks had resided ever since it was built.

Then the stork suddenly asked the geese if they had seen the gray rats who were marching toward Glimminge castle. When Akka replied that she had seen the horrid creatures, he began to tell her about the brave black rats who, for years, had defended the castle. "But this night Glimminge castle will fall into the gray rats' power," sighed the stork.

"And why just this night, Herr Ermenrich?" asked Akka.

"Well, because nearly all the black rats went over to Kullaberg last night," said the stork, "since they had counted on all the rest of the animals also hurrying there. But you see that the gray rats have stayed at home; and now they are mustering to storm the castle to-night, when it will be defended by only a few old creatures who are too feeble to go over to Kullaberg. They'll probably accomplish their purpose. But I have lived here in harmony with the black rats for so many years, that it does not please me to live in a place inhabited by their enemies."

Akka understood now that the stork had become so enraged over the gray rats mode of action, that he had sought her out as an excuse to complain about them. But after the manner of storks, he certainly had done nothing to avert the disaster. "Have you sent word to the black rats, Herr Ermenrich?" she asked. "No," replied the stork, "that wouldn't be of any use. Before they can get back, the castle will be taken." "You mustn't be so sure of that, Herr Ermenrich," said Akka. "I know an old wild goose, I do, who will gladly prevent outrages of this kind."

When Akka said this, the stork raised his head and stared at her. And it was not surprising, for Akka had neither claws nor bill that were fit for fighting; and, in the bargain, she was a day bird, and as soon as it grew dark she fell helplessly asleep, while the rats did their fighting at night.

But Akka had evidently made up her mind to help the black rats. She called Iksi from Vassijaure, and ordered him to take the wild geese over to Vomb Lake; and when the geese made excuses, she said authoritatively: "I believe it will be best for us all that you obey me. I must fly over to the big stone house, and if you follow me, the people on the place will be sure to see us, and shoot us down. The only one that I want to take with me on this trip is Thumbietot. He can be of great service to me because he has good eyes, and can keep awake at night."

The boy was in his most contrary mood that day. And when he heard what Akka said, he raised himself to his full height and stepped forward, his hands behind him and his nose in the air, and he intended to say that he, most assuredly, did not wish to take a hand in the fight with gray rats. She might look around for assistance elsewhere.

But the instant the boy was seen, the stork began to move. He had stood before, as storks generally stand, with head bent downward and the bill pressed against the neck. But now a gurgle was heard deep down in his windpipe; as though he would have laughed. Quick as a flash, he lowered the bill, grabbed the boy, and tossed him a couple of metres in the air. This feat he performed seven times, while the boy shrieked and the geese shouted: "What are you trying to do, Herr Ermenrich? That's not a frog. That's a human being, Herr Ermenrich."

Finally the stork put the boy down entirely unhurt. Thereupon he said to Akka:

"I'll fly back to Glimminge castle now, mother Akka. All who live there were very much worried when I left. You may be sure they'll be very glad when I tell them that Akka, the wild goose, and Thumbietot, the human elf, are on their way to rescue them." With that the stork craned his neck, raised his wings, and darted off like an arrow when it leaves a well-drawn bow. Akka understood that he was making fun of her, but she didn't let it bother her. She waited until the boy had found his wooden shoes, which the stork had shaken off; then she put him on her back and followed the stork. On his own account, the boy made no objection, and said not a word about not wanting to go along. He had become so furious with the stork, that he actually sat and puffed. That long, red-legged thing believed he was of no account just because he was little; but he would show him what kind of a man Nils Holgersson from West Vemminghög was.

A couple of moments later Akka stood in the storks' nest at Glimminge castle. It was a fine, large nest. It had a wheel for

foundation, and over this lay several grass-mats, and some twigs. The nest was so old that many shrubs and plants had taken root up there; and when the mother stork sat on her eggs in the round hole in the middle of the nest, she not only had the beautiful outlook over a goodly portion of Skåne to enjoy, but she had also the wild brier-blossoms and house-leeks to look upon.

Both Akka and the boy saw immediately that something was going on here, which turned up and down—in the most regular order. On the edge of the stork-nest sat two gray owls, an old, gray-streaked cat, and a dozen old, decrepit rats with protruding teeth and watery eyes. They were not exactly the sort of animals one usually finds living peaceably together.

Not one of them turned around to look at Akka, or to bid her welcome. They thought of nothing except to sit and stare at some long, gray lines, which came into sight here and there—on the winter-naked meadows.

All the black rats were silent. One could see that they were in deep despair, and probably knew that they could neither defend

In Glimminge Castle

their own lives—or the castle.   The two owls sat and rolled their big eyes, and twisted their great, encircling eyebrows, and talked in hollow, ghost-like voices, about the awful cruelty of the gray rats, and that they would have to move away from their nest, because they had heard it said of them that they spared neither eggs nor baby birds.   The old gray-streaked cat was positive that the gray rats would bite him to death, since they were coming into the castle in such great numbers, and he scolded the black rats incessantly. " How could you be so idiotic as to let your best fighters go away?" said he.   " How could you trust the gray rats? It is absolutely unpardonable!"

The twelve black rats did not say a word. But the stork, despite his misery, could not refrain from teasing the cat.   " Don't worry so, Monsie house-cat!" said he.   " Can't you see that mother Akka and Thumbietot have come to save the castle?   You can be certain that they'll succeed.   Now I must stand up to sleep—and I do so with the utmost calm. To-morrow, when I awaken, there won't be a single gray rat in Glimminge castle."

The boy winked at Akka, and made a sign
—as the stork stood upon the very edge of the
nest, with one leg drawn up, to sleep—that he
wanted to push him down to the ground; but
Akka restrained him. She did not seem to
be the least bit angry. Instead, she said in a
confident tone of voice: "It would be pretty
poor business if one who is as old as I am could
not manage to get out of worse difficulties than
this. If only Mr. and Mrs. Owl, who can stay
awake all night, will fly off with a couple of
messages for me, I think that all will go well."

Both owls were willing. Then Akka bade
the gentleman owl that he should go and seek
the black rats who had gone off, and counsel
them to hurry home immediately. The lady
owl he sent to Flammea, the steeple-owl,
who lived in Lund cathedral, with a commission which was so secret that Akka only dared
to confide it to her in a whisper.

THE RAT CHARMER

It was getting on toward midnight when
the gray rats after a diligent search succeeded in finding an open air-hole in the

cellar. This was pretty high upon the wall; but the rats got up on one another's shoulders, and it wasn't long before the most daring among them sat in the air-hole, ready to force its way into Glimminge castle, outside whose walls so many of its forebears had fallen.

The gray rat sat still for a moment in the hole, and waited for an attack from within. The leader of the defenders was certainly away, but she assumed that the black rats who were still in the castle wouldn't surrender without a struggle. With thumping heart she listened for the slightest sound, but everything remained quiet. Then the leader of the gray rats plucked up courage and jumped down in the coal-black cellar.

One after another of the gray rats followed the leader. They all kept very quiet; and all expected to be ambushed by the black rats. Not until so many of them had crowded into the cellar that the floor couldn't hold any more, did they venture farther.

Although they had never before been inside the building, they had no difficulty in finding

their way. They soon found the passages in the walls which the black rats had used to get to the upper floors. Before they began to clamber up these narrow and steep steps, they listened again with great attention. They felt more frightened because the black rats held themselves aloof in this way, than if they had met them in open battle. They could hardly believe their luck when they reached the first story without any mishaps.

Immediately upon their entrance the gray rats caught the scent of the grain, which was stored in great bins on the floor. But it was not as yet time for them to begin to enjoy their conquest. They searched first, with the utmost caution, through the sombre, empty rooms. They ran up in the fireplace, which stood on the floor in the old castle kitchen, and they almost tumbled into the well, in the inner room. Not one of the narrow peep-holes did they leave uninspected, but they found no black rats. When this floor was wholly in their possession, they began, with the same caution, to acquire the next. Then they had to venture on a bold and dangerous

climb through the walls, while, with breathless anxiety, they awaited an assault from
the enemy. And although they were tempted by the most delicious odour from the
grain bins, they forced themselves most
systematically to inspect the old-time warriors' pillar-propped kitchen; their stone
table, and fireplace; the deep window-niches,
and the hole in the floor—which in olden
time had been opened to pour down boiling
pitch on the intruding enemy.

All this time the black rats were invisible.
The gray ones groped their way to the third
story, and into the lord of the castle's great
banquet hall—which stood there cold and
empty, like all the other rooms in the old
house. They even groped their way to the
upper story, which had but one big, barren
room. The only place they did not think
of exploring, was the big stork-nest on the
roof—where, just at this time, the lady
owl awakened Akka, and informed her that
Flammea, the steeple owl, had granted her
request, and had sent her the thing she
wished for.

Since the gray rats had so conscientiously inspected the entire castle, they felt at ease. They took it for granted that the black rats had flown, and didn't intend to offer any resistance; and, with light hearts, they ran up into the grain bins.

But the gray rats had hardly swallowed the first wheat-grains, before the sound of a little shrill pipe was heard from the yard. The gray rats raised their heads, listened anxiously, ran a few steps as if they intended to leave the bin, then they turned back and began to eat once more.

Again the pipe sounded a sharp and piercing note—and now something wonderful happened. One rat, two rats—yes, a whole lot of rats left the grain, jumped from the bins and hurried down cellar by the shortest cut, to get out of the house. Still there were many gray rats left. These thought of all the toil and trouble it had cost them to win Glimminge castle, and they did not want to leave it. But again they caught the tones from the pipe, and had to follow them. With wild excitement they rushed

up from the bins, slid down through the narrow holes in the walls, and tumbled over
each other in their eagerness to get out.

In the middle of the courtyard stood a tiny
creature, who blew upon a pipe. All round
him he had a whole circle of rats who listened
to him, astonished and fascinated; and every
moment brought more. Once he took the
pipe from his lips—only for a second—put his
thumb to his nose and wiggled his fingers
at the gray rats; and then it looked as if
they wanted to throw themselves on him and
bite him to death; but as soon as he blew on
his pipe they were in his power.

When the tiny creature had played all the
gray rats out of Glimminge castle, he began
to wander slowly from the courtyard out on
the highway; and all the gray rats followed
him, because the tones from that pipe sounded
so sweet to their ears that they could not
resist them.

The tiny creature walked before them and
charmed them along with him, on the road
to Vallby. He led them into all sorts of
crooks and turns and bends—on through

hedges and down into ditches—and wherever he went they had to follow. He blew continuously on his pipe, which appeared to be made from an animal's horn, although the horn was so small that, in our days, there were no animals from whose foreheads it could have been broken. No one knew, either, who had made it. Flammea, the steeple-owl, had found it in a niche, in Lund cathedral. She had shown it to Bataki, the raven; and they had both figured out that this was the kind of horn that was used in former times by those who wished to gain power over rats and mice. But the raven was Akka's friend; and it was from him she had learned that Flammea owned a treasure like this.

And it was true that the rats could not resist the pipe. The boy walked before them and played as long as the starlight lasted— and all the while they followed him. He played at daybreak; he played at sunrise; and the whole time the entire procession of gray rats followed him, and were enticed farther and farther away from the big grain **loft at** Glimminge castle.

V

THE GREAT CRANE DANCE ON KULLABERG

Tuesday, March twenty-ninth.

ALTHOUGH there are many magnificent buildings in Skåne, it must be acknowledged that there's not one among them that has such pretty walls as old Kullaberg.

Kullaberg is low and rather long. It is not by any means a big or imposing mountain. On its broad summit you'll find woods and grain fields, and one and another heather-heath. Here and there, round heather-knolls and barren cliffs rise up. It is not especially pretty up there. It looks a good deal like all the other upland places in Skåne.

He who walks along the path which runs across the middle of the mountain, can't help feeling a little disappointed. Then he happens, perhaps, to turn away from the path, and wanders off toward the mountain's sides

137

and looks down over the bluffs; and then, all at once, he will discover so much that is worth seeing, he hardly knows how he'll find time to take in the whole of it. For it happens that Kullaberg does not stand on the land, with plains and valleys around it, like other mountains; but it has plunged into the sea, as far out as it could get. Not even the tiniest strip of land lies below the mountain to protect it against the breakers; but these reach all the way up to the mountain walls, and can polish and mould them to suit themselves. This is why the walls stand there as richly ornamented as the sea and its helpmeet, the wind, have been able to effect. You'll find steep ravines that are deeply chiselled in the mountain's sides; and black crags that have become smooth and shiny under the constant lashing of the winds. There are solitary rock-columns that spring right up out of the water, and dark grottoes with narrow entrances. There are barren, perpendicular precipices, and soft, leaf-clad inclines. There are small points, and small inlets, and small rolling stones that are

rattlingly washed up and down with every dash-
ing breaker.   There are majestic cliff-arches
that project over the water.   There are sharp
stones that are constantly sprayed by a
white foam; and others that mirror themselves in unchangeable dark-green still water.
There are giant troll-caverns shaped in the
rock, and great crevices that lure the wan-
derer to venture into the mountain's depths
—all the way to Kullman's Hollow.

And over and around all these cliffs and
rocks crawl entangled tendrils and weeds.
Trees grow there also, but the wind's power
is so great that trees have to transform themselves into clinging vines, that they may get
a firm hold on the steep precipices.   The oaks
creep along on the ground, while their foliage
hangs over them like a low ceiling; and long-
limbed beeches stand in the ravines like great
leaf-tents.

These remarkable mountain walls, with
the blue sea beneath them, and the clear
penetrating air above them, is what makes
Kullaberg so dear to the people that great
crowds of them haunt the place every day

as long as the summer lasts. But it is more difficult to tell what it is that makes it so attractive to animals, that every year they gather there for a big play-meeting. This is a custom that has been observed since time immemorial; and one should have been there when the first sea-wave was dashed into foam against the shore, to be able to explain why just Kullaberg was chosen as a rendezvous, in preference to all other places.

When the meeting is to take place, the stags and roebucks and hares and foxes and all the other four-footers make the journey to Kullaberg the night before, so as not to be observed by the human beings. Just before sunrise they all march up to the playground, which is a heather-heath on the left side of the road, and not very far from the mountain's most extreme point. The playground is inclosed on all sides by round knolls, which conceal it from any and all who do not happen to come right upon it. And in the month of March it is not at all likely that any pedestrians will stray off up there. All the strangers who usually stroll around on the rocks, and

clamber up the mountain's sides the fall storms have driven away these many months past. And the lighthouse keeper out there on the point; the old fru on the mountain farm, and the mountain peasant and his house-folk go their accustomed ways, and do not run about on the desolate heather-fields.

When the four-footers have arrived on the playground, they take their places on the round knolls. Each animal family keeps to itself, although it is understood that, on a day like this, universal peace reigns, and no one need fear attack. On this day a little hare might wander over to the foxes' hill, without losing as much as one of his long ears. But still the animals arrange themselves into separate groups. This is an old custom.

After they have all taken their places, they begin to look around for the birds. It is always beautiful weather on this day. The cranes are good weather prophets, and would not call the animals together if they expected rain. Although the air is clear, and nothing obstructs the vision, the four-footers see no birds. This is strange. The sun stands high in the heavens, and the birds should already be on their way.

But what the animals, on the other hand, observe, is one and another little dark cloud that comes slowly forward over the plain. And look! one of these clouds comes gradually along the coast of Öresund, and up toward Kullaberg. When the cloud has come just over the playground it stops, and, simultaneously, the entire cloud begins to ring and chirp, as if it was made of nothing but tone. It rises and sinks, rises and sinks, but all the while it rings and chirps. At last the whole cloud falls down over a knoll—all at once— and the next instant the knoll is entirely covered with gray larks, pretty red-white-gray bulfinches, speckled starlings and greenish-yellow titmice.

Soon after that, another cloud comes over the plain. This stops over every bit of land; over peasant cottage and palace; over towns and cities; over farms and railway stations; over fishing hamlets and sugar refineries. Every time it stops, it draws to itself a little whirling column of gray dust-grains from the ground. In this way it grows and grows. And at last, when it is all gathered up and heads for Kullaberg it is no longer a cloud but a whole mist, which is so big that it throws a shadow on the ground all the way from Höganäs to Mölle. When it stops over the playground it hides the sun; and for a long while it had to rain gray sparrows on one of the knolls, before those who had been flying in the innermost part of the mist could again catch a glimpse of the daylight.

But still the biggest of these bird-clouds is the one which now appears. This has been formed of birds who have travelled from every direction to join it. It is dark bluish-gray, and no sun-ray can penetrate it. It is full of the ghastliest noises, the most frightful shrieks, the grimmest laughter, and most ill-luck-boding croaking! All on the playground are glad when it finally resolves itself into a storm of fluttering and croaking: of crows and jackdaws and rooks and ravens.

Thereupon not only clouds are seen in the heavens, but a variety of stripes and figures. Then straight, dotted lines appear in the East

and Northeast.   These are forest-birds from
Göinge districts: black grouse and wood
grouse who come flying in long lines a
couple of metres apart.   Swimming-birds
that live around Måkläppen, just out of
Falsterbo, now come floating over Öresund in
many extraordinary figures: in triangular and
long curves; in sharp hooks and semicircles.

To the great reunion held the year that
Nils Holgersson travelled around with the
wild geese, came Akka and her flock—later
than all the others.   And that was not to be
wondered at, for Akka had to fly over the
whole of Skåne to get to Kullaberg.   Beside,
as soon as she awoke, she had been obliged to

go out and hunt for Thumbietot, who, for
many hours, had gone and played to the gray
rats, and lured them far away from Glimminge
castle.   Mr. Owl had returned with the news
that the black rats would be at home immediately after sunrise; and there was no longer
any danger in letting the steeple-owl's pipe
be hushed, and to give the gray rats the
liberty to go where they pleased.

But it was not Akka who discovered the

boy where he walked with his long following, and quickly sank down over him and caught him with the bill and swung into the air with him, but it was Herr Ermenrich, the stork! For Herr Ermenrich had also gone out to look for him; and after he had borne him up to the stork-nest, he begged his forgiveness for having treated him with disrespect the evening before.

This pleased the boy immensely, and the stork and he became good friends. Akka, too, showed him that she felt very kindly toward him; she stroked her old head several times against his arms, and commended him because he had helped those who were in trouble.

But this one must say to the boy's credit: that he did not want to accept praise which he had not earned. "No, mother Akka," he said, "you mustn't think that I lured the gray rats away to help the black ones. I only wanted to show Herr Ermenrich that I was of some consequence."

He had hardly said this before Akka turned to the stork and asked if he thought it was advisable to take Thumbietot along to Kulla-

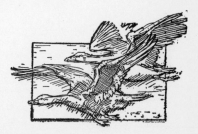

berg. "I mean, that we can rely on him as upon ourselves," said she. The stork at once advised, most enthusiastically, that Thumbietot be permitted to come along. "Certainly you shall take Thumbietot along to Kullaberg, mother Akka," said he. "It is fortunate for us that we can repay him for all that he has endured this night for our sakes. And since it still grieves me to think that I did not conduct myself in a becoming manner toward him the other evening, it is I who will carry him on my back—all the way to the meeting place."

There isn't much that tastes better than to receive praise from those who are themselves wise and capable; and the boy had certainly never felt so happy as he did when the wild goose and the stork talked about him in this way.

Thus the boy made the trip to Kullaberg, riding stork-back. Although he knew that this was a great honour, it caused him much anxiety, for Herr Ermenrich was a master flyer, and started off at a very different pace from the wild geese. While Akka flew her

straight way with even wing-strokes, the
stork amused himself by performing a lot of
flying tricks. Now he lay still in an
immeasurable height, and floated in the air
without moving his wings, now he flung himself downward with such sudden haste that it
seemed as though he would fall to the ground,
helpless as a stone; now he had lots of fun
flying all around Akka, in great and small
circles, like a whirlwind. The boy had never
been on a ride of this sort before; and although he sat there all the while in terror,
he had to acknowledge to himself that he had
never before known what a good flight meant.

Only a single pause was made during the
journey, and that was at Vomb Lake when
Akka joined her travelling companions, and
called to them that the gray rats had been
vanquished. After that, the travellers flew
straight to Kullaberg.

There they descended to the knoll reserved
for the wild geese; and as the boy let his
glance wander from knoll to knoll, he saw on
one of them the many-pointed antlers of the
stags; and on another, the gray herons' neck-

crests. One knoll was red with foxes, one was gray with rats; one was covered with black ravens who shrieked continually, one with larks who simply couldn't keep still, but kept on throwing themselves in the air and singing for very joy.

Just as it has ever been the custom on Kullaberg, it was the crows who began the day's games and frolics with their flying-dance. They divided themselves into two flocks, that flew toward each other, met, turned, and began all over again. This dance had many repetitions, and appeared to the spectators who were not familiar with the dance as altogether too monotonous. The crows were very proud of their dance, but all the others were glad when it was over. It appeared to the animals about as gloomy and meaningless as the winter-storms' play with the snow-flakes. It depressed them to watch it, and they waited eagerly for something that should give them a little pleasure.

They did not have to wait in vain, either; for as soon as the crows had finished, the hares came running. They dashed forward in a

long row, without any apparent order. In
some of the figures, one single hare came; in
others, they ran three and four abreast. They
had all raised themselves on two legs, and they
rushed forward with such rapidity that their
long ears swayed in all directions. As they
ran, they spun round, made high leaps and
beat their forepaws against their hind-paws
so that they rattled. Some performed a long
succession of somersaults, others doubled
themselves up and rolled over like wheels;
one stood on one 'eg and swung round; one
walked upon his forepaws. There was no
regulation whatever, but there was much
that was droll in the hares' play; and the
many animals who stood and watched them
began to breathe faster. Now it was spring;
joy and rapture were advancing. Winter was
over; summer was coming. Soon it was
only play to live.

When the hares had romped themselves out,
it was the great forest birds' turn to perform.
Hundreds of wood-grouse in shining dark-
brown array, and with bright red eyebrows,
flung themselves up into a great oak that

stood in the centre of the playground. The one who sat upon the topmost branch fluffed up his feathers, lowered his wings, and lifted his tail so that the white covert-feathers were seen. Thereupon he stretched his neck and sent forth a couple of deep notes from his thick throat. "Tjack, tjack, tjack," it sounded. More than this he could not utter. It only gurgled a few times way down in the throat. Then he closed his eyes and whispered: "Sis, sis, sis. Hear how pretty! Sis, sis, sis." At the same time he fell into such an ecstasy that he no longer knew what was going on around him.

While the first wood grouse was sissing, the three nearest—under him—began to sing; and before they had finished their song, the ten who sat lower down joined in; and thus it continued from branch to branch, until the entire hundred grouse sang and gurgled and sissed. They all fell into the same ecstasy during their song, and this affected the other animals like a contagious transport. Lately the blood had flowed lightly and agreeably; now it began to grow heavy and hot. "Yes, this is surely spring," thought all the animal folk. "Winter chill has vanished. The fires of spring burn over the earth."

When the black grouse saw that the brown grouse were having such success, they could no longer keep quiet. As there was no tree for them to light on, they rushed down on the playground, where the heather stood so high that only their beautifully turned tail-feathers and their thick bills were visible— and they began to sing; "Orr, orr, orr."

Just as the black grouse began to compete with the brown grouse, something unprecedented happened. While all the animals thought of nothing but the grouse-game, a fox stole slowly over to the wild geese's knoll. He glided very cautiously, and came way up on the knoll before anyone noticed him. Suddenly a goose caught sight of him; and as she could not believe that a fox had sneaked in among the geese for any good purpose, she began to cry: "Have a care, wild geese! Have a care!" The fox struck her across the throat— mostly, perhaps, because he wanted to make her keep quiet—but the wild geese had already

heard the cry, and they all raised themselves
in the air.   And when they had flown up, the
animals saw Smirre Fox standing on the wild
geese's knoll, with a 'dead goose in his mouth.

But because he had in this way broken
the play-day's peace, such a punishment was
meted out to Smirre Fox that, for the rest of
his days, he must regret he had not been
able to control his thirst for revenge, but had
attempted to approach Akka and her flock
in this manner.

He was immediately surrounded by a crowd
of foxes, and doomed in accordance with an
old custom, which demands that whosoever
disturbs the peace on the great play-day, must
go into exile.   Not a fox wished to lighten
the sentence, since they all knew that the
instant they attempted anything of the sort,
they would be driven from the playground,
and would nevermore be permitted to enter
it.   Banishment was pronounced upon Smirre
without opposition.   He was forbidden to
remain in Skåne.   He was banished from wife
and kindred; from hunting grounds, home,
resting places and retreats, which he had

hitherto owned; and he must tempt fortune
in foreign lands. So that all foxes in Skåne
should know that Smirre was outlawed in the
district, the oldest of the foxes bit off his right
earlap. As soon as this was done, all the
young foxes began to yowl from blood-thirst,
and threw themselves on Smirre. For him
there was no alternative except to take flight;
and with all the young foxes in hot pursuit,
he rushed away from Kullaberg.

All this happened while black grouse and
brown grouse were going on with their games.
But these birds lose themselves so completely
in their song, that they neither hear nor see.
Nor had they permitted themselves to be
disturbed.

The forest birds' contest was barely over,
before the stags from Häckeberga came forward to show their wrestling game. There
were several pairs of stags who fought at the
same time. They rushed at each other with
tremendous force, struck their antlers clash-
ingly together, so that their points were
entangled; and tried to force each other backward. The heather-heaths were torn up

beneath their hoofs; the breath came like smoke from their nostrils; out of their throats strained hideous bellowings, and the froth oozed down on their shoulders.

On the knolls round about there was breathless silence while the skilled stag-wrestlers clinched. In all the animals new emotions were awakened. Each and all felt courageous and strong; enlivened by returning powers; born again with the spring; sprightly, and ready for all kinds of adventures. They felt no enmity toward each other, although, everywhere, wings were lifted, neck-feathers raised and claws sharpened. If the stags from Häckeberga had continued another instant, a wild struggle would have arisen on the knolls, for all had been gripped with a burning desire to show that they too were full of life because the winter's impotence was over and strength surged through their bodies.

But the stags stopped wrestling just at the right moment, and instantly a whisper went from knoll to knoll: "The cranes are coming!"

And then came the gray, dusk-clad birds
with plumes in their wings, and red feather-
ornaments on their necks. The big birds with
their tall legs, their slender throats, their
small heads, came gliding down the knoll with
an abandon that was full of mystery. As they
glided forward they swung round—half flying,
half dancing. With wings gracefully lifted,
they moved with an inconceivable rapidity.
There was something marvellous and strange
about their dance. It was as though gray
shadows had played a game which the eye
could scarcely follow. It was as if they had
learned it from the mists that hover over
desolate morasses. There was witchcraft in it.
All those who had never before been on Kullaberg understood why the whole meeting took
its name from the cranes' dance. There was
wildness in it; but yet the feeling which it
awakened was a delicious longing. No one
thought any more about struggling. Instead,
both the winged and those who had no wings,
all wanted to raise themselves eternally, lift
themselves above the clouds, seek that
which was hidden beyond them, leave the

oppresssive body that dragged them down to earth and soar away toward the infinite.

Such longing after the unattainable, after the hidden mysteries back of this life, the animals felt only once a year; and this was on the day when they beheld the great crane dance.

VI

IN RAINY WEATHER

Wednesday, March thirtieth.

IT WAS the first rainy day of the trip. As long as the wild geese had remained in the vicinity of Vomb Lake, they had had beautiful weather; but on the day when they set out to travel farther north, it began to rain, and for several hours the boy had to sit on the goose-back, soaking wet, and shivering with the cold.

In the morning when they started, it had been clear and mild. The wild geese had flown high up in the air—evenly, and without haste—with Akka at the head maintaining strict discipline, and the rest in two oblique lines back of her. They had not taken the time to shout any witty sarcasms to the animals on the ground; but, as it was simply impossible for them to keep perfectly silent, they sang out continually—in rhythm with

the wing-strokes—their usual coaxing-call:
"Where are you? Here am I. Where are
you? Here am I."

They all took part in this persistent calling,
and only stopped, now and then, to show the
goosey-gander the landmarks they were travelling over. The places on this route included
Linderödsosen's dry hills, Ovesholm's manor,
Christianstad's church steeple, Bäckaskog's
royal castle on the narrow isthmus between
Oppmann's lake and Ivös lake, and Ryss
mountain's steep precipice.

It had been a monotonous trip, and when
the rain-clouds made their appearance the
boy thought it was a real diversion. In the
old days, when he had only seen a rain-cloud
from below, he had imagined that they were
gray and disagreeable; but it was a very
different thing to be up amongst them. Now
he saw distinctly that the clouds were enormous carts, which drove through the heavens
with sky-high loads. Some of them were
piled up with huge, gray sacks, some with
barrels; some were so large that they could
hold a whole lake; and a few were filled with

big utensils and bottles which were piled up
to an immense height.   And when so many of
them had driven forward that they filled the
whole sky, it appeared as though someone
had given a signal, for all at once, water commenced to pour down over the earth, from
utensils, barrels, bottles and sacks.

Just as the first spring-showers pattered
against the ground, there arose such shouts of
joy from all the small birds in groves and
pastures, that the whole air rang with them
and the boy leaped high where he sat.   "Now
we'll have rain.   Rain gives us spring; spring
gives us flowers and green leaves; green leaves
and flowers give us worms and insects; worms
and insects give us food; and plentiful, and
good food is the best thing there is," sang the
birds.

The wild geese, too, were glad of the rain
which came to awaken the growing things from
their long sleep, and to drive holes in the
ice-roofs on the lakes.   They were not able
to keep up that seriousness any longer,
but began to send merry calls over the
neighbourhood.

When they flew over the big potato patches, which are so plentiful in the country around Christianstad—and which still lay bare and black—they screamed: "Wake up and be useful! Here comes something that will awaken you. You have idled long enough now."

When they saw people who hurried to get out of the rain, they reproved them saying: "What are you in such a hurry about? Can't you see that it's raining rye-loaves and cookies?"

It was a big, thick mist that moved northward briskly, and followed close upon the geese. They seemed to think that they dragged the mist along with them; and, just now, when they saw great orchards beneath them, they called out proudly: "Here we come with anemones; here we come with roses; here we come with apple blossoms and cherry buds; here we come with peas and beans and turnips and cabbages. He who wills can take them. He who wills can take them."

Thus it had sounded while the first showers fell, and when all were still glad of the rain.

"The wild geese, too, were glad
of the rain"

But when it continued to fall the whole afternoon, the wild geese grew impatient, and cried
to the thirsty forests around Ivös lake:
"Haven't you got enough yet?   Haven't you
got enough yet?"

The heavens were growing grayer and grayer
and the sun hid itself so well that one couldn't
imagine where it was.   The rain fell faster
and faster, and beat harder and harder
against the wings, as it tried to find its way
between the oily outside feathers, into their
skins.   The earth was hidden by fogs; lakes,
mountains, and woods floated together in an
indistinct maze, and the landmarks could not
be distinguished.   The flight became slower
and slower; the joyful cries were hushed; and
the boy felt the cold more and more keenly.

But still he had kept up his courage as long
as he had ridden through the air.   And in
the afternoon, when they had lighted under
a little stunted pine, in the middle of a large
morass, where all was wet, and all was cold;
where some knolls were covered with snow,
and others stood up naked in a puddle of half-
melted ice-water, even then, he had not felt

discouraged, but ran about in fine spirits, and hunted for cranberries and frozen whortle-berries. But then came evening, and darkness sank down on them so close, that not even such eyes as the boy's could see through it; and all the wilderness became so strangely grim and awful. The boy lay tucked in under the goosey-gander's wing, but could not sleep because he was cold and wet. He heard such a lot of rustling and rattling and stealthy steps and menacing voices, that he was terror-stricken and didn't know where he should go. He must go somewhere, where there was light and heat, if he wasn't going to be entirely scared to death.

"If I should venture where there are human beings, just for this night?" thought the boy. "Only so I could sit by a fire for a moment, and get a little food. I could go back to the wild geese before sunrise."

He crept from under the wing and slid down to the ground. He didn't awaken either the goosey-gander or any of the other geese, but stole, silently and unobserved, through the morass.

He didn't know exactly where on earth he was: if he was in Skåne, in Småland, or in Blekinge. But just before he had gotten down in the morass, he had caught a glimpse of a large village, and thither he directed his steps. It wasn't long, either, before he discovered a road; and soon he was on the village street, which was long, and had planted trees on both sides, and was bordered with garden after garden.

The boy had come to one of the big cathedral towns, which are so common on the uplands, but can hardly be seen at all down in the plain.

The houses were of wood, and very prettily constructed. Most of them had gables and fronts, edged with carved mouldings, and glass doors, with here and there a coloured pane, opening on verandas. The walls were painted in light oil-colours; the doors and window-frames shone in blues and greens, and even in reds. While the boy walked about and viewed the houses, he could hear, all the way out to the road, how the people who sat in the warm cottages chattered and laughed. The words he could not distinguish, but he thought it was just lovely to hear human voices. "I wonder what they would say if I knocked and begged to be let in," thought he.

This was, of course, what he had intended to do all along, but now that he saw the lighted windows, his fear of the darkness was gone. Instead, he felt again that shyness which always came over him now when he was near human beings. "I'll take a look around the town for a while longer," thought he, "before I ask anyone to take me in."

On one house there was a balcony. And just as the boy walked by, the doors were thrown open, and a yellow light streamed through the fine, sheer curtains. Then a pretty young fru came out on the balcony and leaned over the railing. "It's raining; now we shall soon have spring," said she. When the boy saw her he felt a strange anxiety. It was as though he wanted to weep. For the first time he was a bit uneasy because he had shut himself out from the human kind.

Shortly after that he walked by a shop.
Outside the shop stood a red corn-drill. He
stopped and looked at it; and finally crawled
up to the driver's place, and seated himself.
When he had got there, he smacked with
his lips and pretended that he sat and drove.
He thought what fun it would be to be
permitted to drive such a pretty machine
over a grainfield. For a moment he forgot what he was like now; then he remembered it, and jumped down quickly from the
machine. Then a greater unrest came over
him. After all, human beings were very
wonderful and clever.

He walked by the post-office, and then he
thought of all the neswpapers which came
every day, with news from all the four corners
of the earth. He saw the apothecary's shop
and the doctor's home, and he thought about
the power of human beings, which was so
great that they were able to battle with sickness and death. He came to the church.
Then he thought how human beings had
built it, that they might hear about another
world than the one in which they lived; of

God and the resurrection and eternal life.
And the longer he walked there, the better
he liked human beings.

It is so with children that they never think
any farther ahead than the length of their
noses. That which lies nearest them, they
want promptly, without caring what it may
cost them. Nils Holgersson had not understood what he was losing when he chose to
remain an elf; but now he began to be
dreadfully afraid that, perhaps, he should
never again get back his right form.

How in all the world should he go to work
in order to become human? This he wanted,
oh! so much, to know.

He crawled up on a doorstep, and seated
himself in the pouring rain and meditated.
He sat there one whole hour—two whole
hours, and he thought so hard that his forehead lay in furrows; but he was none the
wiser. It seemed as though the thoughts
only rolled round and round in his head.
The longer he sat there, the more impossible
it seemed to him to find any solution.

"This thing is certainly much too difficult

for one who has learned as little as I have,"
he thought at last. "It will probably wind
up by my having to go back among human
beings after all. I must ask the minister and
the doctor and the schoolmaster and others
who are learned, and may know a cure for
such things."

This he concluded that he would do at
once, and shook himself—for he was as wet
as a dog that has been in a water-pool.

Just about then he saw that a big owl
came flying along, and alighted on one of the
trees that bordered the village street. The
next instant a lady owl, who sat under the
cornice of the house, began to call out:
"Kivitt, Kivitt! Are you at home again,
Mr. Gray Owl? What kind of a time did you
have abroad?"

"Thank you, Lady Brown Owl. I had a
very comfortable time," said the gray owl.
"Has anything out of the ordinary happened
here at home during my absence?"

"Not here in Blekinge, Mr. Gray Owl; but
in Skåne a marvellous thing has happened!
A boy has been transformed by an elf into a

goblin no bigger than a squirrel; and since then he has gone to Lappland with a tame goose."

"That's a remarkable bit of news, a remarkable bit of news. Can he never be human again, Lady Brown Owl? Can he never be human again?"

"That's a secret, Mr. Gray Owl; but you shall hear it just the same. The elf has said that if the boy watches over the goosey-gander, so that he comes home safe and sound, and——"

"What more, Lady Brown Owl? What more? What more?"

"Fly with me up to the church tower, Mr. Gray Owl, and you shall hear the whole story! I fear there may be someone listening down here in the street." With that, the owls flew their way; but the boy flung his cap in the air, and shouted: "If I only watch over the goosey-gander, so that he gets back safe and sound, then I shall become a human being again, Hurrah! Hurrah! Then I shall become a human being again!"

He shouted "hurrah" until it was strange that they did not hear him in the houses—but they didn't, and he hurried back to the wild geese, out in the wet morass, as fast as his legs could carry him.

VII

THE STAIRWAY WITH THE THREE STEPS

Thursday, March thirty-first.

THE following day the wild geese intended to travel northward through Allbo district, in Småland. They sent Iksi and Kaksi to spy out the land. But when they returned, they said that all the water was frozen, and all the land was snow-covered. "We may as well remain where we are," said the wild geese. "We cannot travel over a country where there is neither water nor food." "If we remain where we are, we may have to wait here until the next moon," said Akka. "It is better to go eastward, through Blekinge, and see if we can't get to Småland by way of Möre, which lies near the coast, and has an early spring."

Thus the boy came to ride over Blekinge the next day. Now, that it was light again, he was in a merry mood once more, and could not comprehend what had come over him the night before. He certainly didn't want to give up the journey and the outdoor life now.

There lay a thick fog over Blekinge. The boy couldn't see how it looked out there. "I wonder if it is a good, or a poor country that I'm riding over," thought he, and tried to search his memory for the things which he had heard about the country at school. But at the same time he knew well enough that this was useless, as he had never been in the habit of studying his lessons.

At once the boy saw the whole school before him. The children sat by the little desks and raised their hands; the teacher sat in the lectern and looked displeased; and he himself stood before the map and should answer some question about Blekinge, but he hadn't a word to say. The schoolmaster's face grew darker and darker for every second that passed, and the boy thought the teacher was more particular that they should know their geography, than anything else. Now he came down from the lectern, took the pointer

from the boy, and sent him back to his seat.
"This won't end well," the boy thought then.

But the schoolmaster had gone over to a
window, and had stood there for a moment
and looked out, and then he had whistled to
himself once. Then he had gone up into the
lectern and said that he would tell them something about Blekinge. And that which he
then talked about had been so amusing that
the boy had listened. When he only stopped
and thought for a moment, he remembered
every word.

"Småland is a tall house with spruce trees
on the roof," said the teacher, "and leading up
to it is a broad stairway with three big steps;
and this stairway is called Blekinge. It is
a stairway that is well constructed. It
stretches forty-two miles along the frontage
of Småland house, and anyone who wishes to
go all the way down to the East sea, by
way of the stairs, has twenty-four miles to
wander.

"A good long time must have elapsed since
the stairway was built. Both days and years
have gone by since the steps were hewn from

gray stones and laid down—evenly and smoothly—for a convenient track between Småland and the East sea.

"Since the stairway is so old, one can, of course, understand that it doesn't look just the same now, as it did when it was new. I don't know how much they troubled themselves about such matters at that time; but big as it was, no broom could have kept it clean. After a couple of years, moss and lichen began to grow on it. In the autumn dry leaves and dry grass blew down over it; and in the spring it was piled up with falling stones and gravel. And as all these things were left there to mould, they finally gathered so much soil on the steps that not only herbs and grass, but even bushes and trees could take root there.

"But, at the same time, a great disparity has arisen between the three steps. The topmost step, which lies nearest Småland, is mostly covered with poor soil and small stones, and no trees except birches and bird-cherry and spruce—which can stand the cold on the heights, and are satisfied with little—

can thrive up there. One understands best
how poor and dry it is there, when one sees
how small the field-plots are, that are ploughed
up from the forest lands; and how many little
cabins the people build for themselves; and
how far it is between the churches. But on
the middle step there is better soil, and it
does not lie bound down under such severe
cold, either. This one can see at a glance,
since the trees are both higher and of finer
quality. There you'll find maple and oak and
linden and weeping-birch and hazel trees
growing, but no cone-trees to speak of. And
it is still more noticeable because of the
amount of cultivated land that you will find
there; and also because the people have built
themselves great and beautiful houses. On
the middle step, there are many churches,
with large towns around them; and in every
way it makes a better and finer appearance
than the top step.

"But the very lowest step is the best of all.
It is covered with good rich soil; and, where
it lies and bathes in the sea, it hasn't the
slightest feeling of the Småland chill. Beeches

and chestnut and walnut trees thrive down
here; and they grow so big that they tower
above the church-roofs.   Here lie also the
largest grain-fields; but the people have not
only timber and farming to live upon, but
they are also occupied with fishing and trading
and seafaring.   For this reason you will find
the most costly residences and the prettiest
churches here; and the parishes have devel-
oped into villages and cities.

"But this is not all that is said of the three
steps.   For one must realise that when it
rains on the roof of the big Småland house, or
when the snow melts up there, the water has
to go somewhere; and then, naturally, a lot
of it is spilled over the big stairway.   In the
beginning it probably oozed over the whole
stairway, big as it was; then cracks appeared
in it, and, gradually, the water has accustomed
itself to flow alongside of it, in well dug-out
grooves.   And water is water, whatever one
does with it.   It never has any rest.   In one
place it cuts and files away, and in another
it adds to.   Those grooves it has dug into
vales, and the walls of the vales it has decked

with soil; and bushes and trees and vines have clung to them ever since—so thick, and in such profusion, that they almost hide the stream of water that winds its way down there in the deep. But when the streams come to the landings between the steps, they throw themselves headlong over them; this is why the water comes with such a seething rush, that it gathers strength with which to move mill-wheels and machinery—these, too, have sprung up by every waterfall.

"But this does not tell all that is said of the land with the three steps. It must also be told that up in the big house in Småland there lived once upon a time a giant, who had grown very old. And it fatigued him in his extreme age, to be forced to walk down that long stairway in order to catch salmon from the sea. To him it seemed much more suitable that the salmon should come up to him, where he lived.

"Therefore, he went up on the roof of his great house; and there he stood and threw stones down into the East sea. He threw them with such force that they flew over the

whole of Blekinge and dropped into the sea.
And when the stones came down, the salmon
got so scared that they came up from the sea
and fled toward the Blekinge streams; ran
through the rapids; flung themselves with high
leaps over the waterfalls, and stopped.

"How true this is, one can see by the number of islands and points that lie along the
coast of Blekinge, and which are nothing in
the world but the big stones that the giant
threw.

"One can also tell because the salmon
always go up in the Blekinge streams and
work their way up through rapids and still
water, all the way to Småland.

"That giant is worthy of great thanks and
much honour from the Blekinge people; for
salmon in the streams, and stone-cutting on
the island—that means work which gives food
to many of them even to this day."

VIII

BY RONNEBY RIVER

NEITHER the wild geese nor Smirre Fox had believed that they should ever run across each other after they had left Skåne. But now it turned out so that the wild geese happened to take the route over Blekinge and thither Smirre Fox had also gone.

So far he had kept himself in the northern parts of the province; and since he had not as yet seen any manor parks, or hunting grounds filled with game and dainty young deer, he was more disgruntled than he could say.

One afternoon, when Smirre tramped around in the desolate forest district of Mellanbygden, not far from Ronneby River, he saw a flock of wild geese fly through the air. Instantly he observed that one of the geese was white and then he knew, of course, with whom he had to deal.

Smirre began immediately to hunt the geese
—just as much for the pleasure of getting a
good square meal, as for the desire to be
avenged for all the humiliation that they had
heaped upon him.   He saw that they flew
eastward until they came to Ronneby River.
Then they changed their course, and followed
the river toward the south.   He understood
that they intended to seek a sleeping-place
along the river-bank, and he thought that
he should be able to get hold of a pair of them
without much trouble.   But when Smirre
finally discovered the place where the wild
geese had taken refuge, he observed they
had chosen such a well-protected spot, that he
couldn't get near them.

Ronneby River isn't any big or important
body of water; nevertheless, it is just as much
talked of, for the sake of its pretty shores.
At several points it forces its way forward
between steep mountain-walls that stand
upright out of the water, and are entirely
overgrown with honeysuckle and bird-cherry,
mountain-ash and osier; and there isn't
much that can be more delightful than to

row out on the little dark river on a pleasant summer day, and look upward on all the soft green that fastens itself to the rugged mountain-sides.

But now, when the wild geese and Smirre came to the river, it was cold and blustery spring-winter; all the trees were nude, and there was probably no one who thought the least little bit about whether the shore was ugly or pretty. The wild geese thanked their good fortune that they had found a sand-strip large enough for them to stand upon, on a steep mountain wall. In front of them rushed the river, which was strong and violent in the snow-melting time; behind them they had an impassable mountain rock wall, and overhanging branches screened them. They couldn't have it better.

The geese were asleep instantly; but the boy couldn't get a wink of sleep. As soon as the sun had disappeared he was seized with a fear of the darkness, and a wilderness-terror, and he longed for human beings. Where he lay—tucked in under the goose-wing—he could see nothing, and only hear a little; and he thought if any harm came to the goosey-gander, he couldn't save him.

Noises and rustlings were heard from all directions, and he grew so uneasy that he had to creep from under the wing and seat himself on the ground, beside the goose.

Long-sighted Smirre stood on the mountain's summit and looked down upon the wild geese. "You may as well give this pursuit up first as last," he said to himself. "You can't climb such a steep mountain; you can't swim in such a wild torrent; and there isn't the tiniest strip of land below the mountain which leads to the sleeping-place. Those geese are too wise for you. Don't ever bother yourself again to hunt them!"

But Smirre, like all foxes, had found it hard to give up an undertaking already begun, and so he lay down on the extremest point of the mountain edge, and did not take his eyes off the wild geese. While he lay and watched them, he thought of all the harm they had done him. Yes, it was their fault that he had been driven from Skåne, and had been obliged to move to poverty-stricken

Blekinge. He worked himself up to such a
pitch, as he lay there, that he wished the
wild geese were dead, even if he, himself
should not have the satisfaction of eating
them.

When Smirre's resentment had reached
this height, he heard rasping in a large pine
that grew close to him, and saw a squirrel
come down from the tree, hotly pursued by
a marten. Neither of them noticed Smirre;
and he sat quietly and watched the chase,
which went from tree to tree. He looked
at the squirrel, who moved among the branches
as lightly as though he'd been able to fly. He
looked at the marten, who was not as skilled
at climbing as the squirrel, but who still ran
up and along the branches just as securely
as if they had been even paths in the forest.
"If I could only climb half as well as either
of them," thought the fox, "those things down
there wouldn't sleep in peace very long!"

As soon as the squirrel had been captured,
and the chase was at an end, Smirre walked
over to the marten, but stopped two steps
away from him, to signify that he did not

wish to cheat him of his prey.   He greeted the
marten in a very friendly manner, and wished
him good luck with his catch.   Smirre chose
his words well—as foxes always do.   The
marten, on the contrary, who, with his long
and slender body, his fine head, his soft skin,
and his light brown neck-piece, looked like
a little marvel of beauty—but in reality was
nothing but a crude forest dweller—hardly
answered him.   "It surprises me," said
Smirre, "that such a fine hunter as you are
should be satisfied with chasing squirrels
when there is much better game within reach."
Here he paused; but when the marten only
grinned impudently at him, he continued:
"Can it be possible that you haven't seen the
wild geese that stand under the mountain
wall? or are you not a good enough climber
to get down to them?"

This time he had no need to wait for an
answer.   The marten rushed up to him with
back bent, and every separate hair on end.
"Have you seen wild geese?" he hissed.
"Where are they? Tell me instantly, or
I'll bite your neck off!"   "No! you must

remember that I'm twice your size—so be a little polite. I ask nothing better than to show you the wild geese."

The next instant the marten was on his way down the steep; and while Smirre sat and watched how he swung his snake-like body from branch to branch, he thought: "That pretty tree-hunter has the wickedest heart in all the forest. I believe that the wild geese will have me to thank for a bloody awakening."

But just as Smirre was waiting to hear the geese's death-rattle, he saw the marten tumble from branch to branch—and plump into the river so the water splashed high. Soon thereafter, wings beat loudly and strongly and all the geese went up in a hurried flight.

Smirre intended to hurry after the geese, but he was so curious to know how they had been saved, that he sat there until the marten came clambering up. That poor thing was soaked in mud, and stopped every now and then to rub his head with his forepaws. "Now wasn't that just what I thought— that you were a booby, and would go and

tumble into the river?" said Smirre, contemptuously.

"I haven't acted boobyishly. You don't
need to scold me," said the marten. "I sat
—all ready—on one of the lowest branches
and thought how I should manage to tear a
whole lot of geese to pieces, when a little
creature, no bigger than a squirrel, jumped
up and threw a stone at my head with such
force, that I fell into the water; and before I
had time to pick myself up——"

The marten didn't have to say any more.
He had no audience. Smirre was already a
long way off in pursuit of the wild geese.

In the meantime Akka had flown southward in search of a new sleeping-place.
There was still a little daylight; and, beside,
the half-moon stood high in the heavens, so
that she could see a little. Luckily, she was
well acquainted in these parts, because it had
happened more than once that she had been
wind-driven to Blekinge when she travelled
over the East sea in the spring.

She followed the river as long as she saw
it winding through the moon-lit landscape

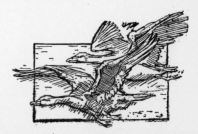

like a black, shining snake. In this way she came way down to Djupafors—where the river first hides itself in an underground channel—and then clear and transparent, as though it were made of glass, rushes down in a narrow cleft, and breaks into bits against its bottom in glittering drops and flying foam. Below the white falls lay a few stones, between which the water rushed away in a wild torrent cataract. Here mother Akka alighted. This was another good sleeping-place—especially this late in the evening, when no human beings moved about. At sunset the geese would hardly have been able to camp there, for Djupafors does not lie in any wilderness. On one side of the falls is a paper factory; on the other— which is steep, and tree-grown—is Djupadal's park, where people are always strolling about on the steep and slippery paths to enjoy the wild stream's rushing movement down in the ravine.

It was about the same here as at the former place; none of the travellers thought the least little bit that they had come to a pretty

and well-known place. They thought rather
that it was ghastly and dangerous to stand
and sleep on slippery, wet stones, in the
middle of a rumbling waterfall. But they
had to be content, if only they were protected
from carnivorous animals.

The geese fell asleep instantly, while the boy
could find no rest in sleep, but sat beside
them that he might watch over the goosey-
gander.

After a while, Smirre came running along
the river-shore. He spied the geese immediately where they stood out in the foaming whirlpools, and understood that he
couldn't get at them here, either. Still he
couldn't make up his mind to abandon them,
but seated himself on the shore and looked
at them. He felt very much humbled, and
thought that his entire reputation as a
hunter was at stake.

All of a sudden, he saw an otter come creeping up from the falls with a fish in his mouth.
Smirre approached him but stopped within
two steps of him, to show him that he didn't
wish to take his game from him.

"You're a remarkable one, who can content yourself with catching a fish, while the stones are covered with geese!" said Smirre. He was so eager, that he hadn't taken the time to arrange his words as carefully as he was wont to do. The otter didn't turn his head once in the direction of the river. He was a vagabond—like all otters—and had fished many times by Vomb Lake, and probably knew Smirre Fox. "I know very well how you act when you want to coax away a salmon-trout, Smirre," said he.

"Oh! is it you, Gripe?" said Smirre, and was delighted; for he knew that this particular otter was a quick and accomplished swimmer. "I don't wonder that you do not care to look at the wild geese, since you can't manage to get out to them." But the otter, who had swimming-webs between his toes, and a stiff tail—which was as good as an oar— and a skin that was water-proof, didn't wish to have it said of him that there was a waterfall that he wasn't able to manage. He turned toward the stream; and as soon as he caught sight of the wild geese, he threw the fish away, and rushed down the steep shore and into the river.

If it had been a little later in the spring, so that the nightingales in Djupafors had been at home, they would have sung for many a day, of Gripe's struggle with the rapid. For the otter was thrust back by the waves many times, and carried down river; but he fought his way steadily up again. He swam forward in still water; he crawled over stones, and gradually came nearer the wild geese. It was a perilous trip, which might well have earned the right to be sung by the nightingales.

Smirre followed the otter's course with his eyes as well as he could. At last he saw that the otter was in the act of climbing up to the wild geese. But just then it shrieked shrill and wild. The otter tumbled backward into the water, and dashed away as if he had been a blind kitten. An instant later, there was a great crackling of geese's wings. They raised themselves and flew away to find another sleeping-place.

The otter soon came on land. He said nothing, but commenced to lick one of his forepaws. When Smirre sneered at him because he hadn't succeeded, he broke out: "It was not the fault of my swimming-art, Smirre. I had raced all the way over to the geese, and was about to climb up to them, when a tiny creature came running, and jabbed me in the foot with some sharp iron. It hurt so, I lost my footing, and then the current took me."

He didn't have to say any more. Smirre was already far away on his way to the wild geese.

Once again Akka and her flock had to take a night fly. Fortunately, the moon had not gone down; and with the aid of its light, she succeeded in finding another of those sleeping-places which she knew in that neighbourhood. Again she followed the shining river toward the south. Over Djupadal's manor, and over Ronneby's dark roofs and white waterfalls she swayed forward without alighting. But a little south of the city and not far from the sea, lies Ronneby health-spring, with its bath house and spring house; with its big hotel and summer cottages for the Spring's guests. All these stand empty and desolate

in winter—which the birds know perfectly
well; and many are the bird-companies who
seek shelter on the deserted buildings' balus-
trades and balconies during hard storm-times.

Here the wild geese lit on a balcony, and,
as usual, they fell asleep at once. The boy,
on the contrary, could not sleep because he
hadn't cared to creep in under the goosey-
gander's wing.

The balcony faced south, so the boy had
an outlook over the sea. And since he could
not sleep, he sat there and saw how pretty it
looked when sea and land meet, here in
Blekinge.

You see that sea and land can meet in many
different ways. In many places the land
comes down toward the sea with flat, tufted
meadows, and the sea meets the land with
flying sand, which piles up in mounds and
drifts. It appears as though they both dis-
liked each other so much that they only
wished to show the poorest they possessed.
But it can also happen that, when the land
comes toward the sea, it raises a wall of hills
in front of it—as though the sea were

something dangerous. When the land does this, the sea comes up to it with fiery wrath, and beats and roars and lashes against the rocks, and looks as if it would tear the land-hill to pieces.

But in Blekinge it is altogether different when sea and land meet. There the land breaks itself up into points and islands and islets; and the sea divides itself into fiords and bays and sounds; and it is, perhaps, this which makes it look as if they must meet in happiness and harmony.

Think now first and foremost of the sea! Far out it lies desolate and empty and big, and has nothing else to do but to roll its gray billows. When it comes toward the land, it happens across the first obstacle. This it immediately overpowers; tears away everything green, and makes it as gray as itself. Then it meets still another obstacle. With this it does the same thing. And still another. Yes, the same thing happens to this also. It is stripped and plundered, as if it had fallen into robbers' hands. Then the obstacles come nearer and nearer together, and then the sea must understand that the land sends toward it her littlest children, in order to move it to pity. It also becomes more friendly the farther in it comes; rolls its waves less high; moderates its storms; lets the green things stay in cracks and crevices; separates itself into small sounds and inlets, and becomes at last so harmless in the land, that little boats dare venture out on it. It certainly cannot recognise itself—so mild and friendly has it grown.

And then think of the hillside! It lies uniform, and looks the same almost everywhere. It consists of flat grain-fields, with one and another birch-grove between them; or else of long stretches of forest ranges. It appears as if it had thought about nothing but grain and turnips and potatoes and spruce and pine. Then comes a sea-fiord that cuts far into it. It doesn't mind that, but borders it with birch and alder, just as if it was an ordinary fresh-water lake. Then still another wave comes driving in. Nor does the hillside bother itself about cringing to this, but it, too, gets the same covering as the first one. Then the

fiords begin to broaden and separate, they
break up fields and woods and then the hillside cannot help but notice them. "I believe
it is the sea itself that is coming," says the
hillside, and then it begins to adorn itself.
It wreathes itself with blossoms, travels up
and down in hills and throws islands into
the sea. It no longer cares about pines and
spruces, but casts them off like old every day
clothes, and parades later with big oaks and
lindens and chestnuts, and with blossoming
leafy bowers, and becomes as gorgeous as a
manor-park. And when it meets the sea, it
is so changed that it doesn't know itself. All
this one cannot see very well until summer-
time; but, at any rate, the boy observed how
mild and friendly nature was; and he began
to feel calmer than he had been before, that
night. Then, suddenly, he heard a sharp
and ugly yowl from the bath-house park; and
when he stood up he saw, in the white moonlight, a fox standing on the pavement under
the balcony. For Smirre had followed the
wild geese once more. But when he had
found the place where they were quartered, he

had understood that it was impossible to get at them in any way; then he had not been able to keep from yowling with chagrin.

When the fox yowled in this manner, old Akka, the leader-goose was awakened. Although she could see nothing, she thought she recognised the voice. "Is it you who are out to-night, Smirre?" said she. "Yes," said Smirre, "it is I; and I want to ask what you geese think of the night that I have given you?"

"Do you mean to say that it is you who have sent the marten and otter against us?" asked Akka. "A good turn shouldn't be denied," said Smirre. "You once played the goose-game with me, now I have begun to play the fox-game with you; and I'm not inclined to let up on it so long as a single one of you still lives even if I have to follow you the world over!"

"You, Smirre, ought at least to think whether it is right for you, who are weaponed with both teeth and claws, to hound us in this way; we, who are without defence," said Akka.

Smirre thought that Akka sounded scared, and he said quickly: "If you, Akka, will take that Thumbietot—who has so often opposed me—and throw him down to me, I'll promise to make peace with you. Then I'll never more pursue you or any of yours." "I'm not going to give you Thumbietot," said Akka. "From the youngest of us to the oldest, we would willingly give our lives for his sake!" "Since you're so fond of him," said Smirre, "I'll promise you that he shall be the first among you that I will wreak vengeance upon."

Akka said no more, and after Smirre had sent up a few more yowls, all was still. The boy lay all the while awake. Now it was Akka's words to the fox that prevented him from sleeping. Never had he dreamed that he should hear anything so great as that anyone was willing to risk life for his sake. From that moment, it could no longer be said of Nils Holgersson that he did not care for anyone.

IX

KARLSKRONA

IT WAS a moonlight evening in Karls-krona—calm and beautiful. But earlier in the day, there had been rain and wind; and the people must have thought that the bad weather still continued, for hardly one of them had ventured out on the streets.

While the city lay there so desolate, Akka, the wild goose, and her flock, came flying toward it over Vemmön and Pantarholmen. They were out in the late evening to seek a sleeping-place on the islands. They couldn't remain inland because they were disturbed by Smirre Fox wherever they lighted.

When the boy rode along high up in the air, and looked at the sea and the islands which spread themselves before him, he thought that everything appeared so strange

and spook-like. The heavens were no longer
blue, but encased him like a globe of green glass.
The sea was milk-white, and as far as he could
see rolled small white waves tipped with
silver ripples. In the midst of all this white
lay numerous little islets, absolutely coal
black. Whether they were big or little,
whether they were as even as meadows, or
full of cliffs they looked just as black. Even
dwelling houses and churches and windmills,
which at other times are white or red, were
outlined in black against the green sky. The
boy thought it was as if the earth had been
transformed, and he was come to another world.

He thought that just for this one night he
wanted to be brave, and not afraid—when
he saw something that really frightened
him. It was a high cliff island, which
was covered with big, angular blocks; and
between the blocks shone specks of bright,
shining gold. He couldn't keep from thinking of Maglestone, by Trolle-Ljungby, which
the trolls sometimes raised upon high gold
pillars; and he wondered if this was some-
thing like that.

"The boy rode along—high up in the air"

But with the stones and the gold it might have gone fairly well, if such a lot of horrid things had not been lying all around the island. It looked like whales and sharks and other big sea-monsters. But the boy understood that it was the sea-trolls, who had gathered around the island and intended to crawl up on it, to fight with the land-trolls who lived there. And those on the land were probably afraid, for he saw how a big giant stood on the highest point of the island and raised his arms—as if in despair over all the misfortune that should come to him and his island.

The boy was not a little terrified when he noticed that Akka began to descend right over that particular island! "No, for pity's sake! We must not light there," said he.

But the geese continued to descend, and soon the boy was astonished that he could have seen things so awry. In the first place, the big stone blocks were nothing but houses. The whole island was a city; and the shining gold specks were street lamps and lighted window-panes. The giant, who stood highest up on the island, and raised his arms, was a church with two cross-towers; all the sea-trolls and monsters, which he thought he had seen, were boats and ships of every description, that lay anchored all around the island. On the side which lay toward the land were mostly row-boats and sail-boats and small coast steamers; but on the side that faced the sea lay armour-clad battleships; some were broad, with very thick, slanting smoke-stacks; others were long and narrow, and so constructed that they could glide through the water like fishes.

Now what city might this be? That, the boy could figure out because he saw all the battle-ships. All his life he had loved ships, although he had had nothing to do with any, except the galleys which he had sailed in the road ditches. He knew very well that this city—where so many battleships lay—couldn't be any place but Karlskrona.

The boy's grandfather had been an old marine; and as long as he had lived, he had talked of Karlskrona every day; of the great warship dock, and of all the other things to be seen in that city. The boy felt perfectly at home, and he was glad that he should see all this of which he had heard so much.

But he only had a glimpse of the towers and fortifications which barred the entrance to the harbour, and the many buildings, and the shipyard—before Akka came down on one of the flat church-towers.

This was a pretty safe place for those who wanted to get away from a fox, and the boy began to wonder if he couldn't venture to crawl in under the goosey-gander's wing for this one night. Yes, that he might safely do. It would do him good to get a little sleep. He should try to see a little more of the dock and the ships after it had grown light.

The boy himself thought it was strange that he could keep still and wait until the next morning to see the ships. He certainly had not slept five minutes before he slipped out from under the wing and slid down the lightning-rod and the water-spout all the way down to the ground.

Soon he stood on a big square which spread itself in front of the church. It was covered

with round stones, and was just as difficult
for him to travel over, as it is for big people to
walk on a tufted meadow. Those who are
accustomed to live in the open—or way out
in the country—always feel uneasy when
they come into a city, where the houses stand
straight and forbidding, and the streets are
open, so that everyone can see who goes there.
And it happened in the same way with the boy.
When he stood on the big Karlskrona square,
and looked at the German church, and town
hall, and the cathedral from which he had
just descended he couldn't do anything but
wish that he was back on the tower again with
the geese.

It was a lucky thing that the square was
entirely deserted. There wasn't a human
being about—unless he counted a statue that
stood on a high pedestal. The boy gazed long
at the statue, which represented a big,
brawny man in a three-cornered hat, long
waistcoat, knee-breeches and coarse shoes,
and wondered what kind of a one he was. He
held a long stick in his hand, and he looked as
if he would know how to make use of it, too—

for he had an awfully severe countenance,
with a big, hooked nose and an ugly mouth.

"What is that long-lipped thing doing
here?" said the boy at last. He had never
felt so small and insignificant as he did that
night. He tried to jolly himself up a bit by
saying something audacious. Then he thought
no more about the statue, but betook himself to a wide street which led down to the sea.

But the boy hadn't gone far before he heard
that someone was following him. Someone
was walking behind him, who stamped on the
stone pavement with heavy footsteps, and
pounded on the ground with a hard stick.
It sounded as if the bronze man up in the
square had gone out for a promenade.

The boy listened after the steps, while he
ran down the street, and he became more and
more convinced that it was the bronze man.
The ground trembled, and the houses shook.
It couldn't be anyone but he, who walked so
heavily, and the boy grew panic-stricken
when he thought of what he had just said to
him. He did not dare to turn his head to
find out if it really was he.

"Perhaps he is only out walking for recreation," thought the boy. "Surely he can't be offended with me for the words I spoke. They were not at all badly meant."

Instead of going straight on, and trying to get down to the dock, the boy turned into a side street which led east. First and foremost, he wanted to get away from the one who tramped after him.

But the next instant he heard that the bronze man had switched off to the same street; and then the boy was so scared that he didn't know what he would do with himself. And how hard it was to find any hiding places in a city where all the gates were closed! Then he saw on his right an old frame church, which lay a short distance away from the street in the centre of a large grove. Not an instant did he pause to consider, but rushed on toward the church. "If I can only get there, then I'll surely be shielded from all harm," thought he.

As he ran forward, he suddenly caught sight of a man who stood on a gravel path and beckoned to him. "There is certainly someone who will help me!" thought the boy; he became intensely happy, and hurried off in that direction.   He was actually so frightened that the heart of him fairly thumped in his breast.

But when he came up to the man who stood on the edge of the gravel path, upon a low pedestal, he was absolutely thunder-struck.   "Surely, it can't have been that one who beckoned to me!" thought he; for he saw that the entire man was made of wood.

He stood there and stared at him. He was a thick-set man on short legs, with a broad, ruddy countenance, shiny, black hair and full black beard. On his head he wore a wooden hat; on his body, a brown wooden coat; around his waist, a black wooden belt; on his legs he had wide wooden knee-breeches and wooden stockings; and on his feet black wooden shoes. He was newly painted and newly varnished, so that he glistened and shone in the moonlight. This undoubtedly had a good deal to do with giving him such a good-natured appearance, that the boy at once placed confidence in him.

In his left hand he held a wooden slate, and there the boy read:

> Most humbly I beg you,
>   Though voice I may lack:
> Come drop a penny, do;
>   But lift my hat!

Oh ho! the man was only a poor-box. The boy felt that he had been done. He had expected that this should be something really remarkable. And now he remembered that grandpa had also spoken of the wooden man, and said that all the children in Karlskrona were so fond of him. And that must have been true, for he, too, found it hard to part with the wooden man. He had something so old-timy about him, that one could well take him to be many hundred years old; and at the same time, he looked so strong and bold, and animated—just as one might imagine that folks looked in olden times.

The boy had so much fun looking at the wooden man, that he entirely forgot the one from whom he was fleeing. But now he heard him. He turned from the street and

came into the churchyard.   He followed him
here too!   Where should the boy go?

Just then he saw the wooden man bend
down to him and stretch forth his big, broad
hand.   It was impossible to believe anything
but good of him; and with one jump, the boy
stood in his hand.   The wooden man lifted
him to his hat—and stuck him under it.

The boy was just hidden, and the wooden
man had just gotten his arm in its right place
again, when the bronze man stopped in front
of him and banged the stick on the ground,
so that the wooden man shook on his pedestal.
Thereupon the bronze man said in a strong
and resonant voice: "Who might this one be?"

The wooden man's arm went up, so that it
creaked in the old woodwork, and he touched
his hat-brim as he replied; "Rosenbom, by
Your Majesty's leave.   Once upon a time boatswain on the man-of-war, *Dristigheten;* after
completed service, sexton at the Admiral's
church—and, lately, carved in wood and
exhibited in the churchyard as a poor-box."

The boy gave a start when he heard that
the wooden man said "Your Majesty."   For

now, when he thought about it, he knew that the statue on the square represented the one who had founded the city. It was probably no less an one than Charles the Eleventh himself, whom he had encountered.

"He gives a good account of himself," said the bronze man. "Can he also tell me if he has seen a little brat who runs around in the city to-night? He's an impudent rascal, if I get hold of him, I'll teach him manners!" With that, he again pounded on the ground with his stick, and looked fearfully angry.

"By Your Majesty's leave, I have seen him," said the wooden man; and the boy was so scared that he commenced to shake where he sat under the hat and looked at the bronze man through a crack in the wood. But he calmed down when the wooden man continued: "Your Majesty is on the wrong track. That youngster certainly intended to run into the shipyard, and conceal himself there."

"Does he say so, Rosenbom? Well then, don't stand still on the pedestal any longer but come with me and help me find him. Four eyes are better than two, Rosenbom."

But the wooden man answered in a doleful voice: "I would most humbly beg to be permitted to stay where I am. I look well and sleek because of the paint, but I'm old and mouldy, and cannot stand moving about."

The bronze man was not one of those who liked to be contradicted. "What sort of notions are these? Come along, Rosenbom!" Then he raised his stick and gave the other one a resounding whack on the shoulder. "Does Rosenbom not see that he holds together?"

With that they broke off and walked forward on the streets of Karlskrona—large and mighty—until they came to a high gate, which led to the shipyard. Just outside and on guard walked one of the navy's jack-tars, but the bronze man strutted past him and kicked the gate open without the jack-tar's pretending to notice it.

As soon as they had gotten into the ship-yard, they saw before them a wide, expansive harbour separated by pile-bridges. In the different harbour basins, lay the warships, which looked bigger, and more awe-inspiring close to, like this, than lately, when the boy had seen them from up above. "Then it wasn't so crazy after all, to imagine that they were sea-trolls," thought he.

"Where does Rosenbom think it most advisable for us to begin the search?" said the bronze man.

"Such an one as he, could most easily conceal himself in the hall of models," replied the wooden man.

On a narrow land-strip which stretched to the right from the gate, all along the harbour, lay ancient structures. The bronze man walked over to a building with low walls, small windows, and a conspicuous roof. He pounded on the door with his stick until it burst open; and tramped up a pair of worn-out steps. Soon they came into a large hall, which was filled with tackled and full-rigged little ships. The boy understood without being told, that these were models for the ships which had been built for the Swedish navy.

There were ships of many different varieties. There were old men-of-war, whose sides bristled with cannon, and which had high structures fore and aft, and their masts weighed down with a network of sails and ropes. There were small island-boats with rowing-benches along the sides; there were undecked cannon sloops and richly gilded frigates, which were models of the ones the kings had used on their travels. Finally, there were also the heavy, broad armour-plated ships with towers and cannon on deck—such as are in use nowadays; and narrow, shining torpedo boats which resembled long, slender fishes.

When the boy was carried around among all this, he was awed. "Fancy that such big, splendid ships have been built here in Sweden!" he thought to himself.

He had plenty of time to see all that was to be seen in there; for when the bronze man saw the models, he forgot everything else. He examined them all, from the first to the last, and asked about them. And Rosenbom, the boatswain on the *Dristigheten*, told as much as he knew of the ships' builders, and of those who had manned them; and of the

fates they had met. He told them about
Chapman and Puke and Trolle; of Hoagland
and Svensksund—all the way along until
1809—after that he had not been there.

Both he and the bronze man had the most
to say about the fine old wooden ships. The
new battleships they didn't exactly appear
to understand.

"I can hear that Rosenbom doesn't know
anything about these new-fangled things,"
said the bronze man. "Therefore, let us go
and look at something else; for this amuses
me, Rosenbom."

By this time he had entirely given up his
search for the boy, who felt calm and secure
where he sat in the wooden hat.

Thereupon both men wandered through
the big establishment: sail-making shops,
anchor smithy, machine and carpenter shops.
They saw the mast sheers and the docks;
the large magazines, the arsenal, the rope-
bridge and the big discarded dock, which
had been blasted in the rock. They went out
upon the pile-bridges, where the naval vessels
lay moored, stepped on board and examined

them like two old sea-dogs; wondered; disapproved; approved; and became indignant.

The boy sat in safety under the wooden hat, and heard all about how they had laboured and struggled in this place, to equip the navies which had gone out from here. He heard how life and blood had been risked; how the last penny had been sacrificed to build the warships; how skilled men had strained all their powers, in order to perfect these ships which had been their fatherland's safeguard. A couple of times the tears came to the boy's eyes, as he heard all this.

And the very last, they went into an open court, where the galley models of old men-of-war were grouped; and a more remarkable sight the boy had never beheld; for these models had inconceivably powerful and terror-striking faces. They were big, fearless and savage: filled with the same proud spirit that had fitted out the great ships. They were from another time than his. He thought that he shrivelled up before them.

But when they came in here, the bronze

man said to the wooden man: "Take off thy
hat, Rosenbom, for those that stand here!
They have all fought for the fatherland."

And Rosenbom—like the bronze man—
had forgotten why they had begun this
tramp. Without thinking, he lifted the
wooden hat from his head and shouted:

"I take off my hat to the one who chose
the harbour and founded the shipyard and
re-created the navy; to the monarch who has
awakened all this into life!"

"Thanks, Rosenbom! That was well
spoken. Rosenbom is a fine man. But what
is this, Rosenbom?"

For there stood Nils Holgersson, right on
the top of Rosenbom's bald pate. He wasn't
afraid any longer; but raised his white toboggan hood, and shouted: "Hurrah for you,
Longlip!"

The bronze man struck the ground hard
with his stick; but the boy never learned
what he had intended to do for now the sun
ran up, and, at the same time, both the
bronze man and the wooden man vanished—
as if they had been made of mists. While he

still stood and stared after them, the wild geese flew up from the church tower, and swayed back and forth over the city. Instantly they caught sight of Nils Holgersson; and then the big white one darted down from the sky and fetched him.

X

THE TRIP TO ÖLAND

Sunday, April third.

THE wild geese went out on a wooded
island to feed. There they happened
to run across a few gray geese, who were surprised to see them—since they knew very
well that their kinsmen, the wild geese,
usually travel over the interior of the country.
They were curious and inquisitive, and
wouldn't be satisfied with less than that the
wild geese should tell them all about the per-
secution which they had to endure from Smirre
Fox. When they had finished, a gray goose,
who appeared to be as old and as wise as
Akka herself, said: "It was a great misfortune for you that Smirre Fox was declared
an outlaw in his own land. He'll be sure to
keep his word, and follow you all the way up
to Lappland. If I were in your place, I
shouldn't travel north over Småland, but

would take the outside route over Öland instead, so that he'll be thrown off the track entirely. To really mislead him, you must remain for a couple of days on Öland's southern point. There you'll find lots of food and lots of company. I don't believe you'll regret it, if you go over there."

It was certainly very sensible advice, and the wild geese concluded to follow it. As soon as they had eaten all they could hold, they started on the trip to Öland. None of them had ever been there before, but the gray goose had given them excellent directions. They only had to travel direct south until they came to a large bird-track, which extended all along the Blekinge coast. All the birds who had winter residences by the West sea, and who now intended to travel to Finland and Russia, flew forward there— and, in passing, they were always in the habit of stopping at Öland to rest. The wild geese would have no trouble in finding guides.

That day it was perfectly still and warm —like a summer's day—the best weather in the world for a sea trip. The only grave

thing about it was that it was not quite clear,
for the sky was gray and veiled. Here and
there were enormous mist-clouds which
hung way down to the sea's outer edge, and
obstructed the view.

When the travellers had gotten away
from the wooded island, the sea spread itself
so smooth and mirror-like, that the boy as
he looked down thought the water had
disappeared. There was no longer any earth
under him. He had nothing but mist and
sky around him. He grew very dizzy, and
held himself tight on the goose-back, more
frightened than when he sat there for the first
time. It seemed as though he couldn't
possibly hold on; he must fall in some
direction.

It was even worse when they reached the
big bird-track, of which the gray goose had
spoken. Actually, there came flock after
flock flying in exactly the same direction.
They seemed to follow a fixed route. There
were ducks and gray geese, surf-scoters and
guillemots, loons and pin-tail ducks and
mergansers and grebes and oyster-catchers

and sea-grouse. But now, when the boy leaned forward, and looked in the direction where the sea ought to lie, he saw the whole bird procession reflected in the water. But he was so dizzy that he didn't understand how this had come about: he thought that the whole bird procession flew with their bellies upside down. Still he didn't wonder at this so much, for he did not himself know which was up, and which was down.

The birds were tired out and impatient to get on. None of them shrieked or said a funny thing, and this made everything seem peculiarly unreal.

"Think, if we have travelled away from the earth!" he said to himself. "Think, if we are on our way up to heaven!"

He saw nothing but mists and birds around him, and began to look upon it as reasonable that they were travelling heavenward. He was glad, and wondered what he should see up there. The dizziness passed all at once. He was so exceedingly happy at the thought that he was on his way to heaven and was leaving this earth.

Just about then he heard a couple of loud shots, and saw two white smoke-columns ascend.

There was a sudden awakening, and an unrest among the birds. "Hunters! Hunters!" they cried. "Fly high! Fly away!"

Then the boy saw, finally, that they were travelling all the while over the sea-coast, and that they certainly were not in heaven. In a long row lay small boats filled with hunters, who fired shot upon shot. The nearest bird-flocks hadn't noticed them in time. They had flown too low. Several dark bodies sank down toward the sea; and for everyone that fell, there arose cries of anguish from the living.

It was strange for one who had but lately believed himself in heaven, to wake up suddenly to such fear and lamentation. Akka shot toward the heights as fast as she could, and the flock followed with the greatest possible speed. The wild geese got safely out of the way, but the boy couldn't get over his amazement. "To think that anyone could wish to shoot upon such as Akka and Yksi and Kaksi and the goosey-gander and the others! Human beings had no conception of what they did."

So it bore on again, in the still air, and everything was as quiet as heretofore—with the exception that some of the tired birds called out every now and then: "Are we not there soon? Are you sure we're on the right track?" Hereupon, those who flew in the centre answered: "We are flying straight to Öland; straight to Öland."

The gray geese were tired out, and the loons flew around them. "Don't be in such a rush!" cried the ducks. "You'll eat up all the food before we get there." "Oh! there'll be enough for both you and us," answered the loons.

Before they had gotten so far that they saw Öland, there came a light wind against them. It brought with it something that resembled immense clouds of white smoke—just as if there was a big fire somewhere.

When the birds saw the first white spiral haze, they became uneasy and increased their speed. But that which resembled smoke blew thicker and thicker, and at last it enveloped them altogether. They smelled no smoke; and the smoke was not dark and dry, but white and damp. Suddenly the boy understood that it was nothing but a mist.

When the mist became so thick that one couldn't see a goose-length ahead, the birds began to carry on like real lunatics. All these, who before had travelled forward in such perfect order, began to play in the mist. They flew hither and thither, to entice one another astray. "Be careful!" they cried. "You're only travelling round and round. Turn back, for pity's sake! You'll never get to Öland in this way."

They all knew perfectly well where the island was, but they did their best to lead each other astray. "Look at those wagtails!" rang out in the mist. "They are going back toward the North Sea!" "Have a care, wild geese!" shrieked someone from another direction. "If you continue like this, you'll get clear up to Rügen."

There was, of course, no danger that the **birds** who were accustomed to travel here, would permit themselves to be lured in a wrong direction. But the ones who had a hard time of it were the wild geese. The jesters observed that they were uncertain as to the way, and did all they could to confuse them.

"Where do you intend to go, good people?" called a swan. He came right up to Akka, and looked sympathetic and serious.

"We shall travel to Öland; but we have never been there before," said Akka. She thought that this was a bird to be trusted.

"It's too bad," said the swan. "They have lured you in the wrong direction. You're on the road to Blekinge. Now come with me, and I'll put you right!"

And so he flew off with them; and when he had taken them so far away from the track that they heard no calls, he disappeared in the mist.

They flew around for a while at random. They had barely succeeded in finding the birds again, when a duck approached them. "It's best that you lie down on the water until the mist clears," said the duck. "It is evident that you are not accustomed to look out for yourselves on journeys."

Those rogues succeeded in making Akka's head swim. As near as the boy could make out, the wild geese flew round and round for a long time.

"Be careful! Can't you see that you are flying up and down?" shouted a loon as he rushed by. The boy positively clutched the goosey-gander around the neck. This was something which he had feared for a long time.

No one can tell when they would have arrived, if they hadn't heard a rolling and muffled sound in the distance.

Then Akka craned her neck, snapped hard with her wings, and rushed on at full speed. Now she had something to go by. The gray goose had told her not to light on Öland's southern point, because there was a cannon there, which the people used to shoot the mist with. Now she knew the way, and now no one in the world should lead her astray again.

XI

ÖLAND'S SOUTHERN POINT

April third to sixth.

ON THE most southerly part of Öland lies a royal demesne, which is called Ottenby. It is a rather large estate which extends from shore to shore, straight across the island; and it is remarkable because it has always been a haunt for large bird-companies. In the Seventeenth Century, when the kings used to go over to Öland to hunt, the entire estate was nothing but a deer park. In the Eighteenth Century there was a stud there, where blooded race-horses were bred; and a sheep farm, where several hundred sheep were maintained. In our days you'll find neither blooded horses nor sheep at Ottenby. In place of them, live great herds of young horses, which are to be used by the cavalry.

In all the land there is certainly no place

that could be a better abode for animals. Along the extreme eastern shore lies the old sheep meadow, which is a mile and a half long, and the largest meadow in all Öland, where animals can graze and play and run about, as free as if they were in a wilderness. And there you will find the celebrated Ottenby grove with the hundred-year-old oaks, which give shade from the sun, and shelter from the severe Öland winds. And we must not forget the long Ottenby wall, which stretches from shore to shore, and separates Ottenby from the rest of the island, so that the animals may know how far the old royal demesne extends, and be careful about getting in on other ground, where they are not so well protected.

You'll find plenty of tame animals at Ottenby, but that isn't all. One could almost believe that the wild ones also felt that on an old crown property both the wild and the tame ones can count upon shelter and protection— since they venture there in such great numbers.

Beside, there are still a few stags of the old descent left; and burrow-ducks and partridges love to live there, and it offers a resting place, in the spring and late summer, for thousands of migratory birds. Above all, it is the swampy eastern shore below the sheep-meadow, where the migratory birds alight, to rest and feed.

When the wild geese and Nils Holgersson had finally found their way to Öland, they came down, like all the rest, on the shore near the sheep meadow. The mist lay thick over the island, just as it had over the sea. But still the boy was amazed at all the birds which he discerned, only on the little narrow stretch of shore which he could see.

It was a low sand-shore with stones and pools, and a lot of cast-up sea-weed. If the boy had been permitted to choose, it isn't likely that he would have thought of alighting there; but the birds probably looked upon this as a veritable paradise. Ducks and geese walked about and fed on the meadow; nearer the water, ran snipe, and other coast-birds. The loons lay in the sea and fished, but the life and movement was upon the long sea-weed banks along the coast. There the birds stood side by side close together and picked grub-worms—which must have been found there in limitless quantities for it was very evident that there was never any complaint over a lack of food.

The great majority were going to travel farther, and had only alighted to take a short rest; and as soon as the leader of a flock thought that his comrades had recovered themselves sufficiently he said, "If you are ready now, we may as well move on."

"No, wait, wait! We haven't had anything like enough," said the followers.

"You surely don't believe that I intend to let you eat so much that you will not be able to move?" said the leader, and flapped his wings and started off. Along the outermost sea-weed banks lay a flock of swans. They didn't bother about going on land, but rested themselves by lying and rocking on the water. Now and then they dived down with their necks and brought up food from the sea-bottom. When they had gotten hold of anything very good, they indulged in loud shouts that sounded like trumpet calls.

When the boy heard that there were swans on the shoals, he hurried out to the sea-weed banks. He had never before seen wild swans at close range. He had luck on his side, so that he got close up to them.

The boy was not the only one who had heard the swans. Both the wild geese and the gray geese and the loons swam out between the banks, laid themselves in a ring around the swans and stared at them. The swans ruffled their feathers, raised their wings like sails, and lifted their necks high in the air. Occasionally one and another of them swam up to a goose, or a great loon, or a diving-duck, and said a few words. And then it appeared as though the one addressed hardly dared raise his bill to reply.

But then there was a little loon—a tiny mischievous baggage—who couldn't stand all this ceremony. He dived suddenly, and disappeared under the water's edge. Soon after that, one of the swans let out a scream, and swam off so quickly that the water foamed. Then he stopped and began to look majestic once more. But soon, another one

shrieked in the same way as the first one, and
then a third.

The little loon wasn't able to stay under
water any longer, but appeared on the water's
edge, little and black and venomous.   The
swans rushed toward him; but when they saw
what a poor little thing it was, they turned
abruptly—as if they considered themselves
too good to quarrel with him.   Then the little
loon dived again, and pinched their feet.   It
certainly must have hurt; and the worst of it
was, that they could not maintain their
dignity.   At once they took a decided stand.
They began to beat the air with their wings
so that it thundered; came forward a bit—as
though they were running on the water—
finally, got wind under their wings, and raised
themselves.

When the swans were gone they were
greatly missed; and those who had lately
been amused by the little loon's antics scolded
him for his thoughtlessness.

The boy walked toward land again.   There
he stationed himself to see how the pool-
snipe played.   They resembled small storks;

like these, they had little .bodies, long legs
and necks, and light, swaying movements;
only they were not gray, but brown. They
stood in a long row on the shore where it
was washed by waves. As soon as a wave
rolled in, the whole row ran backward; as
soon as it receded, they followed it. And
they kept this up for hours.

The showiest of all the birds were the
burrow-ducks. They were undoubtedly
related to the ordinary ducks; for, like these,
they too had a thick-set body, broad bill, and
webbed feet; but they were much more elab-
orately gotten up. The feather dress, itself,
was white; around their necks they wore a
broad gold band; the wing-mirror shone in
green, red, and black; and the wing-edges were
black, and the head was dark green and
shimmered like satin.

As soon as any of these appeared on the
shore, the others said: "Now, just look at
those things! They know how to tog themselves out." "If they were not so conspicuous, they wouldn't have to dig their
nests in the earth, but could lay above ground,

like anyone else," said a brown mallard-duck. "They may try as much as they please, still they'll never get anywhere with such noses," said a gray goose. And this was actually true. The burrow-ducks had a big knob on the base of the bill, which spoiled their appearance.

Close to the shore, sea-gulls and sea-swallows moved forward on the water and fished. "What kind of fish are you catching?" asked a wild goose. "It's a stickle-back. It's Öland stickleback. It's the best stickleback in the world," said a gull. "Won't you taste of it?" And he flew up to the goose, with his mouth full of the little fishes, and wanted to give her some. "Ugh! Do you think that I eat such filth?" said the wild goose.

The next morning it was just as cloudy. The wild geese walked about on the meadow and fed; but the boy had gone to the sea-shore to gather mussels. There were plenty of them; and when he thought that the next day, perhaps, they would be in some place where they couldn't get any food at all, he

concluded that he would try to make himself
a little bag, which he could fill with mussels.
He found an old sedge on the meadow, which
was strong and tough; and out of this he
began to braid a knapsack. He worked at
this for several hours, but he was well satisfied with it when it was finished.

At dinner time all the wild geese came
running and asked him if he had seen anything of the white goosey-gander. "No, he
has not been with me," said the boy. "We
had him with us all along until just lately,"
said Akka, "but now we no longer know
where he's to be found."

The boy jumped up, and was terribly frightened. He asked if any fox or eagle had put
in an appearance, or if any human being had
been seen in the neighbourhood. But no one
had noticed anything dangerous. The
goosey-gander had probably lost his way in
the mist.

But it was just as great a misfortune for the
boy, in whatever way the white one had been
lost, and he started off immediately to hunt
for him. The mist shielded him, so that he

could run wherever he wished without being
seen, but it also prevented him from seeing.
He ran southward along the shore—all the
way down to the lighthouse and the mist
cannon on the island's extreme point.   It
was the same bird confusion everywhere,
but no goosey-gander.   He ventured over to
Ottenby estate, and he searched every one of
the old, hollow oaks in Ottenby grove, but
he saw no trace of the goosey-gander.

He searched until it began to grow dark.
Then he had to turn back again to the eastern
shore.   He walked with heavy steps, and
was fearfully blue.   He didn't know what
would become of him if he couldn't find the
goosey-gander.   There was no one whom he
could spare less.

But when he wandered over the sheep
meadow, what was that big, white thing that
came toward him in the mist if it wasn't
the goosey-gander?   He was all right, and
very glad that, at last, he had been able to
find his way back to the others.   The mist
had made him so dizzy, he said, that he had
wandered around on the big meadow all day

long.   The boy threw his arms around his neck,
for very joy, and begged him to take care of
himself, and not wander away from the others.
And he promised, positively, that he never
would do this again.   No, never again.

But the next morning, when the boy went
down to the beach and hunted for mussels,
the geese came running and asked if he had
seen the goosey-gander.   No, of course he
hadn't.   "Well, then the goosey-gander was
lost again.   He had gone astray in the mist,
just as he had done the day before."

The boy ran off in great terror and began
to search.   He found one place where the
Ottenby wall was so tumble-down that he
could climb over it.   Later, he went about,
first on the shore—which gradually widened
and became so large that there was room for
fields and meadows and farms—then up on
the flat highland, which lay in the middle of
the island, and where there were no buildings
except windmills, and where the turf was so
thin that the white cement shone under it.

Meanwhile, he could not find the goosey-
gander; and as it drew on toward evening,

and the boy must return to the beach, he couldn't believe anything but that his travelling companion was lost. He was so depressed, he did not know what to do with himself.

He had just climbed over the wall again when he heard a stone crash down close beside him. As he turned to see what it was, he thought that he could distinguish something that moved on a stone pile which lay close to the wall. He stole nearer, and saw the goosey-gander come trudging wearily over the stone pile, with several long fibres in his mouth. The goosey-gander didn't see the boy, and the boy did not call to him, but thought it advisable to find out first why the goosey-gander time and again disappeared in this manner.

And he soon learned the reason for it. Up in the stone-pile lay a young gray goose, who cried with joy when the goosey-gander came. The boy crept near, so that he heard what they said; then he found out that the gray goose had been wounded in one wing, so that she could not fly, and that her flock had travelled away from her, and left her alone. She had been near death's door with hunger, when the white goosey-gander had heard her call, the other day, and had sought her out. Ever since, he had been carrying food to her. They had both hoped that she would be well before they left the island, but, as yet, she could neither fly nor walk. She was very much worried over this, but he comforted her with the thought that he shouldn't travel for a long time. At last he bade her good-night, and promised to come the next day.

The boy let the goosey-gander go; and as soon as he was gone, he stole, in turn, up to the stone heap. He was angry because he had been deceived, and now he wanted to say to that gray goose that the goosey-gander was his property. He was going to take the boy up to Lappland, and there would be no talk of his staying here on her account. But now, when he saw the young gray goose close to, he understood, not only why the goosey-gander had gone and carried food to her for two days, but also why he had not wished to mention that he had helped her. She had the prettiest little head; her feather-dress was like soft satin, and the eyes were mild and pleading.

When she saw the boy, she wanted to run away; but the left wing was out of joint and dragged on the ground, so that it interfered with her movements.

"You mustn't be afraid of me," said the boy, and didn't look nearly so angry as he had intended to appear. "I'm Thumbietot, Mor-ten goosey-gander's comrade," he continued. Then he stood there, and didn't know what he wanted to say.

Occasionally one finds something among animals which makes one wonder what sort of creatures they really are. One is almost afraid that they may be transformed human beings. It was something like this with the gray goose. As soon as Thumbietot said who he was, she lowered her neck and head very charmingly before him, and said in a voice that was so pretty that he couldn't believe it was a goose who spoke: "I am very glad that you have come here to help me. The white goosey-gander has told me that no one is as wise and as good as you."

She said this with such dignity, that the boy grew really embarrassed. "This surely can't be any bird," thought he. "It is certainly some bewitched princess."

He was filled with a desire to help her, and ran his hand under the feathers, and felt along the wing-bone. The bone was not broken, but there was something wrong with the joint. He got his finger down into the empty cavity. "Be careful, now!" he said; and got a firm grip on the bone-pipe and fitted it into the place where it ought to be. He did it very quickly and well, considering it was the first time that he had attempted anything of the sort. But it must have hurt very much, for the poor young goose uttered a single shrill cry, and then sank down among the stones without showing a sign of life.

The boy was terribly frightened. He had only wished to help her, and now she was dead. He made a big jump from the stone pile, and ran away. He thought it was as though he had murdered a human being.

The next morning it was clear and free from mist, and Akka said that now they should continue their travels. All the others were willing to go, but the white goosey-gander made excuses. The boy understood well enough that he didn't care to leave the gray goose. Akka did not listen to him, but started off.

The boy jumped up on the goosey-gander's back, and the white one followed the flock—albeit slowly and unwillingly. The boy was mighty glad that they could fly away from the island. He was conscience-stricken on account of the gray goose, and had not cared to tell the goosey-gander how it had turned out when he had tried to cure her. It would probably be best if Morten goosey-gander never found out about this, he thought, though he wondered, at the same time, how the white one had the heart to leave the gray goose.

But suddenly the goosey-gander turned. The thought of the young gray goose had overpowered him. It could go as it would with the Lappland trip: he couldn't go with the others when he knew that she lay alone and ill, and would starve to death.

With a few wing-strokes he was over by the stone pile; but then, there lay no young gray goose between the stones. "Dunfin! Dunfin! Where art thou?" called the goosey-gander.

"The fox has probably been here and taken her," thought the boy. But at that moment he heard a pretty voice answer the goosey-gander. "Here am I, goosey-gander; here am I! I have only been taking a morning bath." And up from the water came the little gray goose—fresh and in good trim— and told how Thumbietot had pulled her wing into place, and that she was entirely well, and ready to follow them on the journey.

The drops of water lay like pearl-dew on her shimmery satin-like feathers, and Thumbietot thought once again that she was a real little princess.

XII

THE BIG BUTTERFLY

THE geese travelled alongside the coast of the long island, which iay distinctly visible under them. The boy felt happy and light of heart during the trip. He was just as pleased and well satisfied as he had been glum and depressed the day before, when he roamed around down on the island, and hunted for the goosey-gander.

He saw now that the interior of the island consisted of a barren high plain, with a wreath of fertile land along the coast; and he began to comprehend the meaning of something which he had heard the other evening.

He had just seated himself to rest a bit by one of the many windmills on the highland, when a couple of shepherds came along with the dogs beside them, and a large herd of sheep in their train. The boy had not been afraid

242

because he was well concealed under the windmill stairs. But as it turned out, the shepherds came and seated themselves on the same stairway, and then there was nothing for him to do but to keep perfectly still.

One of the shepherds was young, and looked about as folks do mostly; the other was an old queer one. His body was large and knotty, but the head was small, and the face had sensitive and delicate features. It appeared as though the body and head didn't want to fit together at all.

One moment he sat silent and gazed into the mist, with an unutterably weary expression. Then he began to talk to his companion. Then the other one took out some bread and cheese from his knapsack, to eat his evening meal. He answered scarcely anything, but listened very patiently, just as if he were thinking: "I might as well give you the pleasure of letting you chatter a while."

"Now I shall tell you something, Eric," said the old shepherd. "I have figured out that in former days, when both human beings and animals were much larger than they are now, that the butterflies, too, must have been uncommonly large. And once there was a butterfly that was many miles long, and had wings as wide as seas. Those wings were blue, and shone like silver, and so gorgeous that, when the butterfly was out flying, all the other animals stood still and stared at it. It had this drawback, however, that it was too large. The wings had hard work to carry it. But probably all would have gone very well, if the butterfly had been wise enough to remain on the hillside. But it wasn't; it ventured out over the East sea. And it hadn't gotten very far before the storm came along and began to tear at its wings. Well, it's easy to understand, Eric, how things would go when the East sea storm commenced to wrestle with frail butterfly-wings. It wasn't long before they were torn away and scattered; and then, of course, the poor butterfly fell into the sea. At first it was tossed backward and forward on the billows, and then it was stranded upon a few cliff-foundations outside of Småland. And there it lay—as large and long as it was.

"Now I think, Eric, that if the butterfly

had dropped on land, it would soon have
rotted and fallen apart. But since it fell into
the sea, it was soaked through and through
with lime, and became as hard as a stone.
You know, of course, that we have found
stones on the shore which were nothing but
petrified worms. Now I believe that it went
the same way with the big butterfly-body. I
believe that it turned where it lay into a
long, narrow mountain out in the East sea.
Don't you?"

He paused for a reply, and the other one
nodded to him. "Go on, so I may hear what
you are driving **at,**" said he.

"And mark you, Eric, "that this very
Öland, upon which you and I live, is nothing
else than the old butterfly-body. If one only
thinks about it, one can observe that the island
is a butterfly. Toward the north, the slender
fore-body and the round head can be seen,
and toward the south, one sees the back-body
—which first broadens out, and then narrows
to a sharp point."

Here he paused once more and looked at
his companion rather anxiously to see

how he would take this assertion. But the young man kept on eating with the utmost calm, and nodded to him to continue.

"As soon as the butterfly had been changed into a limestone rock, many different kinds of seeds of herbs and trees came travelling with the winds, and wanted to take root on it. It was a long time before anything but sedge could grow there. Then came sheep sorrel, and the rock-rose and thorn-brush. But even to-day there is not so much growth on Alvaret, that the mountain is well covered, but it shines through here and there. And no one can think of ploughing and sowing up here, where the earth-crust is so thin. But if you will admit that Alvaret and the strongholds around it, are made of the butterfly-body, then you may well have the right to question where that land which lies beneath the strongholds came from."

"Yes, it is just that," said he who was eating. "That I should indeed like to know."

"Well, you must remember that Öland has lain in the sea for a good many years, and in the course of time all the things which tumble around with the waves—sea-weed and sand and clams—have gathered around it, and remained lying there. And then, stone and gravel have fallen down from both the eastern and western strongholds. In this way the island has acquired broad shores, where grain and flowers and trees can grow.

"Up here, on the hard butterfly-back, only sheep and cows and little horses go about. Only lapwings and plover live here, and there are no buildings except windmills and a few stone huts, where we shepherds crawl in. But down on the coast lie big villages and churches and parishes and fishing hamlets and a whole city."

He looked questioningly at the other one. This one had finished his meal, and was tying the food-sack together. "I wonder where you will end with all this," said he.

"It is only this that I want to know," said the shepherd, as he lowered his voice so that he almost whispered the words, and looked into the mist with his small eyes, which appeared to be worn out from spying after all that which does not exist. "Only this I want to know: if the peasants who live on the built-up farms beneath the strongholds, or the fishermen who take the small herring from the sea, or the merchants in Borgholm, or the bathing guests who come here every summer, or the tourists who wander around in Borgholm's old castle ruin, or the sportsmen who come here in the fall to hunt partridges, or the painters who sit here on Alvaret and paint the sheep and windmills—I should like to know if any of them understand that this island has been a butterfly which flew about with great shimmery wings."

"Ah!" said the young shepherd, suddenly. "It should have occurred to some of them, as they sat on the edge of the stronghold of an evening, and heard the nightingales trill in the groves below them, and looked over Kalmar Sound, that this island could not have come into existence in the same way as the others."

"I want to ask," said the old one, "if no one has had the desire to give wings to the windmills—so large that they could reach to heaven, so large that they could lift the whole island out of the sea and let it fly like a butterfly among butterflies."

"It may be possible that there is something in what you say," said the young one; "for on summer nights, when the heavens widen and open over the island, I have sometimes thought that it was as if it wanted to raise itself from the sea, and fly away."

But when the old one had finally gotten the young one to talk, he didn't listen to him very much. "I would like to know," the old one said in a low tone, "if anyone can explain why one feels such a longing up here on Alvaret. I have felt it every day of my life; and I think it preys upon each and every one who must go about here. I want to know if no one else has understood that all this wistfulness is caused by the fact that the whole island is a butterfly that longs for its wings."

XIII

LITTLE KARL'S ISLAND

THE STORM

Friday, April eighth.

THE wild geese had spent the night on Öland's northern point, and were now on their way to the continent. A strong south wind blew over Kalmar Sound, and they had been thrown northward. Still they worked their way toward land with good speed. But when they were nearing the first islands a powerful rumbling was heard, as if a lot of strong-winged birds had come flying; and the water under them, all at once, became perfectly black. Akka drew in her wings so suddenly that she almost stood still in the air. Thereupon, she lowered herself to light on the edge of the sea. But before the geese had reached the water, the west storm caught up with them. Already, it drove before it

fogs, salt scum and small birds; it also
snatched with it the wild geese, threw them
on end, and cast them toward the sea.

It was a rough storm. The wild geese tried
to turn back, time and again, but they couldn't
do it and were driven out toward the East
sea.   The storm had already blown them past
Öland, and the sea lay before them—empty
and desolate.   There was nothing for them
to do, but to keep out of the water.

When Akka observed that they were unable
to turn back she thought that it was needless
to let the storm drive them over the entire
East sea.   Therefore she sank down to the
water.   Now the sea was raging, and
increased in violence with every second.   The
sea-green billows rolled forward, with seething
foam on their crests.   Each one surged higher
than the other.   It was as though they raced
with each other, to see which could foam the
wildest.   But the wild geese were not afraid
of the swells.   On the contrary, this seemed
to afford them much pleasure.   They did not
strain themselves with swimming, but lay
and let themselves be washed up with the

wave-crests, and down in the water-dales, and had just as much fun as children in a swing. Their only anxiety was that the flock should be separated. The few land-birds who drove by, up in the storm, cried with envy: "There is no danger for you who can swim."

But the wild geese were certainly not out of all danger. In the first place, the rocking made them helplessly sleepy. They wished continually to turn their heads backward, poke their bills under their wings, and go to sleep. Nothing can be more dangerous than to fall asleep in this way; and Akka called out all the while: "Don't go to sleep, wild geese! He that falls asleep will get away from the flock. He that gets away from the flock is lost."

Despite all attempts at resistance one after another fell asleep; and Akka herself came pretty near dozing off, when she suddenly saw something round and dark rise on the top of a wave. "Seals! Seals! Seals!" cried Akka in a high, shrill voice, and raised herself up in the air with resounding wing-strokes. It was just at the crucial moment. Before the last wild goose had time to come up from the water, the seals were so close to her that they made a grab for her feet.

Then the wild geese were once more up in the storm which drove them before it out to sea. No rest did it allow either itself or the wild geese; and no land did they see—only desolate sea.

They lit on the water again, as soon as they dared venture. But when they had rocked upon the waves for a while, they became sleepy again. And when they fell asleep, the seals came swimming. If old Akka had not been so wakeful, not one of them would have escaped.

All day the storm raged; and it caused fearful havoc among the crowds of little birds, which at this time of year were migrating. Some were driven from their course to foreign lands, where they died of starvation; others became so exhausted that they sank down in the sea and were drowned. Many were crushed against the cliff-walls, and many became a prey for the seals.

The storm continued all day, and, at last, Akka began to wonder if she and her flock would perish. They were now dead tired, and nowhere did they see any place where they might rest. Toward evening she no longer dared to lie down on the sea, because now it filled up all of a sudden with large ice-cakes, which struck against each other, and she feared they should be crushed between these. A couple of times the wild geese tried to stand on the ice-crust; but one time the wild storm swept them into the water; another time, the merciless seals came creeping up on the ice.

At sundown the wild geese were once more up in the air. They flew on—fearful for the night. The darkness seemed to come upon them much too quickly this night—which was so full of dangers.

It was terrible that they, as yet, saw no land. How would it go with them if they were forced to stay out on the sea all night? They would either be crushed between the ice-cakes or devoured by seals or separated by the storm.

The heavens were cloud-bedecked, the moon hid itself, and the darkness came quickly. At the same time all nature was filled with a horror which caused the most courageous hearts to quail. Distressed bird-travellers' cries had sounded over the sea all day long, without anyone having paid the slightest attention to them; but now, when one no longer saw who it was that uttered them, they seemed mournful and terrifying. Down on the sea, the ice-drifts crashed against each other with a loud rumbling noise. The seals tuned up their wild hunting songs. It was as though heaven and earth were about to clash.

THE SHEEP

THE boy sat for a moment and looked down into the sea. Suddenly he thought that it began to roar louder than ever. He looked up. Right in front of him—only a couple of metres away—stood a rugged and bare mountain-wall. At its base the waves dashed into a foaming spray. The wild geese flew straight toward the cliff, and the boy did not see how they could avoid being dashed to pieces against it. Hardly had he wondered that Akka hadn't seen the danger in time, when they were over by the mountain. Then he also noticed that in front of them was the half-round entrance to a grotto. Into this the geese steered; and the next moment they were safe.

The first thing the wild geese thought of—before they gave themselves time to rejoice over their safety—was to see if all their comrades were also harboured. Yes, there were Akka, Iksi, Kolmi, Nelja, Viisi, Knusi, all the six goslings, the goosey-gander, Dunfin and Thumbietot; but Kaksi from Nuolja, the first left-hand goose, was missing—and no one knew anything about her fate.

When the wild geese discovered that no one but Kaksi had been separated from the flock, they took the matter lightly. Kaksi was old and wise. She knew all their byways and their habits, and she, of course, would know how to find her way back to them.

Then the wild geese began to look around in the cave. Enough daylight came in through the opening, so that they could see the grotto was both deep and wide. They were delighted to think they had found such a fine night harbour, when one of them caught sight of some shining, green dots, which glittered in a dark corner. "These are eyes!" cried Akka. "There are big animals in here." They rushed toward the opening, but Thumbietot called to them: "There is nothing to run away from! It's only a few sheep who are lying alongside the grotto wall."

When the wild geese had accustomed themselves to the dim daylight in the grotto, they saw the sheep very distinctly. The grown-up ones might be about as many as there were geese; but beside these there were a few little lambs. An old ram with long, twisted horns appeared to be the most lordly one of the flock. The wild geese went up to him with much bowing and scraping. "Well met in the wilderness!" they greeted, but the big ram lay still, and did not speak a word of welcome.

Then the wild geese thought that the sheep were displeased because they had taken shelter in their grotto. "It is perhaps not permissible that we have come in here?" said Akka. "But we cannot help it, for we are wind-driven. We have wandered about in the storm all day, and it would be very good to be allowed to stop here to-night." After that a long time passed before any of the sheep answered with words; but, on the other hand, it could be heard distinctly that a pair of them heaved deep sighs. Akka knew, to be sure, that sheep are always shy and peculiar; but these seemed to have no idea of how they should conduct themselves. Finally an old ewe, who had a long and pathetic face and a doleful voice, said: "There isn't one among us that refuses to let you stay; but this is a house of mourning, and we cannot receive guests as we did in former days." "You needn't worry about anything of that sort," said Akka. "If you knew what we have endured this day, you would surely understand that we are satisfied if we only get a safe spot to sleep on."

When Akka said this, the old ewe raised herself. "I believe that it would be better

for you to fly about in the worst storm than
to stop here.   But, at least, you shall not go
from here before we have had the privilege
of offering you the best hospitality which
the house affords."

She conducted them to a hollow in the
ground, which was filled with water.   Beside
it lay a pile of bait and husks and chaff; and
she bade them make the most of these.   "We
have had a severe snow-winter this year, on
the island," said she.   "The peasants who
own us came out to us with hay and oaten
straw, so we shouldn't starve to death.   And
this trash is all there is left of the good cheer."

   The geese rushed to the food instantly.
They thought that they had fared well, and
were in their best humour.   They must have
observed, of course, that the sheep were
anxious; but they knew how easily scared
sheep generally are, and didn't believe there
was any actual danger on foot.   As soon as
they had eaten, they intended to stand up to
sleep as usual.   But then the big ram got
up, and walked over to them.   The geese
thought that they had never seen a sheep

with such big and coarse horns. In other respects, also, he was noticeable. He had a high, rolling forehead, intelligent eyes, and a good bearing—as though he were a proud and courageous animal.

"I cannot assume the responsibility of letting you geese remain, without telling you that it is unsafe here," said he. "We cannot receive night guests just now." At last Akka began to comprehend that this was serious. "We shall go away, since you really wish it," said she. "But won't you tell us first, what it is that troubles you? We know nothing about it. We do not even know where we are." "This is Little Karl's Island!" said the ram. "It lies outside of Gottland, and only sheep and sea-birds live here." "Perhaps you are wild sheep?" said Akka. "We're not far removed from it," replied the ram. "We have nothing to do with human beings. It's an old agreement between us and some peasants on a farm in Gottland, that they shall supply us with fodder in case we have snow-winter; and as a recompense they are permitted to take

away those of us who become superfluous.
The island is small, so it cannot feed very
many of us. But otherwise we take care of
ourselves all the year round, and we do not
live in houses with doors and locks, but we
reside in grottoes like these."

"Do you stay out here in the winter as
well?" asked Akka, surprised. "We do,"
answered the ram. "We have good fodder
up here on the mountain, all the year around."
"I think it sounds as if you might have it
better than other sheep," said Akka. "But
what is the misfortune that has befallen
you?" "It was bitter cold last winter. The
sea froze, and then three foxes came over here
on the ice, and here they have been ever
since. Otherwise, there are no dangerous
animals here on the island." "Oh, ho! do
foxes dare to attack such as you?" "Oh,
no! not during the day; then I can protect
myself and mine," said the ram, shaking his
horns. "But they sneak upon us at night
when we sleep in the grottoes. We try to
keep awake, but one must sleep some of the
time; and then they come upon us. They

have already killed every sheep in the other grottoes, and there were herds that were just as large as mine."

"It isn't pleasant to tell that we are so helpless," said the old ewe. "We cannot help ourselves any better than if we were tame sheep." "Do you think that they will come here to-night?" asked Akka. "There is nothing else in store for us," answered the old ewe. "They were here last night, and stole a lamb from us. They'll be sure to come again, as long as there are any of us alive. This is what they have done in the other places." "But if they are allowed to keep this up, you'll become entirely exterminated," said Akka. "Oh! it won't be long before it is all over with the sheep on Little Karl's Island," said the ewe.

Akka stood there hesitatingly. It was not pleasant, by any means, to venture out in the storm again, and it wasn't good to remain in a house where such guests were expected. When she had pondered a while, she turned to Thumbietot. "I wonder if you will help us, as you have done so many

times before," said she.   Yes, that he would
like to do, he replied.   "It is a pity for you
not to get any sleep!" said the wild goose,
"but I wonder if you are able to keep awake
until the foxes come, and then to awaken us,
so we may fly away."   The boy was so very
glad of this—for anything was better than to
go out in the storm again—so he promised
to keep awake.

The boy went down to the grotto opening,
crawled in behind a stone, that he might be
shielded from the storm, and sat down to
watch.

When the boy had been sitting there a
while, the storm seemed to abate.   The sky
grew clear, and the moonlight began to play
on the waves.   The boy stepped to the opening to look out.   The grotto was rather high
up on the mountain.   A narrow path led to
it.   It was probably here that he must await
the foxes.

As yet he saw no foxes; but, on the other
hand, there was something which, for the
moment, terrified him much more.   On the
land-strip below the mountain stood some

giants, or other stone-trolls—or perhaps they were actual human beings. At first he thought that he was dreaming, but now he was positive that he had not fallen asleep. He saw the big men so distinctly that it couldn't be an illusion. Some of them stood on the land-strip, and others right on the mountain just as if they intended to climb it. Some had big, thick heads; others had no heads at all. Some were one-armed, and some had humps both before and behind. He had never seen anything so extraordinary.

The boy stood and worked himself into a state of panic because of those trolls, so that he almost forgot to keep his eye peeled for the foxes. But now he heard a claw scrape against a stone. He saw three foxes coming up the steep; and as soon as he knew that he had something real to deal with, he was calm again, and not the least bit scared. It struck him that it was a pity to awaken only the geese, and to leave the sheep to their fate. He thought he would like to arrange things some other way.

He ran quickly to the other end of the grotto, shook the big ram's horns until he awoke, and, at the same time, swung himself upon his back. "Get up, sheep, and we'll try to frighten the foxes a bit!" said the boy.

He had tried to be as quiet as possible, but the foxes must have heard some noise; for when they came up to the mouth of the grotto they stopped and deliberated. "It was certainly someone in there that moved." said one. "I wonder if they are awake." "Oh, go ahead, you!" said another. "At all events, they can't do anything to us."

When they came farther in, in the grotto, they stopped and sniffed. "Who shall we take to-night?" whispered the one who went first. "To-night we will take the big ram," said the last. "After that, we'll have easy work with the rest."

The boy sat on the old ram's back and saw how they sneaked along. "Now butt straight forward!" whispered the boy. The ram butted, and the first fox was thrust—top over tail—back to the opening. "Now butt to the left!" said the boy, and turned the big ram's

head in that direction. The ram measured
a terrific assault that caught the second fox
in the side. He rolled around several times
before he got to his feet again and made
his escape. The boy had wished that the
third one, too, might have gotten a bump,
but this one had already gone.

"Now I think that they've had enough for
to-night," said the boy. "I think so too,"
said the big ram. "Now lie down on my back,
and creep into the wool! You deserve to
have it warm and comfortable, after all the
wind and storm that you have been out in."

HELL'S HOLE

THE next day the big ram went around with
the boy on his back, and showed him the
island. It consisted of a single massive
mountain. It was like a large house with
perpendicular walls and a flat roof. First
the ram walked up on the mountain-roof and
showed the boy the good grazing lands there;
and he had to admit that the island seemed
to be especially created for sheep. There

wasn't much else than sheep-sorrel and such little spicy growths as sheep are fond of that grew on the mountain.

But indeed there was something beside sheep fodder to look at, for one who had gotten well up on the steep. To begin with, the largest part of the sea—which now lay blue and sunlit, and rolled forward in glittering swells—was visible. Only upon one and another point, did the foam spray up. To the east lay Gottland, with even and long-stretched coast; and to the southwest lay Great Karl's Island, which was built on the same plan as the little island. When the ram walked to the very edge of the mountain roof, so the boy could look down the mountain walls, he noticed that they were simply filled with birds' nests; and in the blue sea beneath him, lay surf-scoters and eider-ducks and kittiwakes and guillemots and razor-bills—so pretty and peaceful— busying themselves with fishing for small herring.

"This is really a favoured land," said the boy. "You live in a pretty place, you sheep."

"Oh, yes! it's pretty enough here," said the big ram. It was as if he wished to add something; but he did not, only sighed. "If you go about here alone you must look out for the crevices which run all around the mountain," he continued after a little. And this was a good warning, for there were deep and broad crevices in several places. The largest of them was called Hell's Hole. That crevice was many fathoms deep and nearly one fathom wide. "If anyone fell down there, it would certainly be the last of him," said the big ram. The boy thought it sounded as if he had a special meaning in what he said.

Then he conducted the boy down to the narrow strip of shore. Now he could see those giants which had frightened him the night before, at close range. They were nothing but tall rock-pillars. The big ram called them "cliffs." The boy couldn't see enough of them. He thought that if there had ever been any trolls who had turned into stone they ought to look just like that.

Although it was pretty down on the shore,

the boy liked it still better on the mountain
height. It was ghastly down here; for everywhere they came across dead sheep. It was
here that the foxes had held their orgies.
He saw skeletons whose flesh had been eaten,
and bodies that were half-eaten, and others
which they had scarcely tasted, but had
allowed to lie untouched. It was heart-rend-
ing to see how the wild beasts had thrown
themselves upon the sheep just for sport—
just to hunt them and tear them to death.

The big ram did not pause in front of the
dead, but walked by them in silence. But
the boy, meanwhile, could not help seeing all
the horror.

Then the big ram went up on the mountain
height again; but when he was there he
stopped and said: "If someone who is
capable and wise could see all the misery
which prevails here, he surely would not be
able to rest until these foxes had been pun-
ished." "The foxes must live, too," said the
boy. "Yes," said the big ram, "those who
do not tear in pieces more animals than they
need for their sustenance, they may as well

live. But these are felons." "The peasants
who own the island ought to come here and
help you," insisted the boy. "They have
rowed over a number of times," replied the
ram, "but the foxes always hid themselves
in the grottoes and crevices, so they could not
get near them, to shoot them." "You surely
cannot mean, father, that a poor little creature
like me should be able to get at them, when
neither you nor the peasants have succeeded
in getting the better of them." "He that is
little and spry can put many things to rights,"
said the big ram."

They talked no more about this, and the boy
went over and seated himself among the wild
geese who fed on the highland. Although
he had not cared to show his feelings before
the ram, he was very sad on the sheep's
account, and he would have been glad to
help them. "I can at least talk with Akka
and Morten goosey-gander about the matter,"
thought he. "Perhaps they can help me with
a good suggestion."

A little later the white goosey-gander took
the boy on his back and went over the

mountain plain, and in the direction of Hell's Hole at that.

He wandered, care-free, on the open mountain roof—apparently unconscious of how large and white he was. He didn't seek protection behind tufts, or any other protuberances, but went straight ahead. It was strange that he was not more careful, for it was apparent that he had fared badly in yesterday's storm. He limped on his right leg, and the left wing hung and dragged as if it might be broken.

He acted as if there were no danger, pecked at a grass-blade here and another there, and did not look about him in any direction. The boy lay stretched out full length on the goose-back, and looked up toward the blue sky. He was so accustomed to riding now, that he could both stand and lie down on the goose-back.

When the goosey-gander and the boy were so care-free, they did not observe, of course, that the three foxes had come up on the mountain plain.

And the foxes, who knew that it was well-nigh impossible to take the life of a goose on an open plain, thought at first that they wouldn't chase after the goosey-gander. But as they had nothing else to do, they finally sneaked down on one of the long passes, and tried to steal up to him. They went about it so cautiously that the goosey-gander couldn't see a shadow of them.

They were not far off when the goosey-gander made an attempt to raise himself into the air. He spread his wings, but he did not succeed in lifting himself. When the foxes seemed to grasp the fact that he couldn't fly, they hurried forward with greater eagerness than before. They no longer concealed themselves in the cleft, but came up on the highland. They hurried as fast as they could, behind tufts and hollows, and came nearer and nearer the goosey-gander— without his seeming to notice that he was being hunted. At last the foxes were so near that they could make the final leap. Simultaneously, all three threw themselves, with one long jump at the goosey-gander.

But still at the last moment he must have

noticed something, for he ran out of the way, so the foxes missed him. This, at any rate, didn't mean very much, for the goosey-gander only had a couple of metres headway, and, in the bargain, he limped. Anyway, the poor thing ran ahead as fast as he could.

The boy sat upon the goose-back—backward—and shrieked and called to the foxes. "You have eaten yourselves too fat on mutton, foxes. You can't catch up with a goose even." He teased them so that they became crazed with rage and thought only of rushing forward.

The white one ran right straight to the big cleft. When he was there, he made one stroke with his wings, and got over. Just then the foxes were almost upon him.

The goosey-gander hurried on with the same haste as before, even after he had gotten across Hell's Hole. But he had hardly been running two metres before the boy patted him on the neck, and said: "Now you can stop, goosey-gander."

At that instant they heard a number of wild howls behind them, and a scraping of claws, and heavy falls. But of the foxes they saw nothing more.

The next morning the lighthouse keeper on Great Karl's Island found a bit of bark poked under the entrance-door, and on it had been cut, in slanting, angular letters: "The foxes on the little island have fallen down into Hell's Hole. Take care of them!"

And this the lighthouse keeper did, too.

XIV

TWO CITIES

THE CITY AT THE BOTTOM OF THE SEA

Saturday, April ninth.

IT WAS a calm and clear night. The wild geese did not trouble themselves to seek shelter in any of the grottoes, but stood and slept up on the mountain top; and the boy had lain down in the short, dry grass beside the geese.

It was bright moonlight that night; so bright that it was difficult for the boy to go to sleep. He lay there and thought about just how long he had been away from home; and he figured out that it was three weeks since he had started on the trip. At the same time he remembered that this was Easter-eve.

"It is to-night that all the witches come home from Blakulla," thought he, and laughed

to himself.   For he was just a little afraid of
both the sea-nymph and the elf, but he didn't
believe in witches the least little bit.

If there had been any witches out that
night, he should have seen them, to be sure.
It was so light in the heavens that not the
tiniest black speck could move in the air
without his seeing it.

While the boy lay there with his nose in
the air and thought about this, his eye rested
on something lovely! The moon's disc was
whole and round, and rather high, and over
it a big bird came flying.   He did not fly
past the moon, but he moved just as though
he might have flown out from it.   The bird
looked black against the light background,
and the wings extended from one rim of the
disc to the other.   He flew on, evenly, in the
same direction, and the boy thought that he
was painted on the moon's disc.   The body
was small, the neck long and slender, the legs
hung down, long and thin.   It couldn't be
anything but a stork.

A couple of seconds later Herr Ermenrich,
the stork, lit beside the boy.   He bent down

and poked him with his bill to awaken him.

Instantly the boy sat up. "I'm not asleep, Herr Ermenrich," he said. "How does it happen that you are out in the middle of the night, and how is everything at Glimminge castle? Do you want to speak with mother Akka?"

"It's too light to sleep to-night," answered Herr Ermenrich. "Therefore I concluded to travel over here to Karl's Island and hunt you up, friend Thumbietot. I learned from the seamew that you were spending the night here. I have not as yet moved over to Glimminge castle, but am still living at Pommern."

The boy was simply overjoyed to think that Herr Ermenrich had sought him out. They chatted about all sorts of things, like old friends. At last the stork asked the boy if he wouldn't like to go out riding for a while on this beautiful night.

Oh, yes! that the boy wanted to do, if the stork would manage it so that he got back to the wild geese before sunrise. This he promised, so off they went.

Again Herr Ermenrich flew straight toward the moon. They rose and rose; the sea sank deep down, but the flight went so light and easy that it seemed almost as if the boy lay still in the air.

When Herr Ermenrich began to descend, the boy thought that the flight had lasted an unreasonably short time.

They landed on a desolate bit of seashore, which was covered with fine, even sand. All along the coast ran a row of flying-sand drifts, with lyme-grass on their tops. They were not very high, but they prevented the boy from seeing any of the island.

Herr Ermenrich stood on a sand-hill, drew up one leg and bent his head backward, so he could stick his bill under the wing. "You can roam around on the shore for a while," he said to Thumbietot, "while I rest myself. But don't go so far away but what you can find your way back to me again!"

To start with, the boy intended to climb a sand-hill and see how the land behind it looked. But when he had walked a couple of paces, he stubbed the toe of his wooden shoe against something hard. He stooped down, and saw that a small copper coin lay on the sand, and was so worn with verdigris that it was almost transparent. It was so poor that he didn't even bother to pick it up, but only kicked it out of the way.

But when he straightened himself up once more he was perfectly astounded, for two paces away from him stood a high, dark wall with a big, turreted gate.

The moment before, when the boy bent down, the sea lay there—shimmering and smooth, while now it was hidden by a long wall with towers and battlements. Directly in front of him, where before there had been only a few sea-weed banks, the big gate of the wall opened.

The boy probably understood that it was a spectre-play of some sort; but this was nothing to be afraid of, thought he. It wasn't any dangerous trolls, or any other evil—such as he always dreaded to encounter at night. Both the wall and the gate were so beautifully constructed that he only desired to see what there might be back of them. "I must find

out what this can be," thought he, and went in through the gate.

In the deep archway there were guards, dressed in brocaded and puffed suits, with long-handled spears beside them, who sat and threw dice. They thought only of the game, and took no notice of the boy who hurried past them quickly.

Just within the gate he found an open space, paved with large, even stone blocks. All around this were high and magnificent buildings; and between these opened long, narrow streets. On the square—facing the gate—it fairly swarmed with human beings. The men wore long, fur-trimmed capes over satin suits; plume-bedecked hats sat obliquely on their heads; on their chests hung superb chains. They were all so regally gotten up that the whole lot of them might have been kings.

The women went about in high head-dresses and long robes with tight-fitting sleeves. They, too, were beautifully dressed, but their splendour was not to be compared with that of the men.

This was exactly like the old story-book which mother took from the chest—only once—and showed to him. The boy simply couldn't believe his eyes.

But that which was even more wonderful to look upon than either the men or the women, was the city itself. Every house was built in such a way that a gable faced the street. And the gables were so highly ornamented, that one could believe they wished to compete with each other as to which one could show the most beautiful decorations.

When one suddenly sees so much that is new, he cannot manage to treasure it all in his memory. But at least the boy could recall that he had seen stairway gables on the various landings, which bore images of the Christ and his Apostles; gables, where there were images in niche after niche all along the wall; gables that were inlaid with multi-coloured bits of glass, and gables that were striped and checked with white and black marble. As the boy admired all this, a sudden sense of haste came over him. "Anything like this my eyes have never seen before.

Anything like this, they would never see again," he said to himself. And he began to run in toward the city—up one street, and down another.

The streets were straight and narrow, but not empty and gloomy, as they were in the cities with which he was familiar. There were people everywhere. Old women sat by their open doors and spun without a spinning-wheel—only with the help of a shuttle. The merchants' shops were like market-stalls —opening on the street. All the hand-workers did their work out of doors. In one place they were boiling crude oil; in another tanning hides; in a third there was a long rope-walk.

If only the boy had had time enough he could have learned how to make all sorts of things. Here he saw how armourers hammered out thin breast-plates; how turners tended their irons; how the shoemakers soled soft, red shoes; how the gold-wire drawers twisted gold thread, and how the weavers inserted silver and gold into their weaving.

But the boy did not have the time to stay.

He just rushed on, so that he could manage
to see as much as possible before it would all
vanish again.

The high wall ran all round the city and
shut it in, as a hedge shuts in a field. He
saw it at the end of every street—gable
ornamented and crenulated. On the top of
the wall walked warriors in shining armour;
and when he had run from one end of the city
to the other, he came to still another gate in
the wall. Outside of this lay the sea and
harbour. The boy saw olden-time ships,
with rowing-benches straight across, and high
structures fore and aft. Some lay and took
on cargo, others were just casting anchor.
Carriers and merchants hurried around each
other. All over, it was life and bustle.

But not even here did he seem to have the
time to linger. He rushed into the city
again; and now he came up to the big square.
There stood the cathedral with its three high
towers and deep vaulted arches filled with
images. The walls had been so highly decorated by sculptors that there was not a stone
without its own special ornamentation. And

what a magnificent display of gilded crosses
and gold-trimmed altars and priests in golden
vestments, shimmered through the open gate!
Directly opposite the church there was a
house with a notched roof and a single slender, sky-high tower. That was probably
the courthouse. And between the courthouse and the cathedral, all around the
square, stood the beautiful gabled houses
with their multiplicity of adornments.

The boy had run himself both warm and
tired. He thought that now he had seen the
most remarkable things, and therefore he
began to walk more leisurely. The street
which he had turned into now was surely
the one where the inhabitants purchased
their fine clothing. He saw crowds of people
standing before the little stalls where the
merchants spread brocades, stiff satins, heavy
gold cloth, shimmery velvet, delicate veiling,
and laces as sheer as a spider's web.

Before, when the boy ran so fast, no one
had paid any attention to him. The people
must have thought that it was only a little
gray rat that darted by them. But now,

when he walked down the street, very slowly,
one of the salesmen caught sight of him, and
began to beckon to him.

At first the boy was uneasy and wanted to
hurry out of the way, but the salesman only
beckoned and smiled, and spread out on the
counter a lovely piece of satin damask as
if he wanted to tempt him.

The boy shook his head. "I will never be
so rich that I can buy even a metre of that
cloth," thought he.

But now they had caught sight of him in
every stall, all along the street. Wherever
he looked stood a salesman and beckoned
to him. They left their costly wares, and
thought only of him. He saw how they hurried into the most hidden corner of the stall
to fetch the best that they had to sell, and
how their hands trembled with eagerness
and haste as they laid it upon the counter.

When the boy continued to go on, one of
the merchants jumped over the counter,
caught hold of him, and spread before him
silver cloth and woven tapestries, which shone
with brilliant colours.

The boy couldn't do anything but laugh at him. The salesman certainly must understand that a poor little creature like him couldn't buy such things. He stood still and held out his two empty hands, so they would understand that he had nothing and let him go in peace.

But the merchant raised a finger and nodded and pushed the whole pile of beautiful things over to him.

"Can he mean that he will sell all this for a gold piece?" wondered the boy.

The merchant brought out a tiny worn and poor coin—the smallest that one could see—and showed it to him. And he was so eager to sell that he increased his pile with a pair of large, heavy, silver goblets.

Then the boy began to dig down in his pockets. He knew, of course, that he didn't possess a single coin, but he couldn't help feeling for it.

All the other merchants stood still and tried to see how the sale would come off, and when they observed that the boy began to search in his pockets, they flung themselves over the counters, filled their hands full of gold and silver ornaments, and offered them to him. And they all showed him that what they asked in payment was just one little penny.

But the boy turned both vest and breeches pockets inside out, so they should see that he owned nothing. Then tears filled the eyes of all these regal merchants, who were so much richer than he. At last he was moved because they looked so distressed, and he pondered if he could not in some way help them. And then he happened to think of the rusty coin, which he had but lately seen on the strand.

He started to run down the street, and luck was with him so that he came to the self-same gate which he had happened upon first. He dashed through it, and commenced to search for the little green copper penny which lay on the strand a while ago.

He found it too, very promptly; but when he had picked it up, and wanted to run back to the city with it—he saw only the sea before him. No city wall, no gate, no sentinels,

no streets, no houses could now be seen—
only the sea.

The boy couldn't help that the tears came
to his eyes. He had believed in the beginning,
that that which he saw was nothing but an
hallucination, but this he had already forgotten. He only thought about how pretty
everything was. He felt a genuine, deep
sorrow because the city had vanished.

That moment Herr Ermenrich awoke, and
came up to him. But he didn't hear him,
and the stork had to poke the boy with his bill
to attract attention to himself. "I believe
that you stand here and sleep just as I do,"
said Herr Ermenrich.

"Oh, Herr Ermenrich!" said the boy. "What
was that city which stood here just now?"

"Have you seen a city?" said the stork.
"You have slept and dreamt, as I say."

"No! I have not dreamt," said Thumbietot,
and he told the stork all that he had
experienced.

Then Herr Ermenrich said: "For my part,
Thumbietot, I believe that you fell asleep
here on the strand and dreamed all this.

But I will not conceal from you that Bataki, the raven, who is the most learned of all birds, once told me that in former times there was a city on this shore, called Vineta. It was so rich and so fortunate, that no city has ever been more glorious; but its inhabitants, unluckily, gave themselves up to arrogance and love of display. As a punishment for this, says Bataki, the city of Vineta was overtaken by a flood, and sank into the sea. But these inhabitants cannot die, neither is their city destroyed. And one night in every hundred years, it rises in all its splendour up from the sea, and remains on the surface just one hour."

"Yes, it must be so," said Thumbietot, "for this I have seen."

"But when the hour is up, it sinks again into the sea, if, during that time, no merchant in Vineta has sold anything to a single living creature. If you, Thumbietot, only had had an ever so tiny coin, to pay the merchants, Vineta might have remained up here on the shore; and its people could have lived and died like other human beings."

"Herr Ermenrich," said the boy, "now I understand why you came and fetched me in the middle of the night. It was because you believed that I should be able to save the old city. I am so sorry it didn't turn out as you wished, Herr Ermenrich."

He covered his face with his hands and wept. It wasn't easy to say which one looked the more disconsolate—the boy, or Herr Ermenrich.

THE LIVING CITY

Monday, April eleventh.

ON the afternoon of Easter Monday, the wild geese and Thumbietot were on the wing. They travelled over Gottland.

The large island lay smooth and even beneath them. The ground was checked just as it was in Skåne and there were many churches and farms. But there was this difference, however, that there were more leafy meadows between the fields here, and then the farms were not built up with small houses. And there were no large manors with ancient tower-ornamented castles.

The wild geese had taken the route over Gottland on account of Thumbietot. He had been altogether unlike himself for two days, and hadn't spoken a cheerful word. This was because he had thought of nothing but that city which had appeared to him in such a strange way. He had never seen anything so magnificent and royal, and he could not be reconciled with himself for having failed to save it. Usually he was not chicken-hearted, but now he actually grieved for the beautiful buildings and the stately people.

Both Akka and the goosey-gander tried to convince Thumbietot that he had been the victim of a dream, or an hallucination, but the boy wouldn't listen to anything of that sort. He was so positive that he had really seen what he had seen, that no one could move him from this conviction. He went about so disconsolate that his travelling companions became uneasy for him.

Just as the boy was the most depressed, old Kaksi came back to the flock. She had been blown toward Gottland, and had been compelled to travel over the whole island before she had learned through some crows that her comrades were on Little Karl's Island. When Kaksi found out what was wrong with Thumbietot, she said impulsively: "If Thumbietot is grieving over an old city, we'll soon be able to comfort him. Just come along, and I'll take you to a place that I saw yesterday! You will not need to be distressed very long."

Thereupon the geese had taken farewell of the sheep, and were on their way to the place which Kaksi wished to show Thumbietot. As blue as he was, he couldn't keep from looking at the land over which he travelled, as usual.

He thought it looked as though the whole island had in the beginning been just such a high, steep cliff as Karl's Island—though much bigger of course. But afterward, it had in some way been flattened out. Some-one had taken a big rolling-pin and rolled over it, as if it had been a lump of dough. Not that the island had become altogether flat and even, like a bread-cake, for it wasn't like that. While they had travelled along the coast, he had seen white lime walls with grottoes and crags, in several directions; but in most of the places they were levelled, and sank inconspicuously down toward the sea.

In Gottland they had a pleasant and peaceful holiday afternoon. It turned out to be mild spring weather; the trees had large buds; spring blossoms dressed the ground in the leafy meadows; the poplars' long, thin pendants swayed; and in the little gardens, which one finds around every cottage, the gooseberry bushes were green.

The warmth and the spring-budding had tempted the people out into the gardens and roads, and wherever a number of them were gathered together they were playing. It was not the children alone who played, but the grown-ups also. They were throwing stones at a given point, and they threw balls in the air with such exact aim that they almost touched the wild geese. It looked cheerful and pleasant to see big folks at play; and the boy certainly would have enjoyed it, if he had peen able to forget his grief because he had failed to save the city.

Anyway, he had to admit that this was a lovely trip. There was so much singing and sound in the air. Little children played ring games, and sang as they played. The Salvation Army was out. He saw a lot of people dressed in black and red—sitting upon a wooded hill, playing on guitars and brass instruments. On one road came a great crowd of people. They were Good Templars who had been on a pleasure trip. He recognised them by the big banners with the gold inscriptions which waved above them. They sang song after song as long as he could hear them.

After that the boy could never think of Gottland without thinking of the games and songs at the same time.

He had been sitting and looking down for a long while; but now he happened to raise his eyes. No one can describe his amazement. Before he was aware of it, the wild geese had left the interior of the island and gone westward—toward the sea-coast. Now the wide, blue sea lay before him. However, it was not the sea that was remarkable, but a city which appeared on the sea-shore.

The boy came from the east, and the sun
had just begun to go down in the west.
When he came nearer the city, its walls and
towers and high, gabled houses and churches
stood there, perfectly black, against the light
evening sky. He couldn't see therefore what
it really looked like, and for a couple of
moments he believed that this city was just as
beautiful as the one he had seen on Easter
night.

When he got right up to it, he saw that it
was both like and unlike that city from the
bottom of the sea. There was the same
contrast between them, as there is between a
man whom one sees arrayed in purple and
jewels one day, and on another day one sees him
dressed in rags.

Yes, this city had probably, once upon a
time, been like the one which he sat and
thought about. This one, also, was enclosed
by a wall with towers and gates. But the
towers in this city, which had been allowed
to remain on land, were roofless, hollow and
empty. The gates were without doors; sentinels and warriors had disappeared. All

the glittering splendour was gone. There was
nothing left but the naked, gray stone skeleton.

When the boy came farther into the city,
he saw that the larger part of it was made
up of small, low houses; but here and there
were still a few high gabled houses and
a few cathedrals, which were from the olden
time. The walls of the gabled houses were
whitewashed, and entirely without ornamentation; but because the boy had so lately seen
the buried city, he seemed to understand
how they had been decorated: some with
statues, and others with black and white
marble. And it was the same with the old
cathedrals; the majority of them were roofless with bare interiors. The window open-
ings were empty, the floors were grass-grown,
and ivy clambered along the walls. But
now he knew how they had looked at one
time; that they had been covered with images
and paintings; that the chancel had had
trimmed altars and gilded crosses, and that
there priests had moved about, arrayed in
gold vestments.

The boy saw also the narrow streets, which

were almost deserted on holiday afternoons. He knew, he did, what a stream of stately people had once upon a time sauntered about on them. He knew that they had been like large workshops—filled with all sorts of workmen.

But that which Nils Holgersson did not see was, that the city—even to-day—was both beautiful and remarkable. He saw neither the cheery cottages on the side streets, with their black walls, and white bows and red pelargoniums behind the shining window-panes, nor the many pretty gardens and avenues, nor the beauty in the weed-clad ruins. His eyes were so filled with the preceding glory, that he could not see anything good in the present.

The wild geese flew back and forth over the city a couple of times, so that Thumbietot might see everything. Finally they sank down on the grass-grown floor of a cathedral ruin to spend the night.

When they had arranged themselves for sleep, Thumbietot was still awake and looked up through the open arches, to the pale pink evening sky. When he had been sitting there

a while, he thought he didn't want to gr eve
any more because he couldn't save the
buried city.

No, that he didn't want to do, now that he
had seen this one. If that city, which he
had seen, had not sunk into the sea again,
then it would perhaps become as dilapidated
as this one in a little while. Perhaps it could
not have withstood time and decay, but would
have stood there with roofless churches and
bare houses and desolate, empty streets—just
like this one. Then it was better that it should
remain in all its glory down in the deep.

"It was best that it happened as it happened," thought he. "If I had the power to
save the city, I don't believe that I should
care to do it." Then he no longer grieved
over that matter.

And there are probably many among the
young who think in the same way. But
when people are old, and have become
accustomed to being satisfied with little, then
they are more happy over the Visby that
exists, than over a magnifient Vineta at the
bottom of the sea.

XV

THE LEGEND OF SMÅLAND

Tuesday, April twelfth.

THE wild geese had made a good trip over the sea, and had lighted in Tjust Township, in northern Småland. That township didn't seem able to make up its mind whether it wanted to be land or sea. Fiords ran in everywhere, and cut the land up into islands and peninsulas and points and capes. The sea was so forceful that the only things which could hold themselves above it were hills and mountains. All the lowlands were hidden away under the water exterior.

It was evening when the wild geese came in from the sea; and the land with the little hills lay prettily between the shimmering fiords. Here and there, on the islands, the boy saw cabins and cottages; and the farther inland he came, the bigger and better became

299

the dwelling houses. Finally, they grew into large, white manors. Along the shores there was generally a border of trees; and within this lay field-plots, and on the tops of the little hills there were trees again. He could not help but think of Blekinge. Here again was a place where land and sea met, in such a pretty and peaceful sort of way, just as if they tried to show each other the best and loveliest which they possessed.

The wild geese alighted upon a limestone island a good way in on Goose-fiord. With the first glance at the shore they observed that spring had made rapid strides while they had been away on the islands. The big, fine trees were not as yet leaf-clad, but the ground under them was brocaded with white anemones, gagea, and blue anemones.

When the wild geese saw the flower-carpet they feared that they had lingered too long in the southern part of the country. Akka said instantly that there was no time in which to hunt up any of the stopping places in Småland, By the next morning they must travel northward, over Östergötland.

The boy should then see nothing of Småland, and this grieved him. He had heard more about Småland than he had about any other province, and he had longed to see it with his own eyes.

The summer before, when he had served as goose-boy with a farmer in the neighbour- hood of Jordberga, he had met a pair of Småland children, almost every day, who also tended geese. These children had irritated him terribly with their Småland.

It wasn't fair to say that Osa, the goose- girl, had annoyed him. She was much too wise for that. But the one who could be aggravating with a vengeance, was her brother, little Mats.

"Have you heard, Nils Goose-boy, how it went when Småland and Skåne were created?" he would ask, and if Nils Holgersson said no, he began immediately to relate the old joke- legend.

"Well, it was at that time when our Lord was creating the world. While he was doing his best work, Saint Peter came walking by. He stopped and looked on, and then he asked if it was hard to do. 'Well, it isn't exactly easy,' said our Lord. Saint Peter stood there a little longer, and when he noticed how easy it was to lay out one landscape after another, he too wanted to try his hand at it. 'Perhaps you need to rest yourself a little,' said Saint Peter, 'I could attend to the work in the meantime for you.' But this our Lord did not wish. 'I do not know if you are so much at home in this art that I can trust you to take hold where I leave off,' he answered. Then Saint Peter was angry, and said that he believed he could create just as fine countries as our Lord himself.

"It happened that our Lord was just then creating Småland. It wasn't even half-ready but it looked as though it would be an indescribably pretty and fertile land. It was difficult for our Lord to say no to Saint Peter, and aside from this, he thought very likely that a thing so well begun no one could spoil. Therefore he said: 'If you like, we will prove which one of us two understands this sort of work the better. You, who are only a novice, shall go on with this which I have begun, and I will create a new land.' To this Saint Peter agreed at once; and so they went to work—each one in his place.

"Our Lord moved southward a bit, and there he undertook to create Skåne. It wasn't long before he was through with it, and soon he asked if Saint Peter had finished, and would come and look at his work. 'I had mine ready long ago,' said Saint Peter; and from the sound of his voice it could be heard how pleased he was with what he had accomplished.

"When Saint Peter saw Skåne, he had to acknowledge that there was nothing but good to be said of that land. It was a fertile land and easy to cultivate, with wide plains wherever one looked, and hardly a sign of hills. It was evident that our Lord had really contemplated making it such that people should feel at home there. 'Yes, this is a good country,' said Saint Peter, 'but I think that mine is better.' 'Then we'll take a look at it,' said our Lord.

"The land was already finished in the north

and east when Saint Peter began the work, but the southern and western parts, and the whole interior, he had created all by himself. Now when our Lord came up there, where Saint Peter had been at work, he was so horrified that he stopped short and exclaimed: 'What on earth have you been doing with this land, Saint Peter?'

"Saint Peter, too, stood and looked around— perfectly astonished. He had had the idea that nothing could be so good for a land as a great deal of warmth. Therefore he had gathered together an enormous mass of stones and mountains, and erected a highland, and this he had done so that it should be near the sun, and receive much help from the sun's heat. Over the stone-heaps he had spread a thin layer of soil, and then he had thought that everything was well arranged.

"But while he was down in Skåne, a couple of heavy showers had come up, and more was not needed to show what his work amounted to. When our Lord came to inspect the land, all the soil had been washed away, and the naked mountain foundation shone forth

all over. Where it was about the best,
lay clay and heavy gravel over the rocks, but
it looked so poor that it was easy to understand that hardly anything except spruce
and juniper and moss and heather could
grow there. But what there was plenty of
was water. It had filled up all the clefts
in the mountain; and lakes and rivers and
brooks; these one saw everywhere, to say
nothing of swamps and morasses, which
spread over large tracts. And the most
exasperating thing of all was, that while some
tracts had too much water, it was so scarce
in others, that whole fields lay like dry moors,
where sand and earth whirled up in clouds
with the least little breeze.

" 'What can have been your meaning in
creating such a land as this?' said our Lord.
Saint Peter made excuses, and declared he
had wished to build up a land so high that it
should have plenty of warmth from the sun.
'But then you will also get much of the night
chill,' said our Lord, 'for that too comes
from heaven. • I am very much afraid the
little that can grow here will freeze.'

"This, to be sure, Saint Peter hadn't thought about.

" 'Yes, here it will be a poor and frost-bound land,' said our Lord, 'it can't be helped.' "

When little Mats had gotten this far in his story, Osa, the goose-girl, protested: "I cannot bear, little Mats, to hear you say that it is so miserable in Småland," said she. "You forget entirely how much good soil there is there. Only think of Möre district, by Kalmar Sound! I wonder where you'll find a richer grain region. There are fields upon fields, just like here in Skåne. The soil is so good that I cannot imagine anything that couldn't grow there."

"I can't help that," said little Mats. "I'm only relating what others have said before."

"And I have heard many say that there is not a more beautiful coast land than Tjust. Think of the bays and islets, and the manors, and the groves!" said Osa. "Yes, that's true enough," little Mats admitted. "And don't you remember," continued Osa, "the school teacher said that such a lively and picturesque district as that bit of Småland which lies south of Lake Vettern is not to be found in all Sweden? Think of the beautiful sea and the yellow coast-mountains, and of Grenna and Jönköping, with its match factory, and think of Huskvarna, and all the big establishments there!" "Yes, that's true enough," said little Mats once again. "And think of Visingsö, little Mats, with the ruins and the oak forests and the legends! Think of the valley through which Emån flows, with all the villages and flour-mills and saw-mills, and the carpenter shops!" "Yes, that is true enough," said little Mats, and looked troubled.

All of a sudden he had looked up. "Now we are pretty stupid," said he. "All this, of course, lies in our Lord's Småland, in that part of the land which was already finished when Saint Peter undertook the job. It's only natural that it should be pretty and fine there. But in Saint Peter's Småland it looks as it says in the legend. And it wasn't surprising that our Lord was distressed when he saw it," continued little Mats, as he took

up the thread of his story again. "Saint
Peter didn't lose his courage, at all events,
but tried to comfort our Lord. 'Don't be so
grieved over this!' said he. 'Only wait until
I have created people who can till the swamps
and break up fields from the stone hills.'

"That was the end of our Lord's patience—
and he said: 'No! you can go down to
Skåne and make the Skåninge, but the
Smålander I will create myself.' And so our
Lord created the Smålander, and made him
quick-witted and contented and happy and
thrifty and enterprising and capable, that he
might be able to get his livelihood in his poor
country."

Then little Mats was silent; and if Nils
Holgersson had also kept still, all would have
gone well; but he couldn't possibly refrain
from asking how Saint Peter had succeeded
in creating the Skåninge.

"Well, what do you think yourself?" said
little Mats, and looked so scornful that Nils
Holgersson threw himself upon him, to thrash
him. But Mats was only a little tot, and
Osa, the goose-girl, who was a year older

than he, ran forward instantly to help him.
Good-natured though she was, she sprang like
a lion as soon as anyone touched her brother.
And Nils Holgersson did not care to fight a
girl, but turned his back, and didn't look at
those Småland children for the rest of the day.

XVI

THE CROWS

THE EARTHEN CROCK

IN THE southwest corner of Småland lies a township called Sonnerbo. It is a rather smooth and even country. And one who sees it in winter, when it is covered with snow, cannot imagine that there is anything under the snow but garden-plots, rye-fields and clover-meadows as is generally the case in flat countries. But, in the beginning of April when the snow finally melts away in Sonnerbo, it is apparent that that which lies hidden under it is only dry, sandy heaths, bare rocks, and big, marshy swamps. There are fields here and there, to be sure, but they are so small that they are scarcely worth mentioning; and one also finds a few little red or gray farmhouses hidden away in some beech-coppice—

almost as if they were afraid to show themselves.

Where Sonnerbo township touches the
boundaries of Halland, there is a sandy heath
which is so far-reaching that he who stands
upon one edge of it cannot look across to the
other. Nothing except heather grows on the
heath, and it wouldn't be easy either to coax
other growths to thrive there. To start with,
one would have to uproot the heather; for
it is thus with heather: although it has
only a little shrunken root, small shrunken
branches, and dry, shrunken leaves it fancies
that it's a tree. Therefore it acts just like
real trees—spreads itself out in forest fashion
over wide areas; holds together faithfully, and
causes all foreign growths that wish to crowd
in upon its territory to die out.

The only place on the heath where the
heather is not all-powerful, is a low, stony
ridge which passes over it. There you'll
find juniper bushes, mountain ash, and
a few large, fine oaks. At the time when Nils
Holgersson travelled around with the wild
geese, a little cabin stood there, with a bit of

cleared ground around it. But the people who had lived there at one time, had, for some reason or other, moved away. The little cabin was empty, and the ground lay unused.

When the tenants left the cabin they closed the damper, fastened the window-hooks, and locked the door. But no one had thought of the broken window-pane which was only stuffed with a rag. After the showers of a couple of summers, the rag had moulded and shrunk, and, finally, a crow had succeeded in poking it out.

The ridge on the heather-heath was really not as desolate as one might think, for it was inhabited by a large crow-folk. Naturally, the crows did not live there all the year round. They moved to foreign lands in the winter; in the autumn they travelled from one grain-field to another all over Götaland, and picked grain; during the summer, they spread themselves over the farms in Sonnerbo township, and lived upon eggs and berries and birdlings; but every spring, when nesting time came, they came back to the heather-heath.

The one who had poked the rag from the window, was a crow-cock named Garm White-feather; but he was never called anything but Fumle or Drumle, or out and out Fumle-Drumle, because he always acted awkwardly and stupidly, and wasn't good for anything except to make fun of. Fumle-Drumle was bigger and stronger than any of the other crows, but that didn't help him in the least; he was—and remained—a butt for ridicule. And it didn't profit him, either, that he came from very good stock. If everything had gone smoothly, he should have been leader for the whole flock, because this honour had, from time immemorial, belonged to the oldest Whitefeather. But long before Fumle-Drumle was born, the power had gone from his family, and was now wielded by a cruel wild crow, named Wind-Rush.

This transference of power was due to the fact that the crows on crow-ridge desired to change their manner of living. Possibly there are many who think that everything in the shape of crow lives in the same way; but this is not so. There are entire crow-folk who lead honourable lives—that is to say, they only eat grain, worms, caterpillars, and dead animals; and there are others who lead a regular bandit's life, who throw themselves upon baby-hares and small birds, and plunder every single bird's nest they set eyes on.

The ancient Whitefeathers had been strict and temperate; and as long as they had led the flock, the crows had been compelled to conduct themselves in such a way that other birds could speak no ill of them. But the crows were numerous, and poverty was great among them. They didn't care to go the whole length of living a strictly moral life, so they rebelled against the Whitefeathers, and gave the power to Wind-Rush, who was the worst nest-plunderer and robber that could be imagined—if his wife, Wind-Air, wasn't worse still. Under their government the crows had begun to lead such a life that now they were more feared than pigeon-hawks and leech-owls.

Naturally, Fumle-Drumle had nothing to say in the flock. The crows were all of the

opinion that he did not in the least take after
his forefathers, and that he wouldn't suit as
a leader.   No one would have mentioned him,
if he hadn't constantly committed fresh
blunders.   A few, who were quite sensible,
sometimes said perhaps it was lucky for
Fumle-Drumle that he was such a bungling
idiot, otherwise Wind-Rush and Wind-Air
would hardly have allowed him—who was
of the old chieftain stock—to remain with
the flock.

Now, on the other hand, they were rather
friendly toward him, and willingly took him
along with them on their hunting expeditions.
There all could observe how much more skilful
and daring they were than he.

None of the crows knew that it was Fumle-
Drumle who had pecked the rag out of the
window; and had they known of this, they
would have been very much astonished.
Such a thing as daring to approach a human
being's dwelling, they had never believed of
him.   He kept the thing to himself very
carefully; and he had his own good reasons
for it.   Wind and Air always treated him

well in the daytime, and when the others were around; but one very dark night, when the comrades sat on the night branch, he was attacked by a couple of crows and nearly murdered. After that he moved every night, after dark, from his usual sleeping quarters into the empty cabin.

Now one afternoon, when the crows had put their nests in order on crow-ridge, they happened upon a remarkable find. Wind-Rush, Fumle-Drumle, and a couple of others had flown down into a big hollow in one corner of the heath. The hollow was nothing but a gravel-pit, but the crows could not be satisfied with such a simple explanation; they flew down in it continually, and turned every single sand-grain to get at the reason why human beings had digged it. While the crows were pottering around down there, a mass of gravel fell from one side. They rushed up to it, and had the good fortune to find amongst the fallen stones and stubble— a large earthen crock, which was locked with a wooden clasp! Naturally they wanted to know if there was anything in it, and they tried both to peck holes in the crock, and to bend up the clasp but they had no success.

They stood perfectly helpless and examined the crock, when they heard someone say: "Shall I come down and assist you crows?" They glanced up quickly. On the edge of the hollow sat a fox and blinked down at them. He was one of the prettiest foxes—both in colour and form—that they had ever seen. The only fault with him was that he had lost an ear.

"If you desire to do us a service," said Wind-Rush, "we shall not say nay." At the same time, both he and the others flew up from the hollow. Then the fox jumped down in their place, bit at the jar, and pulled at the lock—but he couldn't open it either.

"Can you make out what there is in it?" said Wind-Rush. The fox rolled the jar back and forth, and listened attentively. "It must be silver money," said he.

This was more than the crows had expected. "Do you think it can be silver?" said they, and their eyes were ready to pop out of their heads with greed; for remarkable as it may sound, there is nothing in the world which crows love as much as silver money.

"Hear how it rattles!" said the fox and rolled the crock around once more. "Only I can't understand how we shall get at it." "That will surely be impossible," said the crows. The fox stood and rubbed his head against his left leg, and pondered. Now perhaps he might succeed, with the help of the crows, in becoming master of that little imp who always eluded him. "Oh! I know someone who could open the crock for you," said the fox. "Then tell us! Tell us!" cried the crows; and they were so excited that they tumbled down into the pit. "That I will do, if you'll first promise me that you will agree to my terms," said he.

Then the fox told the crows about Thumbietot, and said that if they could bring him to the heath he would open the crock for them. But in payment for this counsel, he demanded that they should deliver Thumbietot to him, as soon as he had gotten the silver money for them. The crows had no reason to spare Thumbietot, so agreed to the compact at once. It was easy enough to agree to this; but it was harder to find out where Thumbietot and the wild geese were stopping.

Wind-Rush himself travelled away with fifty crows, and said that he should soon return. But one day after another passed without the crows on crow-ridge seeing a shadow of him.

KIDNAPPED BY CROWS

Wednesday, April thirteenth.

THE wild geese were up at daybreak, so they should have time to get themselves a bite of food before starting out on the journey toward Östergötland. The island in Goose-fiord, where they had slept, was small and barren, but in the water all around it were growths which they could eat their fill upon. It was worse for the boy, however. He couldn't manage to find anything eatable.

As he stood there hungry and drowsy, and looked around in all directions, his glance fell upon a pair of squirrels, who played upon the wooded point, directly opposite the rock island. He wondered if the squirrels still had any of their winter supplies left, and asked the white goosey-gander to take him over to the point, that he might beg them for a couple of hazelnuts.

Instantly the white one swam across the sound with him; but as luck would have it the squirrels had so much fun chasing each other from tree to tree, that they didn't bother about listening to the boy. They drew farther into the grove. He hurried after them, and was soon out of the goosey-gander's sight—who stayed behind and waited on the shore.

The boy waded forward between some white anemone-stems—which were so high they reached to his chin—when he felt that someone caught hold of him from behind, and tried to lift him up. He turned round and saw that a crow had grabbed him by the shirt-band. He tried to break loose, but before this was possible, another crow ran up, gripped him by the stocking, and knocked him over.

If Nils Holgersson had immediately cried

for help, the white goosey-gander certainly
would have been able to save him; but the
boy probably thought that he could protect
himself, unaided, against a couple of crows.
He kicked and struck out, but the crows
didn't let go their hold, and they soon succeeded in raising themselves into the air with
him. To make matters worse, they flew so
recklessly that his head struck against a
branch. He received a hard knock over the
head, it grew black before his eyes, and he
lost consciousness.

When he opened his eyes once more, he
found himself high above the ground. He
regained his senses slowly; at first he knew
neither where he was, nor what he saw.
When he glanced down, he saw that under him
was spread a tremendously big woolly carpet, which was woven in greens and reds, and
in large irregular patterns. The carpet was
very thick and fine, but he thought it was a
pity that it had been so badly used. It was
actually ragged; long tears ran through it;
in some places large pieces were torn away.
And the strangest of all was that it appeared

to be spread over a mirror floor; for under the holes and tears in the carpet shone bright and glittering glass.

The next thing the boy observed was that the sun unrolled itself in the heavens. Instantly, the mirror-glass under the holes and tears in the carpet began to shimmer in red and gold. It looked very gorgeous, and the boy was delighted with the pretty colour-scheme, although he didn't exactly understand what it was that he saw. But now the crows descended, and he saw at once that the big carpet under him was the earth, which was dressed in green and brown cone-trees and naked leaf-trees, and that the holes and tears were shining fiords and little lakes.

He remembered that the first time he had travelled up in the air, he had thought that the earth in Skåne looked like a piece of checked cloth. But this country which resembled a torn carpet—what might this be?

He began to ask himself a lot of questions. Why wasn't he sitting on the goosey-gander's back? Why did a great swarm of crows fly around him? And why was he being pulled

and knocked hither and thither so that he was about to break in pieces?

Then, all at once, the whole thing dawned on him. He had been kidnapped by a couple of crows. The white goosey-gander was still on the shore, waiting, and to-day the wild geese were going to travel to Östergötland. He was being carried southwest; this he understood because the sun's disc was behind him. The big forest-carpet which lay beneath him was surely Småland.

What will become of the goosey-gander now, when I cannot look after him?" thought the boy, and began to call to the crows to take him back to the wild geese instantly. He wasn't at all uneasy on his own account. He believed that they were carrying him off simply in a spirit of mischief.

The crows didn't pay the slightest attention to his exhortations, but flew on as fast as they could. After a bit, one of them flapped his wings in a manner which meant: "Look out! Danger!" Soon thereafter they came down in a spruce forest, pushed their way between prickly branches to the ground, and put the boy down under a thick spruce, where he was so well concealed that not even a falcon could have sighted him.

Fifty crows surrounded him, with bills pointed toward him to guard him. "Now perhaps I may hear, crows, what your purpose is in carrying me off," said he. But he was hardly permitted to finish the sentence before a big crow hissed at him: "Keep still! or I'll bore your eyes out."

It was evident that the crow meant what she said; and there was nothing for the boy to do but obey. So he sat there and stared at the crows, and the crows stared at him.

The longer he looked at them, the less he liked them. It was dreadful how dusty and unkempt their feather dresses were—as though they knew neither baths nor oiling. Their toes and claws were grimy with dried-in mud, and the corners of their mouths were covered with food drippings. These were very different birds from the wild geese—that he observed. He thought they had a cruel, sneaky, watchful, and bold appearance, just like cut-throats and vagabonds.

"It is certainly a real robber-band that I've fallen in with," thought he.

Just then he heard the wild geese's call above him. "Where are you? Here am I. Where are you? Here am I."

He understood that Akka and the others had gone out to search for him; but before he could answer them the big crow who appeared to be the leader of the band hissed in his ear: "Think of your eyes!" And there was nothing else for him to do but to keep still.

The wild geese may not have known that he was so near them, but had just happened, incidentally, to travel over this forest. He heard their call a couple of times more, then it died away. "Well, now you'll have to get along by yourself, Nils Holgersson," he said to himself. "Now you must prove whether you have learned anything during these weeks in the open."

A moment later the crows gave the signal to break up; and since it was still their intention, apparently, to carry him along in such a way that one held on to his shirt-band, and one to a stocking, the boy said: "Is there

not one among you so strong that he can carry
me on his back? You have already travelled
so badly with me that I feel as if I were in
pieces. Only let me ride! I'll not jump from
the crow's back, that I promise you."

"Oh! you needn't think that we care how
you have it," said the leader. But now the
largest of the crows—a dishevelled and
uncouth one, who had a white feather in his
wing—came forward and said: "It would
certainly be best for all of us, Wind-Rush, if
Thumbietot got there whole, rather than half,
and therefore, I shall carry him on my back."
"If you can do it, Fumle-Drumle, I have no
objection," said Wind-Rush. "But don't
lose him!"

With this, much was already gained, and
the boy actually felt pleased again. "There
is nothing to be gained by losing my grit
because I have been kidnapped by the crows,"
thought he. "I'll surely be able to manage
those poor little things."

The crows continued to fly southwest, over
Småland. It was a glorious morning—sunny
and calm; and the birds down on the earth

were singing their best love songs.   In a high,
dark forest sat the thrush himself with drooping wings and swelling throat, and struck up
tune after tune.   "How pretty you are!
How pretty you are! How pretty you are!"
sang he.   "No one is so pretty.   No one is so
pretty.   No one is so pretty."   As soon as he
had finished this song, he began it all over
again.

But just then the boy rode over the forest;
and when he had heard the song a couple of
times, and marked that the thrush knew no
other, he put both hands up to his mouth as a
speaking trumpet, and called down: "We've
heard all this before.   We've heard all this
before."   "Who is it? Who is it? Who is it?
Who makes fun of me?" asked the thrush, and
tried to catch a glimpse of the one who called.
"It is Kidnapped-by-Crows who makes fun
of your song," answered the boy.   At that,
the crow-chief turned his head and said: "Be
careful of your eyes, Thumbietot!" But the
boy thought, "Oh! I don't care about that.
I want to show you that I'm not afraid
of you!"

Farther and farther inland they travelled; and there were woods and lakes everywhere. In a birch-grove sat the wood-dove on a naked branch, and before him stood the lady-dove. He blew up his feathers, cocked his head, raised and lowered his body, until the breast-feathers rattled against the branch. All the while he cooed: "Thou, thou, thou art the loveliest in all the forest. No one in the forest is so lovely as thou, thou, thou!"

But up in the air the boy rode past, and when he heard Mr. Dove he couldn't keep still. "Don't you believe him! Don't you believe him!" cried he.

"Who, who, who is it that lies about me?" cooed Mr. Dove, and tried to get a sight of the one who shrieked at him. "It is Caught-by-Crows that lies about you," replied the boy. Again Wind-Rush turned his head toward the boy and commanded him to shut up, but Fumle-Drumle, who was carrying him, said: "Let him chatter, then all the little birds will think that we crows have become quick-witted and funny birds." "Oh! they're not such fools, either," said Wind-Rush; but he liked the idea just the same, for after that he let the boy call out as much as he liked.

They flew mostly over forests and woodlands, but there were churches and parishes and little cabins in the outskirts of the forest. In one place they saw a pretty old manor. It lay with the forest back of it, and the sea in front of it; had red walls and a turreted roof; great sycamores about the grounds, and big, thick gooseberry-bushes in the orchard. On the top of the weathercock sat the starling, and sang so loud that every note was heard by the wife, who sat on an egg in the heart of a pear tree. "We have four pretty little eggs," sang the starling. "We have four pretty little round eggs. We have the whole nest filled with fine eggs."

When the starling sang the song for the thousandth time, the boy rode over the place. He put his hands up to his mouth, as a pipe, and called: "The magpie will get them. The magpie will get them."

"Who is it that wants to frighten me?" asked the starling, and flapped his wings uneasily. "It is Captured-by-Crows that frightens you," said the boy. This time the crow-chief didn't attempt to hush him up. Instead, both he and his flock were having so much fun that they cawed with satisfaction.

The farther inland they came, the larger were the lakes, and the more plentiful were the islands and points. And on a lake-shore stood a drake and kowtowed before the duck. "I'll be true to you all the days of my life. I'll be true to you all the days of my life," said the drake. "It won't last until the summer's end," shrieked the boy. "Who are you?" called the drake. "My name's Stolen-by-Crows," shrieked the boy.

At dinner time the crows lighted in a food-grove. They walked about and procured food for themselves, but none of them thought about giving the boy anything. Then Fumle-Drumle came riding up to the chief with a dog-rose branch, with a few dried buds on it. "Here's something for you, Wind-Rush," said he. "This is pretty food, and suitable for you." Wind-Rush sniffed contemptuously. "Do you think that I want to eat old, dry buds?" said he. "And I who

thought that you would be pleased with
them!" said Fumle-Drumle; and threw away
the dog-rose branch as if in despair. But
it fell right in front of the boy, and he wasn't
slow about grabbing it and eating until he
was satisfied.

When the crows had eaten, they began to
chatter. "What are you thinking about,
Wind-Rush? You are so quiet to-day," said
one of them to the leader. "I'm thinking
that in this district there lived, once upon a
time, a hen, who was very fond of her mistress;
and in order to really please her, she went
and laid a nest full of eggs, which she hid
under the store-house floor. The mistress
of the house wondered, of course, where the
hen was keeping herself such a long time.
She searched for her, but did not find her.
Can you guess, Longbill, who it was that
found her and the eggs?"

"I think I can guess it, Wind-Rush, but
when you have told about this, I will tell
you something like it. Do you remember
the big, black cat in Hinneryd's parish house?
She was dissatisfied because they always

took the new-born kittens from her, and drowned them. Just once did she succeed in keeping them concealed, and that was when she had laid them in a haystack, out doors. She was pretty well pleased with those young kittens, but I believe that I got more pleasure out of them than she did."

Now they became so excited that they all talked at once. "What kind of an accomplishment is that—to steal little kittens?" said one. "I once chased a young hare who was almost full-grown. That meant to follow him from covert to covert." He got no further before another took the words from him. "It may be fun, perhaps, to annoy hens and cats, but I find it still more remarkable that a crow can worry a human being. I once stole a silver spoon——"

But now the boy thought he was too good to sit and listen to such gabble. "Now listen to me, you crows!" said he. "I think you ought to be ashamed of yourselves to talk about all your wickedness. I have lived amongst wild geese for three weeks, and of them I have never heard or seen any-

thing but good.   You must have a bad chief,
since he permits you to rob and murder in
this way.   You ought to begin to lead new
lives, for I can tell you that human beings
have grown so tired of your wickedness
they are trying with all their might to root
you out.   And then there will soon be an
end of you."

When Wind-Rush and the crows heard this,
they were so furious that they intended to
throw themselves upon him and tear him in
pieces.   But Fumle-Drumle laughed and
cawed, and stood in front of him.   "Oh, no,
no!" said he, and seemed absolutely terrified.
"What think you that Wind-Air will say if
you tear Thumbietot in pieces before he has
gotten that silver money for us?"   "It has to
be you, Fumle-Drumle, that's afraid of women-
folk," said Rush.   But, at any rate, both he
and the others left Thumbietot in peace.

Shortly after that the crows went further.
Until now the boy thought that Småland
wasn't such a poor country as he had heard.
Of course it was woody and full of mountain-
ridges, but alongside the islands and lakes

lay cultivated grounds, and any real desolation he hadn't come upon, But the farther inland they came, the fewer were the villages and cottages. Toward the last, he thought that he was riding over a veritable wilderness where he saw nothing but swamps and heaths and juniper-hills.

The sun had gone down, but it was still perfect daylight when the crows reached the large heather-heath. Wind-Rush sent a crow on ahead, to say that he had met with success; and when it was known, Wind-Air, with several hundred crows from Crow-Ridge, flew to meet the arrivals. In the midst of the deafening cawing which the crows emitted, Fumle-Drumle said to the boy: "You have been so comical and so jolly during the trip that I am really fond of you. Therefore I want to give you some good advice. As soon as we light, you'll be requested to do a bit of work which may seem very easy to you; but beware of doing it!"

Soon thereafter Fumle-Drumle put Nils Holgersson down in the bottom of a sand-pit. The boy flung himself down, rolled over, and lay there as though he was simply done up with fatigue. Such a lot of crows fluttered about him that the air rustled like a wind-storm, but he didn't look up.

"Thumbietot," said Wind-Rush, "Get up now! You shall help us with a matter which will be very easy for you."

The boy didn't move, but pretended to be asleep. Then Wind-Rush took him by the arm, and dragged him over the sand to an earthen crock of old-time make, that was standing in the pit. "Get up, Thumbietot," said he, "and open this crock!" "Why can't you let me sleep?" said the boy. "I'm too tired to do anything to-night. Wait until to-morrow!"

"Open the crock!" said Wind-Rush, shaking him. "How shall a poor little child be able to open such a crock? Why, it's quite as large as I am myself." "Open it!" commanded Wind-Rush once more, "or it will be a sorry thing for you." The boy got up, tottered over to the crock, fumbled the clasp, and let his arms fall. "I'm not usually so weak," said he. "If you will only let me

sleep until morning, I think that I'll be able to manage with that clasp."

But Wind-Rush was impatient, and he rushed forward and pinched the boy in the leg. That sort of treatment the boy didn't care to suffer from a crow. He jerked himself loose quickly, ran a couple of paces backward, drew his knife from the sheath, and held it extended in front of him. "You'd better be careful!" he cried to Wind-Rush.

This one too was so enraged that he didn't dodge the danger. He rushed at the boy, just as though he'd been blind, and ran so straight against the knife, that it entered through his eye into the head. The boy drew the knife back quickly, but Wind-Rush only struck out with his wings, then he fell down—dead.

"Wind-Rush is dead! The stranger has killed our chieftain, Wind-Rush!" cried the nearest crows, and then there was a terrible uproar. Some wailed, others cried for vengeance. They all ran or fluttered up to the boy, with Fumle-Drumle in the lead. But he acted badly as usual. He only fluttered and spread his wings over the boy, and prevented the others from coming forward and running their bills into him.

The boy thought that things looked very bad for him now. He couldn't run away from the crows, and there was no place where he could hide. Then he happened to think of the earthen crock. He took a firm hold on the clasp, and pulled it off. Then he hopped into the crock to hide in it. But the crock was a poor hiding place, for it was nearly filled to the brim with little, thin silver coins. The boy couldn't get far enough down, so he stooped and began to throw out the coins.

Until now the crows had fluttered around him in a thick swarm and pecked at him, but when he threw out the coins they immediately forgot their thirst for vengeance, and hurried to gather the money. The boy threw out handfuls of it, and all the crows— yes, even Wind-Air herself—picked them up. And everyone who succeeded in picking up a coin ran off to the nest with the utmost speed to conceal it.

When the boy had thrown out all the silver pennies from the crock he glanced up. Not more than a single crow was left in the sandpit. That was Fumle-Drumle, with the white feather in his wing; he who had carried Thumbritot. "You have rendered me a greater service than you yourself understand," said the crow —with a very different voice, and a different intonation than the one he had used heretofore—"and I want to save your life. Sit down on my back, and I'll take you to a hiding place where you can be secure for to-night. To-morrow, I'll arrange it so that you will get back to the wild geese."

THE CABIN

Thursday, April fourteenth.

THE following morning when the boy awoke, he lay in a bed. When he saw that he was in a house with four walls around him, and a roof over him, he thought that he was at home. "I wonder if mother will come soon with some coffee," he muttered to himself where he lay half-awake. Then he remembered that he was in a deserted cabin on the crow-ridge,

and that Fumle-Drumle with the white feather
had borne him there the night before.

The boy was sore all over after the journey
he had made the day before, and he thought
it was lovely to lie still while he waited for
Fumle-Drumle who had promised to come
and fetch him.

Curtains of checked cotton hung before the
bed, and he drew them aside to look out into
the cabin. It dawned upon him instantly
that he had never seen the mate to a cabin
like this. The walls consisted of nothing but
a couple of rows of logs; then the roof began.
There was no interior ceiling, so he could look
clear up to the roof-tree. The cabin was so
small that it appeared to have been built
rather for such as he than for real people.
However, the fireplace and chimney were so
large, he thought that he had never seen larger.
The entrance door was in a gable-wall at the
side of the fireplace, and was so narrow that
it was more like a wicket than a door. In the
other gable-wall he saw a low and broad
window with many panes. There was scarcely
any movable furniture in the cabin. The

bench on one side, and the table under the window, were also stationary—also the big bed where he lay, and the many-coloured cupboard.

The boy could not help wondering who owned the cabin, and why it was deserted. It certainly looked as though the people who had lived there expected to return. The coffee-urn and the gruel-pot stood on the hearth, and there was some wood in the fireplace; the oven-rake and baker's peel stood in a corner; the spinning wheel was raised on a bench; on the shelf over the window lay oakum and flax, a couple of skeins of yarn, a candle, and a bunch of matches.

Yes, it surely looked as if those who had lived there had intended to come back. There were bed-clothes on the bed; and on the walls there still hung long strips of cloth, upon which three riders named Kasper, Melchior, and Baltasar were painted. The same horses and riders were pictured many times. They rode around the whole cabin, and continued their ride even up toward the joists.

But in the roof the boy saw something

which brought him to his senses in a jiffy.
It was a couple of loaves of big bread-cakes
that hung there upon a spit. They looked
old and mouldy, but it was bread all the same.
He gave them a knock with the oven-rake
and one piece fell to the floor. He ate, and
stuffed his bag full. It was incredible how
good bread was, anyway.

He looked around the cabin once more, to
try and discover if there was anything else
which he might find useful to take along. "I
may as well take what I need, since no one
else cares about it," thought he. But most
of the things were too big and heavy. The
only things that he could carry might be a
few matches perhaps.

He clambered up on the table, and swung
with the help of the curtains up to the win-
dow-shelf. While he stood there and stuffed
the matches into his bag, the crow with the
white feather came in through the window.
"Well here I am at last," said Fumle-Drumle
as he lit on the table. "I couldn't get here any
sooner because we crows have elected a new
chieftain in Wind-Rush's place." "Whom

have you chosen?" said the boy. "Well, we
have chosen one who will not permit robbery
and injustice. We have elected Garm White-
feather, lately called Fumle-Drumle," answered he, drawing himself up until he looked
absolutely regal. "That was a good choice,"
said the boy and congratulated him. "You
may well wish me luck," said Garm; then he
told the boy about the time they had had
with Wind-Rush and Wind-Air.

During this recital the boy heard a voice
outside the window which he thought sounded
familiar. "Is he here?"—inquired the fox.
"Yes, he's hidden in there," answered a crow-
voice. "Be careful, Thumbietot!" cried
Garm. "Wind-Air stands without with that
fox who wants to eat you." More he didn't
have time to say, for Smirre dashed against
the window. The old, rotten window-frame
gave way, and the next second Smirre stood
upon the window-table. Garm Whitefeather,
who didn't have time to fly away, he killed
instantly. Thereupon he jumped down to
the floor, and looked around for the boy.
He tried to hide behind a big oakum-spiral,

but Smirre had already spied him, and was crouched for the final spring. The cabin was so small, and so low, the boy understood that the fox could reach him without the least difficulty. But just at that moment the boy was not without weapons of defence. He struck a match quickly, touched the curtains, and when they were in flames, he threw them down upon Smirre Fox. When the fire enveloped the fox, he was seized with a mad terror. He thought no more about the boy, but rushed wildly out of the cabin.

But it looked as if the boy had escaped one danger to throw himself into a greater one. From the tuft of oakum which he had flung at Smirre the fire had spread to the bedhangings. He jumped down and tried to smother it, but it blazed too quickly now. The cabin was soon filled with smoke, and Smirre Fox, who had remained just outside the window, began to grasp the state of affairs within. "Well, Thumbietot," he called out, "which do you choose now: to be broiled alive in there, or to come out here to me? Of course, I should prefer to have the pleasure of eating

you; but in whichever way death meets you
it will be dear to me."

The boy could not think but what the fox
was right, for the fire was making rapid headway. The whole bed was now in a blaze, and
smoke rose from the floor; and along the
painted wall-strips the fire crept from rider
to rider. The boy jumped up in the fireplace,
and tried to open the oven door, when he heard
a key which turned around slowly in the lock.
It must be human beings coming. And in
the dire extremity in which he found himself, he
was not afraid, but only glad. He was already
on the threshold when the door opened. He
saw a couple of children facing him; but how
they looked when they saw the cabin in
flames, he took no time to find out; but
rushed past them into the open.

He didn't dare run far. He knew, of
course, that Smirre Fox lay in wait for
him, and he understood that he must
remain near the children. He turned round
to see what sort of folk they were, but he
hadn't looked at them a second before he
ran up to them and cried: "Oh, good-

day, Osa goose-girl! Oh, good day, little Mats!"

For when the boy saw those children he forgot entirely where he was. Crows and burning cabin and talking animals had vanished from his memory. He was walking on a stubble-field, in West Vemminghög, tending a goose-flock; and beside him, on the field, walked those same Småland children, with their geese. As soon as he saw them, he ran up on the stone-hedge and shouted: "Oh, good-day, Osa goose-girl! Oh, good-day, little Mats!"

But when the children saw such a little creature coming up to them with outstretched hands, they grabbed hold of each other, took a couple of steps backward, and looked scared to death.

When the boy noticed their terror he woke up and remembered who he was. And then it seemed to him that nothing worse could happen him, than that those children should see how he had been bewitched. Shame and grief because he was no longer a human being, overpowered him. He turned and fled. He knew not whither.

But a glad meeting awaited the boy when he came down to the heath. For there, in the heather, he spied something white, and toward him came the white goosey-gander, accompanied by Dunfin. When the white one saw the boy running with such speed, he thought that dreadful fiends were pursuing him. He flung him in all haste upon his back and flew off with him.

XVII

THE OLD PEASANT WOMAN

Thursday, April fourteenth.

THREE tired wanderers were out in the late evening in search of a night harbour. They travelled over a poor and desolate portion of northern Småland. But the sort of resting place which they wanted, they should have been able to find; for they were no weaklings who asked for soft beds or comfortable rooms. "If one of these long mountain-ridges had a peak so high and steep that a fox couldn't in any way climb up to it, then we should have a good sleeping-place," said one of them. "If a single one of the big swamps was thawed out, and was so marshy and wet that a fox wouldn't dare venture out on it, this, too, would be a right good night harbour," said the second. "If the ice on one of the large lakes we travel past were loose, so that a fox could not come

out on it, then we should have found just
what we are seeking," said the third.

The worst of it was that when the sun had
gone down, two of the travellers became so
sleepy that every second they were ready to
fall to the ground. The third one, who could
keep himself awake, grew more and more
uneasy as night approached. "Then it was
a misfortune that we came to a land where
lakes and swamps are frozen, so that a fox
can get around everywhere. In other places
the ice has melted away; but now we're well
up in the very coldest Småland, where spring
has not as yet arrived. I don't know how I
shall ever manage to find a good sleeping-
place! Unless I find some spot that is well
protected, Smirre Fox will be upon us before
morning."

He gazed in all directions, but he saw no
shelter where he could lodge. It was a dark
and chilly night, with wind and drizzle. It
grew more terrible and disagreeable around
him every second.

This may sound strange, perhaps, but the
travellers didn't seem to have the least desire

to ask for house-room on any farm. They had already passed many parishes without knocking at a single door. Little hillside cabins on the outskirts of the forest, which all poor wanderers are glad to run across, they took no notice of either. One might almost be tempted to say they deserved to have a hard time of it, since they did not seek help where it was to be had for the asking.

But finally, when it was so dark that there was scarcely a glimmer of light left under the skies and the two who needed sleep journeyed on in a kind of half-sleep, they happened into a farmyard which was a long way off from all neighbours. And not only did it lie there desolate, but it appeared to be uninhabited as well. No smoke rose from the chimney; no light shone through the windows; no human being moved on the place. When the one among the three who could keep awake, saw the place, he thought: "Now come what may, we must try to get in here. Anything better we are not likely to find."

Soon after that, all three stood in the house-yard. Two of them fell asleep the instant they stood still, but the third looked about him eagerly, to find where they could get under cover. It was not a small farm. Beside the dwelling house and stable and smoke-house, there were long ranges with granaries and storehouses and cattlesheds. But it all looked awfully poor and dilapidated. The houses had gray, moss-grown, leaning walls, which seemed ready to topple over. In the roofs were yawning holes, and the doors hung aslant on broken hinges. It was apparent that no one had taken the trouble to drive a nail into a wall on this place for a long time.

Meanwhile, he who was awake had figured out which house was the cowshed. He roused his travelling companions from their sleep, and conducted them to the cowshed door. Luckily, this was not fastened with anything but a hook, which he could easily push up with a rod. He heaved a sigh of relief at the thought that they should soon be in safety. But when the cowshed door swung open with a sharp creaking, he heard a cow begin to bellow. "Are you coming at last, mistress?" said she. "I thought that you didn't propose to give me any supper to-night."

The one who was awake stopped in the doorway, absolutely terrified when he discovered that the cowshed was not empty. But he soon saw that there was not more than one cow, and three or four chickens; and then he took courage again. "We are three poor travellers who want to come in somewhere, where no fox can assail us, and no human being capture us," said he. "We wonder if this can be a good place for us." "I cannot believe but what it is," answered the cow. "To be sure the walls are poor, but the fox does not walk through them as yet; and no one lives here except an old peasant woman, who isn't at all likely to make a captive of anyone. But who are you?" she continued, as she twisted in her stall to get a sight of the newcomers. "I am Nils Holgersson from Vemminghög, who has been transformed into an elf," replied the first of the incomers, "and I have with me a tame goose, whom I generally ride, and a gray goose." "Such rare guests have never before been within my four walls," said the cow, "and you shall be welcome, although I would have preferred that it had been my mistress, come to give me my supper."

The boy led the geese into the cowshed, which was rather large, and placed them in an empty manger, where they fell asleep instantly. For himself, he made a little bed of straw and expected that he, too, should go to sleep at once.

But this was impossible, for the poor cow, who hadn't had her supper, wasn't still an instant. She shook her flanks, moved around in the stall, and complained of how hungry she was. The boy couldn't get a wink of sleep, but lay there and lived over all the things that had happened to him during these last days.

He thought of Osa, the goose-girl, and little Mats, whom he had encountered so unexpectedly; and he fancied that the little cabin which he had set on fire must have been their old home in Småland. Now he recalled that he had heard them speak of just such a cabin, and of the big heather-heath which lay below it. Now they had wandered back there to see their old home again, and then, when they had reached it it was in flames.

It was indeed a great sorrow which he had brought upon them, and it hurt him very much. If he ever again became a human being, he would try to compensate them for the damage and miscalculation.

Then his thoughts wandered to the crows. And when he thought of Fumle-Drumle who had saved his life, and had met his own death so soon after he had been elected chieftain, he was so distressed that tears filled his eyes.

He had had a pretty rough time of it these last few days. But, anyway, it was a rare stroke of luck that the goosey-gander and Dunfin had found him.

The goosey-gander had said that as soon as the wild geese discovered that Thumbietot had disappeared, they had asked all the small animals in the forest about him. They soon learned that a flock of Småland crows had carried him off. But the crows were already

out of sight, and whither they had directed
their course no one had been able to say.
That they might find the boy as soon as possible, Akka had commanded the wild geese
to start out—two and two—in different
directions, to search for him. But after
a two days' hunt, whether or not they had
found him, they were to meet in northwestern
Småland on a high mountain-top, which
resembled an abrupt, chopped-off tower, and
was called Taberg. After Akka had given
them the best directions, and described carefully how they should find Taberg, they had
separated.

The white goosey-gander had chosen Dunfin
as travelling companion, and they had flown
about hither and thither with the greatest
anxiety for Thumbietot. During this ramble
they had heard a thrush, who sat in a tree-top,
cry and wail that someone, who called himself Kidnapped-by-Crows, had made fun of
him. They had talked with the thrush, and
he had shown them in which direction that
Kidnapped-by-Crows had travelled. Afterward, they had met a dove-cock, a starling,

and a drake; they had all wailed about a little culprit who had disturbed their song, and who was named Caught-by-Crows, Captured-by-Crows, and Stolen-by-Crows. In this way, they were enabled to trace Thumbietot all the way to the heather-heath in Sonnerbo township.

As soon as the goosey-gander and Dunfin had found Thumbietot, they had started toward the north, in order to reach Taberg. But it had been a long road to travel, and the darkness was upon them before they had sighted the mountain top. "If we only get there by to-morrow, surely all our troubles will be over," thought the boy, and dug down into the straw to have it warmer. All the while the cow fussed and fumed in the stall. Then, all of a sudden, she began to talk to the boy. "Everything is wrong with me," said the cow. "I am neither milked nor tended. I have no night fodder in my manger, and no bed has been made under me. My mistress came here at dusk, to put things in order for me, but she felt so ill, that she had to go in soon again, and she has not returned."

"It's distressing that I should be little and powerless," said the boy. "I don't believe that I am able to help you." "You can't make me believe that you are powerless because you are little," said the cow. "All the elves that I've ever heard of, were so strong that they could pull a whole load of hay, and strike a cow dead with one fist." The boy couldn't help laughing at the cow. "They were a very different kind of elf from me." said he. "But I'll loosen your halter and open the door for you, so that you can go out and drink in one of the pools on the place, and then I'll try to climb up to the hayloft and throw down some hay in your manger." "Yes, that would be some help," said the cow.

The boy did as he had said; and when the cow stood with a full manger in front of her, he thought that at last he should get some sleep. But he had hardly crept down in the bed before she began, anew, to talk to him.

"You'll be clean put out with me if I ask you for one thing more," said the cow. "Oh, no I won't, if it's only something that I'm able to do," said the boy. "Then I will ask you to go into the cabin, directly opposite, and find out how my mistress is getting along. I fear some misfortune has come to her." "No! I can't do that," said the boy. "I dare not show myself before human beings." "Surely you're not afraid of an old and sick woman," said the cow. "But you do not need to go into the cabin. Just stand outside the door and peep in through the crack!" "Oh! if that is all you ask of me, I'll do it of course," said the boy.

With that he opened the cowshed door and went out in the yard. It was a fearful night! Neither moon nor stars shone; the wind blew a gale, and the rain came down in torrents. And the worst of all was that seven great owls sat in a row on the eaves of the cabin. It was awful just to hear them, where they sat and grumbled at the weather; but it was even worse to think what would happen to him if one of them should set eyes on him. That would be the last of him.

"Pity him who is little!" said the boy as he ventured out in the yard. And he had a right to say this, for he was blown down twice

before he got to the house: once the wind
swept him into a pool, which was so deep that
he came near drowning. But he got there
nevertheless.

He clambered up a pair of steps, scrambled
over a threshold, and came into the hallway.
The cabin door was closed, but down in one
corner a large piece had been cut away, that
the cat might go in and out. It was no difficulty whatever for the boy to see how things
were in the cabin.

He had hardly cast a glance in there before
he staggered back and turned his head away.
An old, gray-haired woman lay stretched out
on the floor within. She neither moved nor
moaned; and her face shone strangely white.
It was as if an invisible moon had thrown a
feeble light over it.

The boy remembered that when his grandfather had died, his face had also become so
strangely white-like. And he understood that
the old woman who lay on the cabin floor
must be dead. Death had probably come
to her so suddenly that she didn't even have
time to lie down on her bed.

As he thought of being alone with the dead in the middle of the dark night, he was terribly afraid. He threw himself headlong down the steps, and rushed back to the cowshed.

When he told the cow what he had seen in the cabin, she stopped eating. "So my mistress is dead," said she. "Then it will soon be over for me as well." "There will always be someone to look out for you," said the boy comfortingly. "Ah! you don't know," said the cow, "that I am already twice as old as a cow usually is before she is laid upon the slaughter-bench. But then I do not care to live any longer, since she, in there, can come no more to care for me."

She said nothing more for a while, but the boy observed, no doubt, that she neither slept nor ate. It was not long before she began to speak again. "Is she lying on the bare floor?" she asked. "She is," said the boy. "She had a habit of coming out to the cowshed," she continued, "and talking about everything that troubled her. I understood what she said, although I could not answer her. These last few days she talked of how afraid

she was lest there would be no one with her
when she died. She was anxious for fear no
one should close her eyes and fold her hands
across her breast, after she was dead. Perhaps you'll go in and do this?'' The boy
hesitated. He remembered that when his
grandfather had died, mother had been very
careful about putting everything to rights.
He knew this was something which had to be
done. But, on the other hand, he felt that
he didn't dare go to the dead, in the ghastly
night. He didn't say no; neither did he take
a step toward the cowshed door. For a
couple of seconds the old cow was silent—just
as if she had expected an answer. But when
the boy said nothing, she did not repeat her
request. Instead, she began to talk with him
of her mistress.

There was much to tell, first and foremost,
about all the children which she had brought
up. They had been in the cowshed every
day, and in the summer they had taken the
cattle to pasture on the swamp and in the
groves so the old cow knew all about them.
They had been splendid, all of them, and

happy and industrious. A cow knew well enough what her caretakers were good for.

There was also much to be said about the farm. It had not always been as poor as it was now. It was very large—although the greater part of it consisted of swamps and stony groves. There was not much room for fields, but there was plenty of good fodder everywhere. At one time there had been a cow for every stall in the cowshed; and the oxshed, which was now empty, had at one time been filled with oxen. And then there was life and gayety, both in cabin and cowhouse. When the mistress opened the cowshed door she would hum and sing, and all the cows lowed with gladness when they heard her coming.

But the good man had died when the children were so small that they could not be of any assistance, and the mistress had to take charge of the farm, and all the work and responsibility. She had been as strong as a man, and had both ploughed and reaped. In the evenings, when she came into the cowshed to milk, sometimes she was so tired that she wept. Then she dashed away her tears, and was cheerful again. "It doesn't matter. Good times are coming again for me too, if only my children grow up. Yes, if they only grow up."

But as soon as the children were grown, a strange longing came over them. They didn't want to stay at home, but went away to a strange country. Their mother never got any help from them. A couple of her children were married before they went away, and they had left their children behind, in the old home. And now these children followed the mistress in the cowshed, just as her own had done. They tended the cows, and were fine, good folk. And, in the evenings, when the mistress was so tired out that she could fall asleep in the middle of the milking, she would rouse herself again to renewed courage by thinking of them. "Good times are coming for me, too," said she—and shook off sleep— "when once they are grown."

But when these children grew up, they went away to their parents in the strange land. No one came back—no one stayed at home—the old mistress was left alone on the farm.

Probably she had never asked them to remain with her. "Think you, Rödlinna, that I would ask them to stay here with me, when they can go out in the world and have things comfortable?" she would say as she stood in the stall with the old cow. "Here in Småland they have only poverty to look forward to."

But when the last grandchild was gone, it was all up with the mistress. All at once she became bent and gray, and tottered as she walked; as if she no longer had the strength to move about. She stopped working. She did not care to look after the farm, but let everything go to rack and ruin. She didn't repair the houses; and she sold both the cows and the oxen. The only one that she kept was the old cow who now talked with Thumbietot. Her she let live because all the children had tended her.

She could have taken maids and farm-hands into her service, who would have helped her with the work, but she couldn't bear to see

strangers around her, since her own had
deserted her. Perhaps she was better satisfied to let the farm go to ruin, since none of
her children were coming back to take it
after she was gone. She did not mind that
she herself became poor, because she didn't
value that which was only hers. But she
was troubled lest the children should find out
how hard she had it. "If only the children
do not hear of this! If only the children do
not hear of this!" she sighed as she tottered
through the cowhouse.

The children wrote constantly, and begged
her to come out to them; but this she did not
wish. She didn't want to see the land that
had taken them from her. She was angry
with it. "It's foolish of me, perhaps, that
I do not like that land which has been so
good for them," said she. "But I don't
want to see it."

She never thought of anything but the
children, and of this—that they must needs
have gone. When summer came, she led
the cow out to graze in the big swamp. All
day she would sit on the edge of the swamp,

her hands in her lap; and on the way home she would say: "You see, Rödlinna, if there had been large, rich fields here, in place of these barren swamps, then there would have been no need for them to leave."

She could become furious with the swamp which spread out so big, and did no good. She could sit and talk about how it was the swamp's fault that the children had left her.

This last evening she had been more trembly and feeble than ever before. She could not even do the milking. She had leaned against the manger and talked about two strangers who had been to see her, and had asked if they might buy the swamp. They wanted to drain it, and sow and raise grain on it. This had made her both anxious and glad. "Do you hear, Rödlinna," she had said, "Do you hear they said that grain can grow on the swamp? Now I shall write to the children to come home. Now they'll not have to stay away any longer; for now they can get their bread here at home." It was this that she had gone into the cabin to do——

The boy heard no more of what the old cow said. He had opened the cowhouse door and gone across the yard, and in to the dead whom he had but lately been so afraid of.

It was not so poor in the cabin as he had expected. It was well supplied with the sort of things one generally finds among those who have relatives in America. In a corner there was an American rocking chair; on the table before the window lay a brocaded plush cover; there was a pretty spread on the bed; on the walls, in carved-wood frames, hung the photographs of the children and grand-children who had gone away; on the bureau stood high vases and a couple of candle-sticks, with thick, spiral candles in them.

The boy searched for a matchbox and lighted these candles, not because he needed more light than he already had; but because he thought that this was one way to honour the dead.

Then he went up to her, closed her eyes, folded her hands across her breast, and stroked back the thin gray hair from her face.

He thought no more about being afraid of her. He was so deeply grieved because she had been forced to live out her old age in loneliness and longing. He, at least, would watch over her dead body this night.

He hunted up the psalm book, and seated himself to read a couple of psalms in an undertone. But in the middle of the reading he paused—because he had begun to think about his mother and father.

Think, that parents can long so for their children! This he had never known. Think, that life can be as though it was over for them when the children are away! Think, if those at home longed for him in the same way that this old peasant woman had longed!

This thought made him happy, but he dared not believe in it. He had not been such an one that anybody could long for him.

But what he had not been, perhaps he could become.

Round about him he saw the portraits of those who were away. They were big, strong men and women with earnest faces. There were brides in long veils, and gentlemen in fine clothes; and there were children with waved hair and pretty white dresses. And he thought that they all stared blindly into vacancy—and did not want to see.

"Poor you!" said the boy to the portraits. "Your mother is dead. You cannot make reparation now, because you went away from her. But my mother is living!"

Here he paused, and nodded and smiled to himself. "My mother is living," said he. "Both father and mother are living."

XVIII

FROM TABERG TO HUSKVARNA

Friday, April fifteenth.

THE boy sat awake nearly all night, but toward morning he fell asleep and then he dreamed of his father and mother. He could hardly recognise them. They had both grown gray, and had old and wrinkled faces. He asked how this had come about, and they answered that they had aged so because they had longed for him. He was both touched and astonished, for he had never believed but what they were glad to be rid of him.

When the boy awoke the morning was come, with fine, clear weather. First, he himself ate a bit of bread which he found in the cabin; then he gave morning feed to both geese and cow, and opened the cowhouse door so that the cow could go over to the nearest farm. When the cow came along

all by herself the neighbours would no doubt
understand that something was wrong with
her mistress. They would hurry over to the
desolate farm to see how the old woman was
getting along, and then they would find her
dead body and bury it.

The boy and the geese had barely raised
themselves into the air, when they caught a
glimpse of a high mountain, with almost
perpendicular walls, and an abrupt, broken-
off top; and they understood that this must
be Taberg. On the summit stood Akka, with
Yksi and Kaksi, Kolmi and Neljä, Viisi and
Knusi, and all six goslings and waited for
them. There was a rejoicing, and a cackling,
and a fluttering, and a calling which no one
can describe, when they saw that the goosey-
gander and Dunfin had succeeded in finding
Thumbietot.

The woods grew pretty high up on Taberg's
sides, but her highest peak was barren; and
from there one could look far out in all
directions. If one gazed toward the east,
or south, or west, then there was hardly anything to be seen but a poor highland with

dark spruce-trees, brown morasses, ice-clad lakes, and bluish mountain-ridges. The boy couldn't keep from thinking it was true that the one who had created this hadn't taken very great pains with his work, but had thrown it together in a hurry. But if one glanced to the north, it was altogether different. Here it looked as if it had been worked out with the utmost care and affection. In this direction one saw only beautiful mountains, soft valleys, and winding rivers, all the way to the big Lake Vettern, which lay ice-free and transparently clear, and shone as if it wasn't filled with water but with blue light.

It was Vettern that made it so pretty to look toward the north, because it looked as though a blue stream had risen up from the lake, and spread itself over land also. Groves and hills and roofs, and the spires of Jönköping City—which shimmered along Vettern's shores—lay enveloped in pale blue which caressed the eye. If there were countries in heaven, they, too, must be blue like this, thought the boy, and imagined that he had gotten a faint idea of how it must look in Paradise.

Later in the day, when the geese continued their journey, they flew up toward the blue valley. They were in holiday humour; shrieked and made such a racket that no one who had ears could help hearing them.

This happened to be the first really fine spring day they had had in this section. Until now, the spring had done its work under rain and bluster; and now, when it had all of a sudden become fine weather, the people were filled with such a longing after summer warmth and green woods that they could hardly perform their tasks. And when the wild geese rode by, high above the ground, cheerful and free, there wasn't one who did not drop what he had in hand, and glance at them.

The first ones who saw the wild geese that day were miners on Taberg, who were digging ore at the mouth of the mine. When they heard them cackle, they paused in their drilling for ore, and one of them called to the birds: "Where are you going? Where are you going?" The geese didn't understand what he said, but the boy leaned forward over the goose-back, and answered for them: "Where there is neither pick nor hammer." When the miners heard the words, they thought it was their own longing that made the goose-cackle sound like human speech. "Take us along with you! Take us along with you!" they cried. "Not this year." shrieked the boy. "Not this year."

The wild geese followed Taber River down toward Monk Lake, and all the while they made the same racket. Here, on the narrow land-strip between Monk and Vettern lakes, lay Jönköping with its great factories. The wild geese rode first over Monksjö paper mills. The noon rest hour was just over, and the big workmen were streaming down to the mill-gate. When they heard the wild geese, they stopped a moment to listen to them. "Where are you going? Where are you going?" called the workmen. The wild geese understood nothing of what they said, but the boy answered for them: "There, where there are neither machines nor steam-boxes." When the workmen heard the answer, they believed it was their own longing that made the goose-cackle sound like human speech. "Take us along with you!" "Not this year," answered the boy. "Not this year."

Next, the geese rode over the well-known match factory, which lies on the shores of Vettern—large as a fortress—and lifts its high chimneys toward the sky. Not a soul moved out in the yards; but in a large hall young working-women sat and filled match-boxes. They had opened a window on account of the beautiful weather, and through it came the wild geese's call. The one who sat nearest the window, leaned out with a match-box in her hand, and cried: "Where are you going? Where are you going?" "To that land where there is no need of either light or matches," said the boy. The girl thought that what she had heard, was only goose-cackle; but since she thought she had distinguished a couple of words, she called out in answer: "Take me along with you!" "Not this year, replied the boy. "Not this year."

East of the factories rises Jönköping, on the

most glorious spot that any city can occupy. The narrow Vettern has high, steep sand-shores, both on the eastern and western sides; but straight south, the sand-walls are broken down, just as if to make room for a large gate, through which one reaches the lake. And in the middle of the gate—with mountains to the left, and mountains to the right; with Monk Lake behind it, and Vettern in front of it—lies Jönköping.

The wild geese travelled forward over the long, narrow city, and behaved themselves here just as they had done in the country. But in the city there was no one who answered them. It was not to be expected that city folks should stop out in the streets, and call to the wild geese.

The trip extended further along Vettern's shores; and after a little they came to Sanna Sanitarium. Some of the patients had gone out on the veranda to enjoy the spring air, and in this way they heard the goose-cackle. "Where are you going?" asked one of them with such a feeble voice that he was scarcely heard. "To that land where there is neither

sorrow nor sickness," answered the boy.
"Take us along with you!" said the sick
ones. "Not this year," answered the boy.
"Not this year."

When they had travelled still farther on,
they came to Huskvarna. It lay in a valley.
The mountains around it were steep and
beautifully formed. A river rushed along
the heights in long and narrow falls. Big
workshops and factories lay below the mountain walls; and scattered over the valley-
bottom were the workingmen's homes,
encircled by little gardens; and in the centre
of the valley lay the schoolhouse. Just as
the wild geese came along, a bell rang, and a
crowd of school children marched out in line.
They were so numerous that the whole school-
yard was filled with them. "Where are you
going? Where are you going?" the children
shouted when they heard the wild geese.
"Where there are neither books nor lessons
to be found," answered the boy. "Take
us along!" shrieked the children. "Not this
year, but next," cried the boy. "Not this
year, but next."

XIX

THE BIG BIRD-LAKE

JARRO, THE WILD DUCK

O N THE eastern shore of Vettern lies
Mount Omberg; east of Omberg lies
Dagmosse; east of Dagmosse lies Lake Takern.
Around the whole of Takern spreads the big,
even Östergöta plain.

Takern is a pretty large lake and in olden
times it must have been still larger.   But then
the people thought it covered entirely too
much of the fertile plain, so they attempted
to drain the water from it, that they might
sow and reap on the lake-bottom. But they
did not succeed in laying waste the entire
lake—which had evidently been their intention—therefore it still hides a lot of land.
Since the draining the lake has become
so shallow that hardly at any point is it
more than a couple of metres deep. The

shores have become marshy and muddy;
and out in the lake, little mud-islets stick up
above the water's surface.

Now, there is one who loves to stand with
his feet in the water, if he can just keep his
body and head in the air, and that is the
reed. And it cannot find a better place
to grow upon, than the long, shallow
Takern shores, and around the little mud-
islets. It thrives so well that it grows
taller than a man's height, and so thick that
it is almost impossible to push a boat through
it. It forms a broad green enclosure around
the whole lake, so that it is only accessible
in a few places where the people have taken
away the reeds.

But if the reeds shut the people out, they
give, in return, shelter and protection to many
other things. In the reeds there are a lot of
little dams and canals with green, still water,
where duckweed and pondweed run to seed;
and where gnat-eggs and blackfish and worms
are hatched out in uncountable masses. And
all along the shores of these little dams and
canals, there are many well-concealed places,

where seabirds hatch their eggs, and bring up their young without being disturbed, either by enemies or food worries.

An incredible number of birds live in the Takern reeds; and more and more gather there every year, as it becomes known what a splendid abode it is. The first who settled there were the wild ducks; and they still live there by thousands. But they no longer own the entire lake, for they have been obliged to share it with swans, grebes, coots, loons, fen-ducks, and a lot of others.

Takern is certainly the largest and choicest bird lake in the whole country; and the birds may count themselves lucky as long as they own such a retreat. But it is uncertain just how long they will be in control of reeds and mud-banks, for human beings cannot forget that the lake extends over a considerable portion of good and fertile soil; and every now and then the proposition to drain it comes up among them. And if these propositions were carried out, the many thousands of water-birds would be forced to move from this quarter.

At the time when Nils Holgersson travelled around with the wild geese, there lived at Takern a wild duck named Jarro. He was a young bird, who had only lived one summer, one fall, and a winter; now, it was his first spring. He had just returned from South Africa, and had reached Takern in such good season that the ice was still on the lake.

One evening, when he and the other young wild ducks played at racing backward and forward over the lake, a hunter fired a couple of shots at them, and Jarro was wounded in the breast. He thought he should die; but in order that the one who had shot him shouldn't get him into his power, he continued to fly as long as he possibly could. He didn't think whither he was directing his course, but only struggled to get far away. When his strength failed him, so that he could not fly any farther, he was no longer on the lake. He had flown a bit inland, and now he sank down before the entrance to one of the big farms which lie along the shores of Takern.

A moment later a young farm-hand

happened along. He saw Jarro, and came
and lifted him up. But Jarro, who asked for
nothing but to be let die in peace, gathered
his last powers and nipped the farm-hand in
the finger, so he should let go of him.

Jarro didn't succeed in freeing himself.
The encounter had this good in it at any rate:
the farm-hand noticed that the bird was
alive. He carried him very gently into the
cottage, and showed him to the mistress of
the house—a young woman with a kindly
face. At once she took Jarro from the farm-
hand, stroked him on the back and wiped
away the blood which trickled down through
the neck-feathers. She looked him over very
carefully; and when she saw how pretty he
was, with his dark-green, shining head, his
white neck-band, his brownish-red back, and
his blue wing-mirror, she must have thought
that it was a pity for him to die. She promptly
put a basket in order, and tucked the bird
into it.

All the while Jarro fluttered and struggled
to get loose; but when he understood that
the people didn't intend to kill him, he

settled down in the basket with a sense of pleasure. Now it was evident how exhausted he was from pain and loss of blood. The mistress carried the basket across the floor to place it in the corner by the fireplace; but before she put it down Jarro was already fast asleep.

In a little while Jarro was awakened by someone who nudged him gently. When he opened his eyes he experienced such an awful shock that he almost lost his senses. Now he was lost! for there stood *the* one who was more dangerous than either human beings or birds of prey. It was no less a thing than Cæsar himself—the long-haired dog—who nosed around him inquisitively.

How pitifully scared had he not been last summer, when he was still a little yellow-down duckling, every time it had sounded over the reed-stems: "Cæsar is coming! Cæsar is coming!" When he had seen the brown and white spotted dog with the teeth-filled jowls come wading through the reeds, he had believed that he beheld death itself. He had always hoped that he would never have to live through that moment when he should meet Cæsar face to face.

But, to his sorrow, he must have fallen down in the very yard where Cæsar lived, for there he stood right over him. "Who are you?" he growled. "How did you get into the house? Don't you belong down among the reed banks?"

It was with great difficulty that he gained the courage to answer. "Don't be angry with me, Cæsar, because I came into the house!" said he. "It isn't my fault. I have been wounded by a gunshot. It was the people themselves who laid me in this basket."

"Oho! so it's the folks themselves that have placed you here," said Cæsar. "Then it is surely their intention to cure you; although, for my part, I think it would be wiser for them to eat you up, since you are in their power. But, at any rate, you are tabooed in the house. You needn't look so scared. Now, we're not down on Takern."

With that Cæsar laid himself to sleep in front of the blazing log-fire. As soon as Jarro understood that this terrible danger was past, extreme lassitude came over him, and he fell asleep anew.

The next time Jarro awoke, he saw that a dish with grain and water stood before him. He was still quite ill, but he felt hungry nevertheless, and began to eat. When the mistress saw that he ate, she came up and petted him, and looked pleased. After that, Jarro fell asleep again. For several days he did nothing but eat and sleep.

One morning Jarro felt so well that he stepped from the basket and wandered along the floor. But he hadn't gone very far before he keeled over, and lay there. Then came Cæsar, opened his big jaws and grabbed him. Jarro believed, of course, that the dog was going to bite him to death; but Cæsar carried him back to the basket without harming him. Because of this, Jarro acquired such a confidence in the dog Cæsar, that on his next walk in the cottage, he went over to the dog and lay down beside him. Thereafter Cæsar and he became good friends, and every day, for several hours, Jarro lay and slept between Cæsar's paws.

But an even greater affection than he felt
for Cæsar, did Jarro feel toward his mistress.
Of her he had not the least fear; but rubbed
his head against her hand when she came and
fed him. Whenever she went out of the
cottage he sighed with regret; and when she
came back he cried welcome to her in his own
language.

Jarro forgot entirely how afraid he had been
of both dogs and humans in other days. He
thought now that they were gentle and kind,
and he loved them. He wished that he were
well, so he could fly down to Takern and
tell the wild ducks that their enemies were
not dangerous, and that they need not fear
them.

He had observed that the human beings,
as well as Cæsar, had calm eyes, which it did
one good to look into. The only one in the
cottage whose glance he did not care to meet,
was Clawina, the house cat. She did him no
harm, either, but he couldn't place any confidence in her. Then, too, she quarrelled
with him constantly, because he loved human
beings. "You think they protect you because

they are fond of you," said Clawina. "You just wait until you are fat enough! Then they'll wring the neck off you. I know them, I do."

Jarro, like all birds, had a tender and affectionate heart; and he was unutterably distressed when he heard this. He couldn't imagine that his mistress would wish to wring the neck off him, nor could he believe any such thing of her son, the little boy who sat for hours beside his basket, and babbled and chattered. He seemed to think that both of them had the same love for him that he had for them.

One day. when Jarro and Cæsar lay on the usual spot before the fire, Clawina sat on the hearth and began to tease the wild duck.

"I wonder, Jarro, what you wild ducks will do next year, when Takern is drained and turned into grain fields?" said Clawina. "What's that you say, Clawina?" cried Jarro, and jumped up—scared through and through. "I always forget, Jarro, that you do not understand human speech, like Cæsar and myself," answered the cat. "Or else you surely would have heard how the men, who were here in the cottage yesterday, said that all the water was going to be drained from Takern, and that next year the lake-bottom would be as dry as a house-floor. And now I wonder where you wild ducks will go." When Jarro heard this talk he was so furious that he hissed like a snake. "You are just as mean as a common coot!" he screamed at Clawina. "You only want to incite me against human beings. I don't believe they want to do anything of the sort. They must know that Takern is the wild ducks' property. Why should they make so many birds homeless and unhappy? You have certainly hit upon all this to scare me. I hope that you may be torn in pieces by Gorgo, the eagle! I hope that my mistress will chop off your whiskers!"

But Jarro couldn't shut Clawina up with this outburst. "So you think I'm lying," said she. "Ask Cæsar, then! He was also in the house last night. Cæsar never lies."

"Cæsar," said Jarro, "you understand human speech much better than Clawina.

Say that she hasn't heard aright! Think
how it would be if the people drained Takern,
and changed the lake-bottom into fields!
Then there would be no more pond-weed or
duck-food for the grown wild ducks, and no
blackfish or worms or gnat-eggs for the ducklings. Then the reed-banks would disappear
—where now the ducklings conceal themselves until they are able to fly. All ducks
would be compelled to move away from here
and seek another home. But where shall they
find a retreat like Takern? Cæsar, say that
Clawina has not heard aright!"

It was extraordinary to watch Cæsar's
behaviour during this conversation. He had
been wide-awake the whole time before, but
now, when Jarro turned to him, he panted,
laid his long nose on his forepaws, and was
sound asleep within the wink of an eyelid.

The cat looked down at Cæsar with a knowing smile. "I believe that Cæsar doesn't care
to answer you," she said to Jarro. "It is
with him as with all dogs; they will never
acknowledge that humans can do any wrong.
But you can rely upon my word, at any rate.

I shall tell you why they wish to drain the lake just now. As long as you wild ducks still had the power on Takern, they did not wish to drain it, for, at least, they got some good out of you; but now, grebes and coots and other birds who are no good as food, have infested nearly all the reed-banks, and the people don't think they need let the lake remain on their account."

Jarro didn't trouble himself to answer Clawina, but raised his head, and shouted in Cæsar's ear: "Cæsar! You know that on Takern there are still so many ducks left that they fill the air like clouds. Say it isn't true that human beings intend to make all of these homeless!"

Then Cæsar sprang up with such a sudden outburst at Clawina that she had to save herself by jumping up on a shelf. "I'll teach you to keep quiet when I want to sleep," bawled Cæsar. "Of course I know that there is some talk about draining the lake this year. But there's been talk of this many times before without anything coming of it. And that draining business is a matter in which I

take no stock whatever. For how would it
go with the game if Takern were laid waste.
You're a donkey to gloat over a thing like that.
What will you and I have to amuse ourselves
with, when there are no more birds on
Takern?"

THE DECOY-DUCK

Sunday, April seventeenth.

A couple of days later Jarro was so well
that he could fly all about the house. Then
he was petted a good deal by the mistress, and
the little boy ran out in the yard and plucked
the first grass-blades for him which had
sprung up. When the mistress caressed him,
Jarro thought that, although he was now so
strong that he could fly down to Takern at
any time, he shouldn't care to be separated
from the human beings. He had no objection
to remaining with them all his life.

But early one morning the mistress placed
a halter, or noose, over Jarro, which prevented
him from using his wings, and then she turned
him over to the farm-hand who had found
him in the yard. The farm-hand poked him

under his arm, and went down to Takern with him.

The ice had melted away while Jarro had been ill. The old, dry fall leaves still stood along the shores and islets, but all the water-growths had begun to take root down in the deep; and the green stems had already reached the surface. And now nearly all the migratory birds were at home. The curlews' hooked bills peeped out from the reeds. The grebes glided about with new feather-collars around the neck; and the jack-snipes were gathering straws for their nests.

The farm-hand got into a scow, laid Jarro in the bottom of the boat, and began to pole himself out on the lake. Jarro, who had now accustomed himself to expect only good of human beings, said to Cæsar, who was also in the party, that he was very grateful toward the farm-hand for taking him out on the lake. But there was no need to keep him so closely guarded, for he did not intend to fly away. To this Cæsar made no reply. He was very close-mouthed that morning.

The only thing which struck Jarro as being

a bit peculiar was that the farm-hand had
taken his gun along. He couldn't believe
that any of the good folk in the cottage would
want to shoot birds. And, beside, Cæsar
had told him that the people didn't hunt at
this time of the year. "It is a prohibited
time," he had said, "although this doesn't
concern me, of course."

The farm-hand went over to one of the
little reed-enclosed mud-islets. There he
stepped from the boat, gathered some old
reeds into a pile, and lay down behind it.
Jarro was permitted to wander around on
the ground, with the halter over his wings,
and tethered to the boat, with a long string.

Suddenly Jarro caught sight of some young
ducks and drakes, in whose company he had
formerly raced backward and forward over the
lake. They were a long way off, but Jarro
called them to him with a couple of loud
shouts. They responded, and a large and
beautiful flock approached. Before they got
there, Jarro began to tell them about his
marvellous rescue, and of the kindness of
human beings. Just then, two shots sounded

behind him. Three ducks sank down in the reeds—lifeless—and Cæsar bounced out and captured them.

Then Jarro understood. The human beings had only saved him that they might use him as a decoy-duck. And they had also succeeded. Three ducks had died on his account. He thought he should die of shame. He thought that even his friend Cæsar looked contemptuously at him; and when they came home to the cottage, he didn't dare lie down and sleep beside the dog.

The next morning Jarro was again taken out on the shallows. This time, too, he saw some ducks. But when he observed that they flew toward him, he called to them: "Away! Away! Be careful! Fly in another direction! There's a hunter hidden behind the reed-pile. I'm only a decoy-bird!" And he actually succeeded in preventing them from coming within shooting distance.

Jarro had scarcely had time to taste of a grass-blade, so busy was he in keeping watch. He called out his warning as soon as a bird drew nigh. He even warned the grebes,

although he detested them because they
crowded the ducks out of their best hiding-
places. But he did not wish that any bird
should meet with misfortune on his account.
And, thanks to Jarro's vigilance, the farm-
hand had to go home without firing off a single
shot.

Despite this fact, Cæsar looked less displeased than on the previous day; and when
evening came he took Jarro in his mouth,
carried him over to the fireplace, and let him
sleep between his forepaws.

Nevertheless Jarro was no longer contented
in the cottage, but was grievously unhappy.
His heart suffered at the thought that humans
never had loved him. When the mistress,
or the little boy, came forward to caress him,
he stuck his bill under his wing and pretended
that he slept.

For several days Jarro continued his dis-
tressful watch-service; and already he was
known all over Takern. Then it happened
one morning, while he called as usual: "Have
a care, birds! Don't come near me! I'm only
a decoy-duck," that a grebe-nest came floating

toward the shallows where he was tied. This was nothing especially remarkable. It was a nest from the year before; and since grebe-nests are built in such a way that they can move on water like boats, it often happens that they drift out toward the lake. Still Jarro stood there and stared at the nest, because it came so straight toward the islet that it looked as though someone had steered its course over the water.

As the nest came nearer, Jarro saw that a little human being—the tiniest he had ever seen—sat in the nest and rowed it forward with a pair of sticks. And this little human called to him: "Go as near the water as you can, Jarro, and be ready to fly. You shall soon be freed."

A few seconds later the grebe-nest lay near land, but the little oarsman did not leave it, but sat huddled up between branches and straw. Jarro too held himself almost immovable. He was actually paralysed with fear lest the rescuer should be discovered.

The next thing which occurred was that a flock of wild geese came along. Then Jarro woke up to business, and warned them with loud shrieks; but in spite of this they flew backward and forward over the shallows several times. They held themselves so high that they were beyond shooting distance; still the farm-hand let himself be tempted to fire a couple of shots at them. These shots were hardly fired before the little creature ran up on land, drew a tiny knife from its sheath, and, with a couple of quick strokes, cut loose Jarro's halter. "Now fly away, Jarro, before the man has time to load again!" cried he, while he himself ran down to the grebe-nest and poled away from the shore.

The hunter had had his gaze fixed upon the geese, and hadn't observed that Jarro had been freed; but Cæsar had followed more carefully that which happened; and just as Jarro raised his wings, he dashed forward and grabbed him by the neck.

Jarro cried pitifully; and the boy who had freed him said quietly to Cæsar: "If you are just as honourable as you look, surely you cannot wish to force a good bird to sit here and entice others into trouble."

When Cæsar heard these words, he grinned viciously with his upper lip, but the next second he dropped Jarro. "Fly, Jarro!" said he. "You are certainly too good to be a decoy-duck. It wasn't for this that I wanted to keep you here; but because it will be lonely in the cottage without you."

THE LOWERING OF THE LAKE

Wednesday, April twentieth.

IT WAS indeed very lonely in the cottage without Jarro. The dog and the cat found the time long, when they didn't have him to wrangle over; and the housewife missed the glad quacking which he had indulged in every time she entered the house. But the one who longed most for Jarro, was the little boy, Per Ola. He was but three years old, and the only child; and in all his life he had never had a playmate like Jarro. When he heard that Jarro had gone back to Takern and the wild ducks, he couldn't be satisfied with this, but thought constantly of how he should get him back again.

Per Ola had talked a good deal with Jarro

while he lay still in his basket, and he was certain that the duck understood him. He begged his mother to take him down to the lake that he might find Jarro, and persuade him to come back to them. Mother wouldn't listen to this; but the little one didn't give up his plan on that account.

The day after Jarro had disappeared, Per Ola was running about in the yard. He played by himself as usual, but Cæsar lay on the stoop; and when mother let the boy out, she said: "Take care of Per Ola, Cæsar!"

Now if all had been as usual, Cæsar would also have obeyed the command, and the boy would have been so well guarded that he couldn't have run the least risk. But Cæsar was not like himself these days. He knew that the farmers who lived along Takern had held frequent conferences about the lowering of the lake; and that they had almost settled the matter. The ducks must leave, and Cæsar should nevermore behold a glorious chase. He was so preoccupied with thoughts of this misfortune, that he did not remember to watch over Per Ola.

And the little one had scarcely been alone in the yard a minute, before he realised that now the right moment was come to go down to Takern and talk with Jarro. He opened a gate, and wandered down toward the lake on the narrow path which ran along the banks. As long as he could be seen from the house, he walked slowly; but afterward he increased his pace. He was very much afraid that mother, or someone else, should call to him that he couldn't go. He didn't wish to do anything naughty, only to persuade Jarro to come home; but he felt that those at home would not have approved of the undertaking.

When Per Ola came down to the lakeshore, he called Jarro several times. Thereupon he stood for a long time and waited, but no Jarro appeared. He saw several birds that resembled the wild duck, but they flew by without noticing him, and he could understand that none among them was the right one.

When Jarro didn't come to him, the little boy thought that it would be easier to find him if he went out on the lake. There were several good craft lying along the shore, but they were tied. The one that lay loose, and at liberty, was an old leaky scow which was so unfit that no one thought of using it. But Per Ola scrambled up in it without caring that the whole bottom was filled with water. He had not strength enough to use the oars, but instead, he seated himself to swing and rock in the scow. Certainly no grown person would have succeeded in moving a scow out on Takern in that manner; but when the tide is high—and ill-luck to the fore—little children have a marvellous faculty for getting out to sea. Per Ola was soon riding around on Takern, and calling for Jarro.

When the old scow was rocked like this —out to sea—its cracks opened wider and wider, and the water actually streamed into it. Per Ola didn't pay the slightest attention to this. He sat upon the little bench in front and called to every bird he saw, and wondered why Jarro didn't appear.

At last Jarro caught sight of Per Ola. He heard that someone called him by the name which he had borne among human beings, and he understood that the boy had gone out on Takern to search for him. Jarro was unspeakably happy to find that one of the humans really loved him. He shot down toward Per Ola, like an arrow, seated himself beside him, and let him caress him. They were both very happy to see each other again, But suddenly Jarro noticed the condition of the scow. It was half-filled with water, and was almost ready to sink. Jarro tried to tell Per Ola that he, who could neither fly nor swim, must try to get upon land; but Per Ola didn't understand him. Then Jarro did not wait an instant, but hurried away to get help.

Jarro came back in a little while, and carried on his back a tiny thing, who was much smaller than Per Ola himself. If he hadn't been able to talk and move, the boy would have believed that it was a doll. Instantly, the little one ordered Per Ola to pick up a long, slender pole that lay in the bottom of the scow, and try to pole it toward one of the reed-islands. Per Ola obeyed him, and he and the tiny creature, together, steered the scow. With a couple of strokes they were on a little reed-encircled island, and now Per Ola was told that he must step on land. And just the very moment that Per Ola set foot on land, the scow was filled with water, and sank to the bottom.

When Per Ola saw this he was sure that father and mother would be very angry with him. He would have started in to cry if he hadn't found something else to think about soon; namely, a flock of big, gray birds, who lighted on the island. The little midget took him up to them, and told him their names, and what they said. And this was so funny that Per Ola forgot everything else.

Meanwhile the folks on the farm had discovered that the boy had disappeared, and had started to search for him. They searched the outhouses, looked in the well, and hunted through the cellar. Then they went out into the highways and by-paths; wandered to the neighbouring farm to find out if he had strayed over there, and searched for him also

down by Takern.   But no matter how much
they sought they did not find him.

Cæsar, the dog, understood very well that
the farmer-folk were looking for Per Ola, but
he did nothing to lead them on the right
track; instead, he lay still as though the
matter didn't concern him.

Later in the day, Per Ola's footprints were
discovered down by the boat-landing.   And
then came the thought that the old, leaky
scow was no longer on the strand.   Then one
began to understand how the whole affair
had come about.

The farmer and his helpers immediately
took out the boats and went in search of the
boy.   They rowed around on Takern until
way late in the evening, without seeing the
least shadow of him.   They couldn't help
believing that the old scow had gone down,
and that the little one lay dead on the lake-
bottom.

In the evening, Per Ola's mother hunted
around on the strand.   Everyone else was
convinced that the boy was drowned, but
she could not bring herself to believe this.

She searched all the while. She searched between reeds and bulrushes; tramped and tramped on the muddy shore, never thinking of how deep her foot sank, and how wet she had become. She was unspeakably desperate. Her heart ached in her breast. She did not weep, but wrung her hands and called for her child in loud piercing tones.

Round about her she heard swans' and ducks' and curlews' shrieks. She thought that they followed her, and moaned and wailed—they too. "Surely, they, too, must be in trouble, since they moan so," thought she. Then she remembered: these were only birds that she heard complain. They surely had no worries.

It was strange that they did not quiet down after sunset. But she heard all these uncountable bird-throngs, which lived along Takern, send forth cry upon cry. Several of them followed her wherever she went; others came rustling past on light wings. All the air was filled with moans and lamentations.

But the anguish which she herself was suffering, opened her heart. She thought that she was not as far removed from all other living creatures as people usually think. She understood much better than ever before, how birds fared. They had their constant worries for home and children; they, as she. There was surely not such a great difference between them and her as she had heretofore believed.

Then she happened to think that it was as good as settled that these thousands of swans and ducks and loons would lose their homes here by Takern. "It will be very hard for them," she thought. "Where shall they bring up their children now?"

She stood still and mused on this. It appeared to be an excellent and agreeable accomplishment to change a lake into fields and meadows, but let it be some other lake than Takern; some other lake, which was not the home of so many thousand creatures.

She remembered how on the following day the proposition to lower the lake was to be decided, and she wondered if this was why her little son had been lost—just to-day.

Was it God's meaning that sorrow should come and open her heart—just to-day—before it was too late to avert the cruel act?

She walked rapidly up to the house, and began to talk with her husband about this. She spoke of the lake, and of the birds, and said that she believed it was God's judgment on them both. And she soon found that he was of the same opinion.

They already owned a large place, but if the lake-draining was carried into effect, such a goodly portion of the lake-bottom would fall to their share that their property would be nearly doubled. For this reason they had been more eager for the undertaking than any of the other shore owners. The others had been worried about expenses, and anxious lest the draining should not prove any more successful this time than it was the last. Per Ola's father knew in his heart that it was he who had influenced them to undertake the work. He had exercised all his eloquence, so that he might leave to his son a farm as large again as his father had left to him.

He stood and pondered if God's hand was
back of the fact that Takern had taken his
son from him on the day before he was to
draw up the contract to lay it waste. The
wife didn't have to say many words to him,
before he answered: "It may be that God
does not want us to interfere with His order.
I'll talk with the others about this to-morrow,
and I think we'll conclude that all may
remain as it is."

While the farmer-folk were talking this
over, Cæsar lay before the fire. He raised
his head and listened very attentively. When
he thought that he was sure of the outcome,
he walked up to the mistress, took her by
the skirt, and led her to the door. "But
Cæsar!" said she, and wanted to break
loose. "Do you know where Per Ola is?"
she exclaimed. Cæsar barked joyfully, and
threw himself against the door. She opened
it, and Cæsar dashed down toward Takern.
The mistress was so positive he knew where
Per Ola was, that she rushed after him.
And no sooner had they reached the shore
than they heard a child's cry out on the lake.

Per Ola had had the best day of his life, in company with Thumbietot and the birds; but now he had begun to cry because he was hungry and afraid of the darkness. And he was glad when father and mother and Cæsar came for him.

XX

ULVÅSA-LADY

THE PROPHECY

Friday, April twenty-second.

ONE night when the boy lay and slept on an island in Takern, he was awakened by oar-strokes. He had hardly gotten his eyes open before there fell such a dazzling light on them that he began to blink.

At first he couldn't make out what it was that shone so brightly out here on the lake; but he soon saw that a scow with a big burning torch stuck up on a spike, aft, lay near the edge of the reeds. The red flame from the torch was clearly reflected in the night-dark lake; and the brilliant light must have lured the fish, for round about the flame in the deep a mass of dark specks were seen, that moved continually, and changed places.

There were two old men in the scow.

One sat at the oars, and the other stood on a bench in the stern and held in his hand a short spear which was coarsely barbed. The one who rowed was apparently a poor fisherman. He was small, dried-up and weather-beaten, and wore a thin, threadbare coat. One could see that he was so used to being out in all sorts of weather that he didn't mind the cold. The other was well fed and well dressed, and looked like a prosperous and self-complacent farmer.

"Now, stop!" said the farmer, when they were opposite the island where the boy lay. At the same time he plunged the spear into the water. When he drew it out again, a long, fine eel came with it.

"Look at that!" said he as he released the eel from the spear. "That was one who was worth while. Now I think we have so many that we can turn back."

His comrade did not lift the oars, but sat and looked around. "It is lovely out here on the lake to-night," said he. And so it was. It was absolutely still, so that the entire water-surface lay in undisturbed rest with the exception of the streak where the boat had gone forward. This lay like a path of gold, and shimmered in the firelight. The sky was clear and dark blue and thickly studded with stars. The shores were hidden by the reed islands except toward the west. There Mount Omberg loomed up high and dark, much more impressive than usual, and cut away a big, three-cornered piece of the vaulted heavens.

The other one turned his head to get the light out of his eyes, and looked about him. "Yes, it is lovely here in Östergylln," said he. "Still the best thing about the province is not its beauty." "Then what is it that's best?" asked the oarsman. "That it has always been a respected and honoured province." "That may be true enough." "And then this, that one knows it will always continue to be so." "But how in the world can one know this?" said the one who sat at the oars.

The farmer straightened up where he stood and braced himself with the spear. "There is an old story which has been handed down from father to son in my family; and in it one learns what will happen to Östergötland." "Then you may as well tell it to me," said the oarsman. "We do not tell it to anyone and everyone, but I do not wish to keep it a secret from an old comrade.

"At Ulvåsa, here in Östergötland," he continued (and one could tell by the tone of his voice that he talked of something which he had heard from others, and knew by heart), "many, many years ago, there lived a lady who had the gift of looking into the future, and telling people what was going to happen to them—just as certainly and accurately as though it had already occurred. For this she became widely noted; and it is easy to understand that people would come to her, both from far and near, to find out what they were going to pass through of good or evil.

"One day, when Ulvåsa-lady sat in her hall and spun, as was customary in former days, a poor peasant came into the room and seated himself on the bench near the door.

" 'I wonder what you are sitting and

thinking about, dear lady,' said the peasant after a little.

" 'I am sitting and thinking about high and holy things,' answered she. 'Then it is not fitting, perhaps, that I ask you about something which weighs on my heart,' said the peasant.

" 'It is probably nothing else that weighs on your heart than that you may reap much grain on your field. But I am accustomed to receive communications from the Emperor about how it will go with his crown; and from the Pope, about how it will go with his keys.' 'Such things cannot be easy to answer,' said the peasant. 'I have also heard that no one seems to go from here without being dissatisfied with what he has heard.'

"When the peasant said this, he saw that Ulvåsa-lady bit her lip, and moved higher up on the bench. 'So this is what you have heard about me,' said she. 'Then you may as well tempt fortune by asking me about the thing you wish to know; and you shall see if I can answer so that you will be satisfied.'

After this the peasant did not hesitate to

state his errand. He said that he had come
to ask how it would go with Östergötland in
the future. There was nothing which was
so dear to him as his native province, and he
felt that he should be happy until his dying
day if he could get a satisfactory reply to
his query.

" 'Oh! is that all you wish to know,' said
the wise lady; 'then I think that you will be
content.   For here where I now sit, I can tell
you that it will be like this with Östergötland:
it will always have something to boast of
ahead of other provinces.'

" 'Yes, that was a good answer, dear lady,'
said the peasant, 'and now I would be
entirely at peace if I could only comprehend
how such a thing should be possible.'

" 'Why should it not be possible?' said
Ulvåsa-lady. 'Don't you know that Östergötland is already renowned?   Or think you
there is any place in Sweden that can boast
of owning, at the same time, two such cloisters
as the ones in Alvastra and Vreta, and such
a beautiful cathedral as the one in Linköping?'

" 'That may be so,' said the peasant. 'But

I'm an old man, and I know that people's minds are changeable. I fear that there will come a time when they won't want to give us any glory, either for Alvastra or Vreta or for the cathedral.'

"'Herein you may be right,' said Ulvåsa-lady, 'but you need not doubt prophecy on that account. I shall now build up a new cloister on Vadstena, and that will become the most celebrated in the North. Thither both the high and the lowly shall make pilgrimages, and all shall sing the praises of the province because it has such a holy place within its confines.'

"The peasant replied that he was right glad to know this. But he also knew, of course, that everything was perishable; and he wondered much what would give distinction to the province, if Vadstena Cloister should once fall into disrepute.

"'You are not easy to satisfy,' said Ulvåsa-lady, 'but surely I can see so far ahead that I can tell you, before Vadstena Cloister shall have lost its splendour, there will be a castle erected close by, which will be the most

magnificent of its period.   Kings and dukes
will be guests there, and it shall be accounted
an honour to the whole province, that it owns
such an ornament.''

" 'This I am also glad to hear,' said the peasant. 'But I'm an old man, and I know how
it generally turns out with this world's glories.
And if the castle goes to ruin, I wonder much
what there will be that can attract the people's
attention to this province.'

" 'It's not a little that you want to know,'
said Ulvåsa-lady, 'but, certainly, I can look
far enough into the future to see that there
will be life and movement in the forests around
Finspång.   I see how cabins and smithies
arise there, and I believe that the whole
province shall be renowned because iron will
be moulded within its confines.'

" The peasant didn't deny that he was
delighted to hear this.   'But if it should go
so badly that even Finspång's foundry went
down in importance, then it would hardly
be possible that any new thing could arise
of which Östergötland might boast.'

" 'You are not easy to please,' said Ulvåsa-lady, 'but I can see so far into the future that I mark how, along the lake-shores, great manors—large as castles—are built by gentlemen who have carried on wars in foreign lands. I believe that the manors will bring the province just as much honour as anything else that I have mentioned.'

" 'But if there comes a time when no one lauds the great manors?' insisted the peasant.

" 'You need not be uneasy at all events,' said Ulvåsa-lady. 'I see how health-springs bubble on Medevi meadows, by Vätter's shores. I believe that the wells at Medevi will bring the land as much praise as you can desire.'

" 'That is a mighty good thing to know,' said the peasant. 'But if there comes a time when people will seek their health at other springs?'

" 'You must not give yourself any anxiety on that account,' answered Ulvåsa-lady. 'I see how people dig and labour, from Motala to Mem. They dig a canal right through the country, and then Östergötland's praise is again on everyone's lips.'

"But, nevertheless, the peasant looked **distraught.**

" 'I see that the rapids in Motala stream begin to draw wheels,' said Ulvåsa-lady— and now two bright red spots came to her cheeks, for she began to be impatient—'I hear hammers resound in Motala, and looms clatter in Norrköping.'

" 'Yes, that's good to know,' said the peasant, 'but everything is perishable, and I'm afraid that even this can be forgotten, and go into oblivion.'

"When the peasant was not satisfied even now, there was an end to the lady's patience. 'You say that everything is perishable,' said she, 'but now I shall still name something which will always be like itself; and that is that such arrogant and pig-headed peasants as you will always be found in this province —until the end of time.'

"Hardly had Ulvåsa-lady said this before the peasant rose—happy and satisfied—and thanked her for a good answer. Now, at last, he was satisfied, he said.

" 'Verily, I understand now how you look at it,' then said Ulvåsa-lady.

" 'Well, I look at it in this way, dear lady,'

said the peasant, 'that everything which kings and priests and noblemen and merchants build and accomplish, can only endure for a few years. But when you tell me that in Östergötland there will always be peasants who are honour-loving and persevering, then I know also that it will be able to keep its ancient glory. For it is only those who go bent under the eternal labour with the soil, who can hold this land in good repute and honour—from one time to another.' "

XXI

THE HOMESPUN CLOTH

Saturday, April twenty-third.

THE boy rode forward—way up in the air. He had the great Östergötland plain under him, and sat and counted the many white churches which towered above the small leafy groves around them. It wasn't long before he had counted fifty. After that he became confused and couldn't keep track of the counting.

Nearly all the farms were built up with large, whitewashed two-story houses, which looked so imposing that the boy couldn't help admiring them. "There can't be any peasants in this land," he said to himself, "since I do not see any peasant farms."

Immediately all the wild geese shrieked: "Here the peasants live like gentlemen. Here the peasants live like gentlemen."

On the plains the ice and snow ad

420

disappeared, and the spring work had begun. "What kind of long crabs are those that creep over the fields?" asked the boy after a bit. "Ploughs and oxen. Ploughs and oxen," answered the wild geese.

The oxen moved so slowly down on the fields, that one could scarcely perceive they were in motion, and the geese shouted to them: "You won't get there before next year. You won't get there before next year." But the oxen were equal to the occasion. They raised their muzzles in the air and bellowed: "We do more good in an hour than such as you do in a whole lifetime."

In a few places the ploughs were drawn by horses. They went along with much more eagerness and haste than the oxen; but the geese couldn't keep from teasing these either. "Ar'n't you ashamed to be doing ox-duty?" cried the wild geese. "Ar'n't you ashamed yourselves to be doing lazy man's duty?" the horses neighed back at them.

But while horses and oxen were at work in the fields, the stable ram walked about in the barnyard. He was newly clipped and

touchy, knocked over the small boys, chased
the shepherd dog into his kennel, and then
strutted about as though he alone were lord of
the whole place. "Rammie, rammie, what
have you done with your wool?" asked the
wild geese, who rode by up in the air. "That
I have sent to Drag's woollen mills in Norrköping," replied the ram with a long, drawn-
out bleat. "Rammie, rammie, what have
you done with your horns?" asked the geese.
But any horns the rammie had never possessed, to his sorrow, and one couldn't offer
him a greater insult than to ask after them.
He ran around a long time, and butted at the
air, so furious was he.

On the country road came a man who
drove a flock of Skåne pigs that were not more
than a few weeks old, and were going to be
sold up country. They trotted along bravely,
as little as they were, and kept close together
—as if they sought protection. "Nuff, nuff,
nuff, we came away too soon from father and
mother. Nuff, nuff, nuff, how will it go with
us poor children?" said the little pigs. The
wild geese didn't have the heart to tease such

poor little creatures. "It will be better for you than you can ever believe," they cried as they flew past them.

The wild geese were never so merry as when they flew over a flat country. Then they did not hurry themselves, but flew from farm to farm, and joked with the tame animals.

As the boy rode over the plain, he happened to think of a legend which he had heard a long time ago. He didn't remember it exactly, but it was something about a petticoat— half of which was made of gold-woven velvet, and half of gray homespun cloth. But the one who owned the petticoat adorned the homespun cloth with such a lot of pearls and precious stones that it looked richer and more gorgeous than the gold-cloth.

He remembered this about the homespun cloth, as he looked down on Östergötland, because it was made up of a large plain, which lay wedged in between two mountainous forest-tracts—one to the north, the other to the south. The two forest-heights lay there, a lovely blue, and shimmered in the morning

light, as if they were decked with golden veils;
and the plain, which simply spread out one
winter-naked field after another, was, in and
of itself, prettier to look upon than gray
homespun.

But the people must have been contented
on the plain, because it was generous and kind,
and they had tried to decorate it in the best
way possible.   High up—where the boy rode
by—he thought that cities and farms,
churches and factories, castles and railway
stations were scattered over it, like large and
small trinkets.   It shone on the roofs, and the
window-panes glittered like jewels. Yellow
country roads, shining railway-tracks and
blue canals ran along between the districts,
like embroidered loops.   Linköping lay
around its cathedral like a pearl-setting around
a precious stone; and the gardens in the
country were like little brooches and buttons.
There was not much regulation in the pattern,
but it was a display of grandeur which one
could never tire of looking at.

The geese had left Öberg district, and
travelled toward the east along Göta Canal.

This was also getting itself ready for the summer. Workmen laid canal-banks, and tarred the huge lock-gates. They were working everywhere to receive spring fittingly, even in the cities. There, masons and painters stood on scaffoldings and made fine the exteriors of the houses while maids were cleaning the windows. Down at the harbour, sailboats and steamers were being washed and dressed up.

At Norrköping the wild geese left the plain, and flew up toward Kolmården. For a time they had followed an old, hilly country road, which wound around cliffs, and ran forward under wild mountain-walls—when the boy suddenly let out a shriek. He had been sitting and swinging his foot back and forth, and one of his wooden shoes had slipped off.

"Goosey-gander, goosey-gander, I have dropped my shoe!" cried the boy. The goosey-gander turned about and sank toward the ground; then the boy saw that two children, who were walking along the road, had picked up his shoe. "Goosey-gander, goosey-gander," screamed the boy excitedly, "fly

upward again! It is too late. I cannot get
my shoe back again."

Down on the road stood Osa, the goose-
girl, and her brother, little Mats, looking
at a tiny wooden shoe that had fallen from
the skies.

Osa, the goose-girl, stood silent a long
while, and pondered over the find. At last
she said, slowly and thoughtfully: "Do you
remember, little Mats, that when we went
past Övid Cloister, we heard that the folks in
a farmyard had seen an elf who was dressed
in leather breeches, and had wooden shoes on
his feet, like any other working man? And
do you recollect when we came to Vittskövle,
a girl told us that she had seen a Goa-Nisse
with wooden shoes, who flew away on the
back of a goose? And when we ourselves came
home to our cabin, little Mats, we saw a goblin
who was dressed in the same way, and who
also straddled the back of a goose—and flew
away. Maybe it was the same one who
rode along on his goose up here in the air and
dropped his wooden shoe."

"Yes, it must have been," said little Mats.

"A tiny wooden shoe that had fallen
from the skies"

They turned the wooden shoe about and examined it carefully—for it isn't every day that one happens across a Goa-Nisse's wooden shoe on the highway.

"Wait, wait, little Mats!" said Osa, the goose-girl. "There is something written on one side of it."

"Why, so there is! but they are such tiny letters."   .

"Let me see! It says—it says: 'Nils Holgersson from W. Vemminghög.'   That's the most wonderful thing I've ever heard!" said little Mats.

END OF BOOK I

APPENDIX

The final *e* is sounded in Skåne, Sirle, Gripe, etc.

The *å* in Skane and Småland is pronounced like *o* in ore.

j is like the English *y*. Nuolja, Oviks-fjällen, Sjangeli, Jarro, etc., should sound as if they were spelled like this: Nuolya, Oviks-fyellen, Syang[one syllable]elee, Yarro, etc.

g, when followed by *e*, *i*, *y*, *ä*, *ö*, is also like *y*. Example, Göta is pronounced Yöta.

When *g* is followed by *a*, *o*, *u*, or *å*, it is hard, as in go.

k in Norrköping, Linköping, Kivik (pronounced Cheeveek), etc., is like *ch* in cheer.

k is hard when it precedes *a*, *o*, *u*, or *å*. Example, Kaksi, Kolmi, etc.

ä is pronounced like *ā* in fare. Example, Färs.

There is no sound in the English language

which corresponds to the Swedish ö.   It is like the French *eu* in jeu.

Gripe is pronounced Greep-e.

In Sirle, the first syllable has the same sound as *sir*, in sirup.

The names which Miss Lagerlöf has given to the animals are descriptive.

Smirre Fox, is cunning fox.

Sirle Squirrel, is graceful, or nimble squirrel.

Gripe Otter, means grabbing or clutching otter.

Mons is a pet name applied to cats; like our tommy and pussy.   Monsie house-cat is equivalent to Tommy house-cat.

Mårten gåskarl (Morten Goosie-gander) is a pet name for a tame gander, just as we use Dickie-bird for a pet bird.

Fru is the Swedish for Mrs.   This title is usually applied to gentlewomen only.   The author has used this meaning of "fru."

A Goa-Nisse is an elf-king, and corresponds to the English Puck or Robin Goodfellow.

VELMA SWANSTON HOWARD.